To Me

Many thanks in advance for your review!

Best,

Aaron

2012

For Keeps

– A Sam Moore Mystery –

By Aaron Paul Lazar

Twilight Times Books
Kingsport Tennessee

For Keeps

This is a work of fiction. All concepts, characters and events portrayed in this book are used fictitiously and any resemblance to real people or events is purely coincidental.

Twilight Times Books
P O Box 3340
Kingsport TN 37664
http://twilighttimesbooks.com/

First Edition, July 2012

Library of Congress Control Number: 2012942969

ISBN: 978-1-60619-174-3

Cover art by Ardy M. Scott

Printed in the United States of America.

This book is dedicated to Don Harman, who knows better than most what it's like to lose a beloved wife. Thank you, Don, for your years of friendship and support. And thanks to Peg Harman, who rescued my dear friend when life seemed pretty bleak. You two make an amazing couple, and I'm proud to be counted among your friends.

Acknowledgments

Special thanks to Sonya Bateman, Sheila Deeth, Nancy Luckhurst, Joan Miller, Nancy Robertson and Marta Stephens, who provided extraordinary editing assistance.

Thank you to Jude Hardin for the title suggestion of *For Keeps.* He recommended it for the first book in this series, which would have worked very well, but it fit even better for the third book in the series. Thanks, Jude, and best of luck with your new release.

Thanks to my Twilight Times editor, Jennifer Styskal. I'm trying to learn from your patient corrections.

And finally, thank you to my publisher, Lida Quillen Twilight Times Books is a shining example of how to achieve and maintain excellence. I salute your passion for doing things right and for the relentless pursuit of great stories.

Chapter One

"MURDERED?" SAM JUGGLED FOUR POTS OF YELLOW DAYLILIES IN HIS arms, squeezing the cell phone between his shoulder and ear. "Where? And why in the world do you need *me?*"

Lou sighed. "I told you. The Twin Sisters Inn. And I can't say over the phone, I just need your...expertise."

My expertise? Sam had practiced family medicine in East Goodland, New York for over thirty years, but couldn't imagine how treating runny noses and chicken pox qualified him to help with a murder. And why was Lou being so damned secretive about the whole thing?

"Hold on a sec, Lou." He dropped the flowerpots on the counter and barely caught them before they toppled. Flashing the clerk an apologetic smile, he swept the spilled dirt into a pile and mumbled into the phone. "I'm at Palmiter's. Just checking out."

Lou groaned. "Why am I not surprised? Since you retired, that's all you've done. Flowers and more flowers. Holy Mother Mary. Don't you get sick of it? Or are you trying to get your place on the Home and Garden network?"

Sam slid the plants toward the clerk. "You're just jealous."

"Damn right I am. I can't retire for another coupla years. Remember, I was two years behind you in med school."

"Just because I'm retired doesn't mean I've lost my marbles. Of course I remember." Sam thought back to the coroner when she was a student at the University of Rochester. Short strawberry blond hair, willowy figure, high cheekbones, and a ready smile. Aside from her gray hair, Louise Reardon hadn't changed much after forty years and five kids. Except she was a hell of a lot pushier.

The freckled teen behind the counter looked bored. "That'll be fourteen ninety-two."

Sam dug out fifteen bucks and paid her. "Thanks. Keep the change."

She raised her eyebrows as if she couldn't believe he'd actually try to tip her with eight lousy cents. "Gee. Thanks, mister."

He shrugged, loaded his plants into a green wagon, and pulled it toward the Highlander. He'd bought enough plants here to put all their kids through college. Anyway, who tipped sales clerks? "Lou? You still there? I'm almost at the car."

"I'm here." She let loose another frustrated sigh. "How long 'til you get here?"

Sam loaded his plants in the back, got in, and turned the key. The SUV purred to life. "Not long. I'm putting you on speaker. Just a sec." He slid the phone into his breast pocket and backed out of the parking spot. None of those new-fangled blue tooth gadgets for him. It was hard enough to keep up with cell phones, laptops, iPods, and every new device that came out each year. "On my way."

"Geez. *Finally.* Watch out for the news vultures when you get here, though. They're everywhere."

"Will do. Be there in a few."

He hung up and pushed his silver forelock back from his forehead. Shouldering his way through a pack of hungry journalists to view a dead body had not been in today's plans. Today was supposed to be devoted to gardening, to feeding his insatiable need to dig in rich loam while the sun warmed his back. If Lou weren't such a good friend, he'd have blown her off.

Turning south on Route 39, he imagined the ribbing he'd get if she knew about his aversion to cadavers. A doctor? Afraid of bodies?

He'd dealt with dead people before, but not a great deal. Med school, of course. He'd barfed his way through that ordeal. And when Mrs. Tupple had died in her bed ten years ago, he'd gone to the house at Mr. Tupple's request. Reluctantly. But he'd gone. The most recent experience had been last fall, at his brother's funeral.

Well, it hadn't really been a *body*...it was Billy's bones, bones pinned underwater for fifty years. Submerged with heavy stones deposited by Sam's three best friends. Billy's disappearance had remained a mystery, until it was finally revealed last year. When things happened. Things he couldn't explain to anyone, except Rachel. He couldn't even tell *her* the whole story. But Billy connecting with him from beyond and helped him get to the truth.

A familiar sadness took hold, and as if in response, Billy's green marble hummed and warmed in his pocket. His brother's face floated across his mind's eye. Freckles. Clear hazel eyes. Sandy hair. Impish smile.

Billy wanted to talk.

Not now. I can't. Later, buddy. He thought the words in his head, knowing Billy could hear him if he said them out loud or imagined them.

Sam turned left at the Mobil Station on the corner of Main Street and Route 20A and headed for the historic brick building housing The Twin Sisters Inn. Willing the marble to be quiet, he forced himself to think of what lay ahead.

A murder victim? Why the heck did Lou need his help? It didn't make any sense, but in spite of his reservations, a trickle of excitement ran down his spine.

News vans and squad cars jammed the lot. He parked on the side of the road and headed toward the building. The marble pulsed twice, then grew cold.

Was it a warning?

The green glass talisman had linked Sam to Billy since he unearthed it in his garden last year. He'd learned to respect it, and through it, Billy's interventions had helped with a number of sticky situations. He'd saved the life of his friend, Senator Bruce McDonald, after the sudden collapse of Healey's Cave. And more important, he'd found his daughter, Beth, after she'd been kidnapped.

He locked his car and headed toward the building, skirting around vehicles and people. He brushed against the back of a policeman when several news reporters pushed past him. The officer swung his head around and stared.

"Er. Sorry." He smiled at the patrolman and kept going.

If they had any idea. If they knew I talked to Billy, traveled back in time with him... A lace dragged from his shoe, threatening to trip him. He stopped to tie it. *If they knew, they'd put me back in the asylum, just like they did when I was twelve.*

A chill stole over him. Memories of the day Billy disappeared assaulted him. Billy, on his brand new bicycle, driving down the road, never to return. Guilt coiled in his stomach. He'd answered a phone call from a damned girl, instead of following his brother on the bike ride like he'd promised. He'd never forgive himself for that.

That moment had been the end of life as he knew it, and the beginning of his tortured life to come. The insane asylum had been the worst, though. He hated to remember the way they talked to him, the stupid pills they'd made him take that doped him up, and the disgusting smell of antiseptic that had followed him everywhere, even seeped onto his pillowcase at night. He shuddered and tried to put it out of his mind. Best to forget it and see what the hell Lou wanted.

Chapter Two

Lou hailed him from the front steps. "Over here, Doctor Moore." She said it loud enough to discourage the eager journalists who craned their heads to see if he was anyone they cared about. When they realized he wasn't a detective, they lost interest and swarmed toward the police chief's car that just pulled in behind Sam's SUV.

Lou took his arm and steered him inside. The inn boasted antiques and wide plank floorboards. Inside the door, a pine bench with a stenciled backboard lined the wall; an old-fashioned pie cabinet anchored the opposite wall beside a mahogany sideboard, on which an essential oils diffuser sat, filling the air with the scent of balsam. Sam breathed it in, relieved it wasn't one of those chemical smelling, fake candles. It bolstered his spirits and reminded him of the deep woods in the Adirondacks. He was damned sure it smelled a hell of a lot better than what he'd find upstairs in the crime scene.

Mary and Alice Peterson, the inn owners and former patients of his, had been encouraging him to investigate the oils for years, and he'd meant to, but had been too swamped with patients to check them out. He'd always regretted that, and had resolved to do some research in his retirement that might help merge traditional approaches with those steeped in Eastern medicine. Time would tell if he could fit it in between the gardening, babysitting, and spending time with Rachel. She needed more care now that her MS had worsened, but he was up to the challenge. It was one of the reasons he'd retired a little early.

He shuffled after Lou. Tin chandeliers hung over a long trestle table, decorated with dried crabapples and fresh flowers. The twins reportedly served scrumptious breakfasts to guests at that table, and he'd been invited more than a few times to partake of their homemade breads, jams, and other goodies. Again, he'd had to decline his patients' generous invitations. There just hadn't been enough hours in the day to socialize and run his practice. But now that he was retired, he wanted to find time for more of that kind of thing.

A policeman sat in the corner, interviewing the hotel owners. Alice's hands shook when she took a pen from the officer to sign a statement, and her complexion seemed unusually pale. Sam wondered if her blood sugar was low. She'd been his patient forever. He started toward her with concern, but Lou grabbed his sleeve.

"Come on, it's this way."

"But Alice—"

"For crying out loud, you're retired now. She's not your patient anymore, Sam. It's not your job. Come on."

Sam dug in his heels. He shook his arm loose and spun around. "Alice. Are you feeling okay?"

Alice's face lit up. "Oh, Doc! I'm so glad you're here. It's awful. Just awful. A woman was killed in the Maple Nut room!"

Mary put an arm around her sister's shoulders. "She's shook up, Doc."

Sam felt her pulse. "I think she's more than shook up. Let's get her some orange juice. She needs something to get her sugar back up."

"I'm fine, Doc. Just a little light-headed."

When Mary brought the juice, he sat while she drank it, sputtering the whole time about not needing such a fuss made over her. He waited another ten minutes, making small talk, while Lou fumed. When he was sure she seemed stable, he turned to Lou. "Okay. I'm ready."

Lou blew up a lock of her gray bangs and made a face. "Geez, Sam. You'll never be able to leave it alone, will you?"

"It's not like I died when I retired. Alice has been my patient since I started my practice. I couldn't just walk past her, for God's sake. I'm not a monster." He followed Lou up the stairs to the second floor, ticked off now. Did being a coroner make you callous toward the living? He shook his head, mulling it over while they threaded around police, through a carpeted hallway, and into a room already marked with yellow tape. The room crawled with technicians.

Lou spoke through tight lips. "Just be careful not to touch anything."

Sam nodded and followed her across the suite, around a coffee table, past a fireplace, and into a bedroom.

"She's in the bathroom," Lou said. "You'll have to stand in the doorway to see. They're still taking photos of the blood spatter."

Blood spatter.

Sam's insides churned. There was a reason he didn't become an emergency room doctor. And blood spatter had a lot to do with it. He took a deep breath and forced himself to focus.

Inside the black and pink bathroom, a woman lay on her side, facing away. A three-foot long gray braid curled behind her on the floor, fastened at the top and bottom with elastic bands and fake daisies. She had been slim, and wore a silky Japanese dressing gown, covered with pink and black dragons that matched the floor tiles. Three technicians crowded around the body. Camera flashes blinded Sam as he tried to absorb the scene.

Lou whispered in his ear. "She was hit from behind with that phone."

An old-fashioned beige rotary phone perched on the edge of the tub. Red smudges stained its edges. Blood soiled the back of the woman's head and neck and splashed about the room on the walls and floor. A particularly large spot smeared the pink shower curtain. He felt sick and hoped he wouldn't lose it in front of all these professionals.

Lou leaned on his shoulder to look past him at the body. "Looks like it happened last night, sometime between midnight and four. We think she let him in, recognized him, since there was no sign of forced entry. The sisters didn't see anything. Lights are out at ten, but guests are free to admit family or friends whenever they like."

One well-toned leg extended back from her body, with toes pointed toward the sink. An anklet glistened in the light of the camera flashes. Four silver stars marched around her slim ankle, separated by black pearls.

A technician lifted the hem of the dead woman's gown to reveal a vivid pentagram tattoo, circled with black roses. The photographer shot it from all angles.

Sam caught a glimpse of painted pink toenails. One hand, nails unpolished, rested on the cold tile, as if the victim was ready to push herself into a sitting position. A bottle of nail polish had spilled on the floor by the tub.

"She never saw it coming," Lou said. The skinny, bald technician looked up and nodded as if he agreed, then went back to work dusting the edges of the phone and tub.

"Maybe we should let these gentlemen finish their jobs," Sam said. He backed up into the bedroom. "And I still don't get—"

Lou shushed him with steely eyes. "Wait. Just *wait a minute*, for God's sake."

She'd been testy with him since she called, and he was starting to get sick of it. He'd come here to help her. He'd much rather be in his garden, or better yet, having lunch with Rachel.

In ten minutes, the room cleared. One of the techs nodded to Lou on the way out. "She's all yours, Doc. Let us know if you need anything."

"Thanks." Lou shot him a grim smile and motioned for Sam to follow her to the nightstand.

"Look at this." She flipped through the white pages using the eraser end of a yellow pencil. "There. There it is. The book was opened to this page when they found her."

Sam stared at the circled entry. "Are you sure she did this?"

Lou shook her head. "No. But it's pretty damned likely."

The name and address circled shouted at him. *Dr. Samuel J. and Rachel S. Moore. 5125 Maple Beach Road. East Goodland, New York.*

Sam stared at the phone book, then glanced around the room. It was tidy, as if the occupant had just arrived. The suitcase lay unpacked and opened on a stand near the television. "Am I a suspect?"

"Hell, no. I just want to see if you knew her. I didn't exactly broadcast the information to the police." She gestured to the phone book. "I wanted to show you first. I'm not sure if they picked up on it."

"Thanks, Lou." The last thing he needed was to be part of a murder investigation. He thought back to last night. He didn't even have a good alibi—Rachel had fallen asleep early, and he'd read until he'd drifted off.

He leaned over and looked at the books on the nightstand. Standard fare. The newest Dean Koontz novel and a women's magazine.

"According to the detective, the ID she gave at the front desk comes up bogus in the system, and her purse is missing. If she carried one, that is. No wallet, no identifying papers." Lou's voice softened. "You ready to see if you recognize her?"

Sam squared his shoulders and nodded, feeling less confident than he sounded. "Sure. But what makes you think I'll know her? Maybe she was just looking for a local doctor."

They walked toward the bathroom. "Maybe." Lou led the way. She crouched beside the victim and carefully rolled her onto her back. "But take a look anyway."

Chapter Three

THE WOMAN LAY ON THE TILE FLOOR, HER LIMBS FROZEN IN AWKWARD positions since her body had been flipped. Her kimono fell back, revealing a pendulous breast. Sam averted his eyes, and Lou drew the gown together at the neckline.

"Sorry," Lou said.

"Are you saying that to me or her?"

She shrugged, but pain etched her face. Lou wasn't as hard boiled as she pretended to be.

"Both of you, I guess," she said.

Sam took a second look at the dead woman, then stared at her face. Memories pricked at him, urging him to remember. The long braid. The square jaw. The arched eyebrows. The pouty lips.

God damn it. He *knew* this woman. Or he had known her, years ago. Decades ago.

Something about the curve of her cheek niggled at his memory banks, pushing him back, back in time. He reached back, digging into his past. Why did she look so familiar?

He scanned her body again, this time taking in the chunky topaz ring on her right hand. With a start, he moved closer and studied it.

Good God.

He recognized the amber topaz. Remembered it flashing over his body as the woman had purred atop him and stroked him into oblivion. It had been a sexual nirvana, the hottest night of his young life.

Spring break. Senior year of medical school. Miami.

The weather had hung heavy with humidity, making breathing difficult and movement an instant sweat bath. His friends had met up with three willing coeds and pushed him into the arms of this girl the night they arrived. While his friends balled their brains out in their respective rooms, eliciting shrieks and ungodly screams from their nubile partners, Sam tried to get to know his "date." They'd talked about politics, music, organic foods, and books. She'd been interested in the occult and chatted animatedly about her Ouija board. He especially remembered her crystal green eyes.

I really was a nerd. So scared. So inexperienced. Especially for my age.

He glanced at the body, so completely different from his memories. The crow's feet that flanked her eyes, the large pores on her cheeks and nose, the ragged split in her bottom lip, the sagging pouch of skin under her chin. His eyes took in the rest. Knobby knuckles, indicative of arthritis.

Her eyes hadn't been closed. Sam wondered when they actually closed them for murder victims. Did they plant pennies on her lids? Was it after the legions of photos had blinded her already dead orbs? After ten men had crawled around her poor body and detailed every beautiful and ugly detail? After the whole official police and ambulance roster had drifted past the door, staring at the poor woman whose privacy, complete and quiet only hours ago, now had been violated like a frog's dissection in Biology 101? Sam sighed. The poor woman had wanted only to paint her fingernails pink.

Those eyes would never see sunlight again. Flat and dulled, even in the fluorescent light of the bathroom, they looked olive green, not pretty emerald like they had so many eons ago.

Raking back through memories, Sam recalled the episode. The previous six years, he'd focused only on school, hadn't had time for girls, and still ached over the loss of his little brother. There had been no women in his life. Only the ones who invaded his dreams and occasionally followed him into his mind in the shower stall. They'd been easy to appease, easy to dispatch, and easy to forget. The relationship, if you could call self-satisfaction such a thing, was perfect for him.

It wasn't that he didn't like real, live, hot-breathed girls who oozed sexuality and whose curves jostled him in the crowded hallways of the university. He liked them plenty. But he'd never quite recovered from the guilt he harbored after his brother's disappearance. He'd frozen into a social recluse, a boring study hog who bent over textbooks instead of pretty coeds. He'd used medical school as a convenient excuse to avoid most human contact. Until his friends had virtually forced the spring break vacation on him, that is.

Sam sat back on his heels, his eyes unfocused. What *was* her name?

He thought back to the moment they'd met. She'd giggled with her girlfriends, fooling around on the beach with a purple Frisbee. He remembered that long braid. It had been reddish then, copper-colored. Thick and lustrous, it tickled his skin when it flitted over his chest when she straddled him on the beach or in the hotel room.

She'd worn a lime green bikini. Silver flip-flops. And her bronzed legs had eagerly clamped around him when she dragged him into her bedroom at night. Her name came to him in a flash.

Ginger.

That was it. Ginger. Ginger. Ginger…Kennedy. He'd teased her about being related to the Kennedys, though she swore there was no connection.

The memories flooded him now. Three solid days of glorious sex. Sweaty, sultry nights on perspiration soaked sheets that smelled of lavender, the sea, and girl. Salt rimmed marguerītas. Running naked on the beach at two in the morning. Falling into the sand and coupling like randy wildcats. She'd nearly worn him out with her passion, and it had been…incredible.

He flushed as he remembered, embarrassed he'd been such a shallow hedonist, and even more embarrassed that he remembered it with such longing. Several years after the encounter, he'd met his dear Rachel. He'd fallen head over heels for her, married her, and they'd started their family. But it had been completely different from the tryst in Miami. Their relationship had been filled with a healthy dose of lovemaking, but it had been almost wholesome, based on mutual adoration.

Lou jolted him out of his reverie. "You know her, don't you?"

Sam nodded. "I do. I mean, I did." He stood and stretched his back. "It was years ago, when I was just a kid. I met her on spring break. Her name is Ginger Kennedy."

Lou stared at him. "And?"

Sam huffed. "And what? I knew her for a few days. We partied. No big deal."

Lou kept her eyes on him, pushing for more.

"So we had a brief fling. It was before I met Rachel. It didn't mean anything."

Lou raised her eyebrows and shot him a crooked smile. "Doctor Moore. I'm shocked. And we all thought you were the unapproachable celibate in med school."

Sam grimaced. "Right. I'm sure I was on every woman's mind back then."

Her expression grew serious. "You'd be surprised, Doctor." Lou's eyes flooded with something Sam hadn't seen before, or if he had, he hadn't recognized it as anything close to attraction. It made him squirm. He stopped breathing for a moment, then composed himself.

Her fingers fluttered as she covered with an embarrassed laugh. "Oh, hell. That was forty years ago. But there was a time, dear doctor, when I had it bad for you."

Sam stared at her. *"What?"*

She hurriedly covered her words. "Don't feel awkward about it. It was before I met Mel. A very long time ago, Sam."

He rubbed his lips with his hand and looked away. "Um. Okay. This is a little weird for me."

"Sorry, Sam. The last thing I want to do is make you uncomfortable." Her voice caught when she spoke the last few words, but she turned back to Ginger's body, and Sam couldn't be sure if it was his imagination.

"Okay, let's get back to business. Ginger Kennedy. Well, now that we know her name, the police can dig up more info on her." She cleared her throat and assumed her coroner demeanor. "I'll discuss it with Detective Marlin. He's just outside. You okay with me briefing him?"

Sam took a deep breath. "I guess so. I told Rachel about Ginger years ago. We don't have any secrets between us."

"Did you ever hear from her after your...er...tryst?"

Sam dropped into a chair, suddenly tired. "No. We never even pretended we'd write. I think she had a steady guy back home, maybe a fiancé. She mentioned him a few times, but implied she was having one last fling before she settled down. Of course, I was a hormone-crazed guy. I didn't question her ethics."

"Uh huh." Lou eyed him with a sardonic smile.

Sam almost blushed. "Come on. Don't tell me you never let loose on spring break."

She chuckled. "Oh, yeah. I sure did. I went hog friggin' wild. I worked double shifts at my dad's pharmacy and made eye contact with all the geriatric customers. Those were the days, I'll tell ya. Raunchy Bohemian parties where I covered the old geezers with Pepto Bismol and spoon-fed them Metamucil. I'll never forget it."

"I knew it. Wild times behind the drugstore counter. How exotic." He laughed, feeling more comfortable, especially now that the topic didn't include her awkward revelations about having a crush on him. Damn, that had been weird. He raised an eyebrow in her direction, gilding the lily. "And how *did* you manage to survive all those years living on the edge with wild senior citizens? Melvin sure settled you down, didn't he?"

Lou snorted, but covered her mouth before she could attract the attention of the men in the hallway.

"Settled *me* down? That party animal? I had to tame him like a wild beast. He still gets the urge to paint the town red on Friday nights. Kind of interferes with our pizza night for the kids, you know?" She chuckled. "You're killin' me, Sam. Come on. Let's get out of here. Can I buy you lunch? My treat."

Though lunch was the last thing on Sam's mind, he agreed. "I've got to call Rachel and let her know what's up."

Lou linked arms with him for the second time that day. "Sure. Give her a buzz so she won't worry."

Sam gently disengaged his arm, turning in the opposite direction to phone his wife. After a brief conversation, he returned to Lou's side. "How about Clara's?"

She grinned. "Best burgers in town. Come on, you drive. My ride's gonna be tied up for a while."

He noticed the old fashioned black coroner's van backed up to the side door of the inn when he'd arrived. "Oh. Right. Well, then, let's go."

The marble pulsed again in Sam's pocket, warming his thigh. He covered it with his hand to hide the green glow.

Not now, Billy. Not now.

Chapter Four

The parking lot at Clara's was packed. When they entered, Sam was assaulted with the aroma of french fries and bacon; coffee and hamburgers. He liked the cozy feel of the place, with an unpretentious staff, friendly owners, and the homey feel of the fifties-style interior. Gray vinyl stools hugged the counter, and booths with jukebox controls lined the broad windows. Farmers, local businessmen, store clerks, students, professors, mothers and babies, and a large contingent of seniors filled the booths and crowded along the counter. Lou grabbed the only empty stools and waved hello to the waitress.

He watched the new girl balance heavy plates on one arm while juggling mugs of coffee. A bead of sweat rolled down her temple and she rubbed it away with her arm, but kept moving. Sam's heart went out to her. His daughter Beth had waited tables at Denny's during college. She'd worked nights and gone to school during the day. It had been a rough shift, with drunks and partiers coming in for sober-up coffee. She'd come home with blisters on her feet, aches in her shoulders from the heavy trays she carried, and very little cash.

Sam shrugged out of his coat, took Lou's jacket, and backtracked to the coat rack by the door to hang them up. A chubby two-year-old boy escaped from his mother and ran directly in front of him. Sam skidded to a stop just in time, held up his hands as if in defense, and laughed.

"Oh, I'm sorry!" A petite redhead scooped the boy up in her arms. "Jordan's always doing this." She nuzzled him on his belly, elicited peals of giggles, and took him back to the booth.

"It's quite all right." Sam laughed and rejoined Lou at the counter. He swung onto the stool and motioned toward the waitress. "Who's the new girl? And where's Hattie?"

"Not sure about the new gal. But Hattie's taking a leave of absence to help her daughter with triplets."

He turned to Lou with raised eyebrows. "Seriously?"

Lou nodded, studying the specials scribbled on the white board. "Seriously. Annie just had three little boys. Out in Minnesota. So

Hattie's gone for a couple of months. They're still in the neonatal intensive care unit, but Annie's gotta heal from the C-section. She needs her mom's help."

Sam picked up a menu, but he knew what he wanted. The waitress swished past in her pink uniform and deposited a plate of bacon and fried eggs in front of a beefy farmer dressed in overalls and a John Deere baseball cap who sat two stools down.

Sam caught a glimpse of the nametag on her uniform. *Lacey.*

She called to them over her shoulder. "Be right with you folks." After refilling coffee for the elderly couple at the end of the counter, she stopped and whisked out an order pad. "What'll ya have?"

Lou didn't hesitate. She squinted as if she'd forgotten her glasses and peered at the white board. "A bowl of tomato soup and a grilled swiss on rye."

"And to drink?" Lacey asked.

"Coffee's fine."

Lacey scribbled a bit on the pad, then turned to Sam. "And you, sir?"

"I'll have the turkey and bacon club on marble rye. Extra mayo. An order of sweet potato fries. And a large milk."

"Want that rye toasted?"

Sam nodded. "Please."

"Okay. Back in a flash." Lacey slid the pencil behind her ear and whisked off to the kitchen.

Sam watched her work, impressed with her efficiency. In her early forties, she wore her black hair shorn like a boy's; short enough that Sam wondered if maybe she'd undergone chemo recently. Her pale brown eyes shifted quickly from customer to customer as she wiped tables, took orders, and delivered meals with expertise. She didn't miss a beat.

"She seems to know what she's doing," Sam said as she disappeared into the kitchen with a tray full of dirty dishes.

Lou nodded. "Guess so. I—"

A loud crash sounded from the kitchen in the back. All heads swiveled in the direction of splintered dishes. A few shards of china flew out the swinging door and clattered against the wall.

Expletives shot from the kitchen. Sam caught a glimpse of a red-faced Lacey, hands gesturing wildly in the air. "I can't friggin' believe it!"

Clara, the owner of the diner, raised her voice above the din. "Lacey! For goodness sakes! The customers can hear you."

Every head turned, every ear cocked, and all eyes widened in surprise.

"*Please* don't fire me. I really need this job." Lacey's voice changed from hot fury to tearful wheedling. Sam couldn't hear what Clara said in response, but a minute later, he heard the sounds of someone sweeping glass and china shards into a dustpan. Lacey finally emerged, her cheeks flushed red and lips compressed. She set their drinks on the counter.

"Thanks," Sam and Lou muttered at once.

Lacey nodded, brushing at her eyes. "You're welcome."

"You okay, honey?" Lou asked.

Lacey tried to shrug it off, but the tension remained in the muscles around her mouth. "I'll be fine. Just have to be more careful is all."

Distinctly subdued, Lacey went about her work while they dug into their lunch. When she refilled Lou's coffee, she ripped the bill off her pad and laid it down. "Whenever you're ready."

Lou reached over to touch the back of her hand. "Listen, honey. I know it's hard when you start a new job. I used to run the counter at my father's pharmacy. Broke a lot of dishes."

Lacey grimaced. "It's coming out of my check this week. Twenty bucks at least. I don't know how I'll manage."

Her voice cracked. Sam exchanged a glance with Lou, who knew what he was about to do and nodded before he did it. "Listen. We don't want your first week in Conaroga to be like this. Let us pay for the dishes."

He laid a ten and a five on the counter, followed by Lou who slapped down another ten.

"I'm Sam, and this is Lou. I used to be a doctor, and she's the county coroner. Will you let us help you?"

Lacey's eyes flitted back and forth between them as if she didn't think they were serious. "But...why would you do that? You don't even *know* me." A few tears spilled down her cheeks.

Lou held up a hand to stop her. "Now, honey. It's not too hard to understand. Sam and me here, we just want special treatment. When we come in, we want coffee. Lots of hot coffee." She winked at Clara, who watched from the kitchen door.

"I..." Lacey dabbed at her eyes. "Thank you. But I insist on paying you back. I swear, I will."

Sam waved a hand in the air. "No, no. It's a done deal. Just consider it a welcome from the hungry citizens of Conaroga. We both come here a lot, me with my wife, and the coroner here with her husband and brood of five kids."

Lacey's eyebrows rose in twin arcs. She sniffed and straightened her shoulders. "Oh. I thought you two were married."

Lou snorted. "Hell, no. I wouldn't marry a guy like Sam if you paid me. All he wants to do is dig in the dirt all day. Give me my nice old teddy bear, Mel, any day. I always know where he'll be. Right in front of the T.V. set."

Relieved that Lou had reverted to her usual bantering instead of confessing long lost affection, he slapped down another twenty on the bill to cover the lunch. "Same here. My wife's at home and she's expecting me, matter of fact. We've gotta get a move on."

"Er. Thanks, you two. I still don't hardly know what to say." Lacey took off her apron and handed her order pad and pencil to a Sandy, a blue-haired lady who appeared from the kitchen. "My shifts over, but I'll watch for you folks. You can count on it."

After Lacey left, Lou vented about her job and nursed her third cup of coffee until Sam thought he'd go nuts. Finally, she pushed back and swung off the stool, jabbing him in the side with her elbow. "Geez, Sam. I thought you'd *never* finish. Come on, I've got work to do."

They headed for Sam's Toyota and got inside. Two rows over, Lacey sat in a rusty Honda Civic with a missing bumper and cracked side window. She leaned over the steering wheel, slamming her fists against it and sobbing. Sam was about to get out to see if she needed help, when the Honda's engine roared to life and the vehicle flew past them.

They stared as she skidded out of the driveway and watched her car huff and puff down Main Street, leaving a plume of black smoke.

Lou's mouth hung open. "Wow. Lacey's got some real issues."

Sam took a left on Main Street and merged with the light traffic. "Or real problems."

Lou shook her head. "Think she takes drugs?"

"I don't think so. She seemed pretty clear-headed before she dropped those dishes." Sam put on the blinker and waited for the light to switch to green. "Or maybe she just needs someone to listen. Poor thing."

"Judging by her car, she needs to win the lottery."

"Or get some damn good tips. It's hard to make tips on the breakfast shift. The meals are so cheap to start with."

Lou cracked her window open. "If she lets loose like that again, Clara will fire her ass. She doesn't put up with any crapola."

When they arrived back at the inn, Sam pulled up as close as he could to the still mobbed building. Murder was a rare commodity in this quiet farming community, and the news hounds were hungry for more blood.

Sam shifted into park, but left the engine running. "Thanks for calling today."

"No problem, Sam. But don't get too comfortable. If they pick up on your name circled in the phone book, they might need to question you and Rachel."

Sam's eyebrows shot up. "You really think so?"

"Don't worry. I'm sure they won't think of you as a suspect. They *know* you. But just for the record, they'll probably need a statement."

He relaxed. "Okay. I'll warn Rachel not to panic if the men in blue show up at the door."

Lou chuckled, and her eyes softened. She brushed a lock of hair back from her eyes and rested a hand on Sam's arm. Her fingers lingered a little too long for comfort and stroked his flesh. "Say hi to her for me, Sam." She squeezed his arm. "I don't know how you do it, big guy. It's gotta be so hard on you."

Her eyes flooded with empathy, but it rubbed him the wrong way. He didn't *need* sympathy. Most people didn't realize how ridiculously happy he and Rachel were, in spite of Rachel's disability. It wasn't hard on him, it was hard on Rachel. She was the one who suffered every single day when the rest of the world whirled about her, going to work, driving their cars, jogging down the street. She'd had many losses over the years, one by one. And it was only getting worse.

He couldn't smile back at Lou. His face felt wooden. "It's not 'hard' on me, Lou. I'm luckiest damned guy in the world. She's my whole life." *And get your hand off my arm. What the hell are you doing batting your eyelashes at me, for crying out loud?*

Lou's smile faltered when he pulled his arm back abruptly. "Oh, crap. I'm sorry, Sam. I didn't mean any harm." She jumped out of the SUV and closed the door with an embarrassed wave.

Sam backed around the driveway and pushed away the feelings of uneasiness that churned in his stomach and threatened to choke him. This bouncing back and forth between professional camaraderie and...whatever was getting to him.

What was she thinking? I'm a married man. And she's married, too. With five kids and a bunch of grandkids. She's losing it.

He headed home for the comfort of his well-established life and ignored the feeling of the marble pulsing against his leg.

Chapter Five

When Sam got home, he hurried into the living room, scooted up behind Rachel's chair, and bent over her shoulder to hug her from behind. "Hi, baby." He rubbed the back of his hand across her soft cheek.

"What was that for?" She set aside the strand of cane she'd been weaving into the seat of the antique chair and peered at him over her reading glasses. Her soft gray bangs had grown too long, and she'd brushed them to the side.

Walking around to the front, he moved her caning project aside and crouched in front of her. "I missed you."

She laughed and put her glasses into the case. "You missed me? You left just a few hours ago, you silly man."

His smile faded. "I know. But a lot happened since then."

Her expression changed from a gentle chiding smile to concern. She motioned to Sam's favorite leather armchair. "Honey, what happened? Sit here, dear. Talk to me."

He plopped onto the chair and sighed. "Damn. I didn't expect the morning to turn out like this." He fidgeted and cleared his throat. How could he tell her about the dead woman who'd circled their names in the phone book? But more importantly, how could he tell her Lou had practically made a pass at him? Good old Lou. College buddy Lou. Professional colleague Lou.

Damn.

Rachel stared at him. "Like what? Was it that body Lou asked you to look at?" She maneuvered her chair even closer.

In a sudden wave, his hesitation dissipated, evaporating like drops of rain on a sizzling tarmac. He turned to look into her chocolate brown eyes. He reached for her hand. "Yeah. I recognized the dead woman."

A hand shot to Rachel's mouth. "Who was it?"

"Someone from my past, actually."

One eyebrow shot up. "What past? You didn't have much of a life before you married me." She reached over to take his chin in one of her hands and gently squeezed. "Did you, Dr. Moore?"

"Well. There were a few years before you, my dear. Do you remember my confession about spring break, senior year in med school?"

"Oh, my God. How could I forget? She was the woman in the bikini who rocked your world before I stole your heart, wasn't she?" She smiled mischievously and chuckled.

He snorted. "Yeah. You remember me telling you about her?"

"Hot and sultry evenings in Miami on the beach. Your first real experience with a woman. Totally sensuous and totally meaningless. At first I was so jealous I thought I'd permanently turn green. But as the years passed and she never showed up, I figured I was safe."

He squeezed her hand. "You'd have been safe even if she'd shown up in that skimpy green bikini with a cold margarita in her hand. There's no one for me but you, hon."

Rachel smiled with her eyes. "Aw, Sammy. You are a prince among men." She leaned in for a kiss. "What was it like, seeing her now, after all these years?"

He pushed on the chair arms and back, forcing the footrest to move up and out. With legs stretched out all the way now, he kicked off his shoes and sighed. "It was absolutely bizarre. At first I had an inkling of knowing her, like brief flashes of memory that came so quick I couldn't catch them."

"Oh, I know exactly what you mean. Like your brain is teasing you about a memory, but won't let you see it?"

"Yes! Exactly. I saw her long gray braid. That was the first clue."

"She was a redhead back then, right?"

"Uh huh. And there was something about the curve of her cheek, the way her lips looked. It niggled at me, drove me nuts."

"I'd be jealous again if she wasn't dead. When did it finally hit you?"

"When I saw her ring."

"Really? Was it a diamond?"

"No. A chunky topaz. She'd had it on when I knew her, and for some reason, that ring was the thing that opened up the floodgates. I remembered it all, in one big whoosh."

"So, Ginger Kennedy came home to roost. So to speak."

Sam looked at her with surprise. "You remember her *name*?"

A sly smile appeared. "Why, yes. I remember everything you told me about her, and probably made up more stuff in my mind over the years. I love to hate her. At least her memory."

Sam slapped his thigh. "By golly, woman. You amaze me."

"'By golly?' I haven't heard that expression since my grandfather died when I was twenty-two. What are you, turning into an old geezer?"

He started to smile, but it withered when he thought of Lou. "Uh. Sometimes I feel like one. But…"

She leaned forward. "But what?"

"Something else happened."

"On top of seeing the dead body of your first lover?"

"Er. Yeah."

"Well, don't keep me wondering, honey. Spill it."

Sam put his footrest down and sat up straighter. His eyes closed, then opened. "It was Lou."

"What? Does she have cancer or something? You look positively gray."

He shook his head. "No, no. She's fine. It's just what she said to me." He sighed, then let the words rush out in one huge breath. "She told me she used to have a crush on me in med school."

Rachel's jaw dropped. "Huh?"

He met her eyes with a level stare. "Yep. That's what she said."

"Maybe she was kidding with you."

"No. She wasn't kidding, because she laid her damned hand on my arm and didn't take it off. For way too long. Made me insane."

Her jaw tightened and her eyes shot steel. "You've got to be kidding. She made a *pass* at you?"

"Yes. In a way. It wasn't so obvious, but it made me so damned uncomfortable. It was brutal. I couldn't wait to shake her off me."

"What did you *do*? Did you tell her to leave my husband alone?"

Sam leaned over and took Rachel's hands in his. "I did. I told her I was supremely happy with you in no uncertain terms. She seemed pretty subdued when I left. I'm sure I got my point across."

Rachel huffed. "Good. That witch has a husband and five children, for God's sake! What in the world was she thinking?"

Sam shrugged. "God only knows."

She looked into the distance with a furrowed brow. "Come to think of it, I did overhear something about her in the supermarket yesterday."

Sam looked up, startled. "You did?"

"Uh huh. Something about Mel filing for divorce. Rumors about a younger woman."

Sam pushed up from his chair. "Damn. If it's true, Mel's an absolute idiot."

"I know. And I think I did see him with a pretty little brunette. Driving past in his new red sports car. I didn't connect it at the time, thought maybe it was one of his daughters. But I'll bet..."

Sam shook his head in disgust. "Poor Lou."

"Maybe that's why she acted so out of character today, honey. If it's true, she's in the middle of a major trauma. And she could be reaching out to her past, trying to comfort herself with memories of other men in her life."

Sam put out a hand as if to ward off the idea. "She was never in my life, Rach. She was just a fellow underclassman in med school. A girl in my study group. That's it."

Rachel rolled up to Sam and took his hand, holding it against her cheek. "Oh, honey. I know. I'm not worried. You're mine. For keeps, remember?"

Sam crouched down before her and looked into her dark eyes, remembering their wedding. Rachel had worn a simple white dress, with few adornments. With her gorgeous dark hair framing her pretty oval face, her creamy skin lustrous in the light of the church candles, she had needed no accoutrements. And after they both read their handwritten vows, they'd grabbed each other's hands and said, "For keeps." It had been spontaneous. And it had felt so right.

"I remember, honey."

She released his hand and sat up straighter. "Good. Now that we have that settled, I need you to pick some veggies for dinner."

"Okay. What do you need?"

"I'm making scalloped ham and potatoes. So dig me up a dozen, sweet little yellow potatoes that I can slice in their skins. And some beets. Cukes. Tomatoes. And yellow squash."

"Is that all?" Sam laughed. "Planning a feast, are we? Who's coming for dinner?"

She chuckled and wheeled into the kitchen. "Beth's bringing the baby over. And she's got a new friend she wants us to meet."

"I knew it! Okay. I'll get out there and start digging. How long do I have?"

She pulled a cookbook from the low shelves Sam had designed for her when she'd been forced to use the wheelchair due to her weakened legs. She pulled her glasses case from her pocket and put them on again. "You can play in the dirt for a few hours before I need them, hon. I'm going to make a chocolate cake first."

"Sounds good." He smiled, already giving in to the lure of the outdoors. His mind worked overtime, listing the chores he could accomplish in two sun-drenched hours.

"Shoo. Go on. I've got work to do here." She flashed him a smile, then bent over her cookbook.

"Okay. Be back around two-thirty."

He grabbed his black Velcro back brace from the hook by the door and slid into it as he hurried outside.

Chapter Six

Sam put all thoughts of past lovers and amorous coroners out of his head. The garden called to him, luring him to the earth filled with abundant early August produce. A breeze rustled the cottonwoods overhead, calming him and ruffling the hair on his brow.

In the barn, he grabbed his favorite double-headed weeding tool, with a spade on one end and a fork on the other. He hefted it and looked toward the rows of onions with purpose. The thickly clustered weeds were about to meet their destiny. Something had to be done. The golden globes they nearly obscured would be harvested in a few weeks.

He passed the swing set he'd erected for his grandsons and noticed Lila trotting out from the woods to greet him. She emitted a sharp mew, then wove around his ankles. He leaned over to pat her soft white fur, stroking her back and encircling her tail in his fingers as he swept them up to the tip, over and over again. She rubbed her head against his hand, purring as if she'd just discovered a saucer of cream.

"You like that, don't ya, girl?"

The cat rose on both hind feet and tapped his arm with her forefeet, crying again.

"Okay. You win. Come on up."

He held his arms out and she leapt into them, jumping to his shoulders and rubbing her face against his. He chuckled and let her wind from shoulder to shoulder.

"Okay, okay. Come on now. I've got work to do." He leaned over, urging her to jump down. She landed lightly on her feet and immediately began to wash up.

Sam chuckled. "Was I that dirty?"

Lila ignored him this time, and started to work on her face, licking her paw, then rubbing her whiskers.

He walked on the soft soil between the kale and potatoes, then ducked under an archway festooned with morning glory vines to enter the main garden surrounded by a post and board fence with bushes and trees crowding the perimeter. A strong pulse thrummed against his leg.

The marble.

He'd ignored Billy all day. Hurrying now, he turned left and walked along the strip of mowed lawn that surrounded the massive plot of fruits and vegetables. This "secret garden," as his grandson Evan called it, was safe from prying eyes. Nobody could see him sweating when he raked along the rows of beans or bent over the beet plants to pluck them from the soft earth. He liked it that way.

He hung his tool on the top board of the wooden plank fence. The strong sun beat on his hair and face. Alone now, and free to scratch ungentlemanly places or just sit and think, Sam sank onto the soft grass near the fence. He leaned back against the cushion of riotous morning glories, willing Billy to come to him.

He reached into his pocket and took out the cat's eye. It glowed jade green, pulsing and warming in his hand. He studied it, seeing his own reflection. Where would Billy take him today? To their past, when they were children? Would he talk to him this time, treat Sam to a ghostly visit? Or would he whisk Sam to the seashore, mountains, or their old bedroom they'd shared as boys?

In a flash, a wave of green smoke engulfed him, wrapping him in an ethereal mist that twisted seamlessly away from the present. The garden faded, and Sam woke in a dark room.

He wasn't exactly *in* the room. He floated above it, somewhere near the ceiling. Just like the dozens of excursions Billy took him on in the past through the marble's magic, once again he was pinned somewhere between the present and past, hovering on the edge of time.

Below him sat a dark haired child—a girl dressed in pink leotards and a ratty purple sweatshirt. She had to be at least two. Maybe three. Her large brown eyes were filled with fright. And she was crying buckets.

She shrieked through tears, calling for her parents, battering her fists against a wooden door. Tangled hair covered half her face. Sam's heart clenched, and he wanted to scoop up the poor little girl in his arms and take her to safety.

Through a high opened window came sounds of chanting. Screams. Singing. Scents of woodsmoke. Incense. Many voices. Guttural and shrill. A medley of almost unholy sounds. He wanted to float toward the window to look outside, but Billy wouldn't allow it.

The child wept again, calling for the parents who had deserted her.

Sam wanted to comfort her, reach out to her. Yet he remained glued within a green web that pushed him back against the ceiling, immobilizing him. He strained and pulled against the green force, helpless. The little girl finally gave up and curled onto a blanket in the corner of the room. Her shoulders heaved while she cried herself to sleep.

With a final wrench, Sam tried once more to free himself. Instead, he was propelled back to his garden in a sudden thrust through time and space.

He woke on his side, face pressed against the grass. The rich scent of soil and flowers assailed him, as if he'd never smelled them before. They swirled within him, brightening his spirit and squeezing his heart in a strange twist of passion. With heightened senses, he sat up and tried to collect himself. What in the world had happened?

Who was the girl? And why had Billy tried so hard all day to put him in this scene? The marble had pulsed three times today before he'd finally been able to give in and be transported.

And what *the hell* had been going on outside that window?

It had sounded like a ceremony of some kind, but with an uncomfortable twist. There had been a wildness to it, a sense of barbarism or...savagery. It was hard to pin down, but the whole thing made him shudder.

And why was the poor child abandoned in that room? Without a bed, a toy, or even a teddy bear. It clearly wasn't her bedroom or home. There had been very little furniture. A wooden table. A warped chest of drawers with a rotting doily under a thick leather book. No lit lamp. Just the moonlight streaming through the single window. It looked more like an abandoned cabin than a home. So why was the child left alone there? Had her parents been outside?

With a deep sigh, Sam tabled his concern for the little girl. Billy would show him more when the time was right. For now, he couldn't help her. He didn't know where she lived, what her name was, or anything about her. For all he knew, it could be in California, Russia, or 1932. Time and location were subject to no rules where Billy was concerned.

He stood and grabbed his weeding tool. It was time to get to work.

℘℘

The memory of the child in the locked room haunted Sam as he sat in the sun on his garden scooter and pulled stubborn weeds from three rows of onions. After he'd freed the onions from their stranglehold, he dug warm potatoes from the earth. The basket piled high with spuds before he realized he'd probably unearthed three dozen, far more than Rachel requested.

Shaking off his worries about the child, he next focused on the beets. Two wide rows of Lutz beets stretched forty feet, billowing with eighteen-inch high greens that arched over the walkways separating the rows. The red roots jammed too close to each other, growing huge even in early August. This particular variety, dubbed "long season beets," grew to massive size, yet retained their candied sweetness whether harvested small in July or monstrous in November.

Sam poked around the row, pulling the largest to make room for their struggling neighbors. He always planted the beets close together, thinning the row as the season progressed. He and Rachel had tasted the first buttery sweet beets on July Fourth this year.

When he'd pulled six hefty samples, he wandered back to the secret garden, where black plastic covered a third of the eighty-foot long patch. Originally home to their two horses, the garden offered rich soil from which all plants burst with vigor. Three-foot high bushes with elephant-ear-sized leaves shaded the squash proliferating beneath. Sam stepped high to avoid trampling the vines. Leaning over to brush aside the prickly leaves, he ignored the overgrown fruits and chose a tender selection of Middle Eastern squash, the cousa variety. His particular favorite was a light green-skinned beauty named Ghada. He selected four prime specimens.

The temperature had moderated this week, down from the nineties the previous week that melted everyone and everything. Today, with the highs reaching only eighty, he felt human again, and ready to work.

He picked a long European cucumber and slid his fingers down its length, dislodging the tiny, sharp barbs. After he set it next to the overfilled basket, he walked toward the tomato patch, choosing the ripest of the red and yellow fruits. Anticipating dinner with Beth, he chose a number of grape tomatoes, her favorites. A vision of her as a ten-year-old flashed across his mind. Copper-colored pigtails. Pretty sundress. Eyes alive with questions. Popping cherry tomatoes into her mouth as she followed him around the garden and chatted like a magpie.

Beth's own baby girl, born in April, had created a fresh stir of excitement in the family. Isabel was their third grandchild, after his son Andrew and Maryellen's two boys, Evan and Timmy. Rachel's tired eyes sparkled anew with this precious addition in spite of the less-than-perfect circumstances of the child's conception. There was no daddy in the picture, only a lab that provided anonymous sperm donations. But Beth had thrived. She'd moved in with Rachel and Sam for the first three months of her daughter's life, and had just recently rented a cottage on Conesus Lake, only two miles from the farmhouse. Tiny, but immaculate, it served her purpose. She'd always loved water, and claimed the lapping sound of the lake on the shore lulled her and the baby to sleep at night.

Beth hadn't dated since she moved home from New York City to take a job at her advertising firm's Rochester office. She'd dutifully cared for her child, working in the evenings from home while Isabel slept. Thankful that her job allowed telecommuting, she had progressed into a workable schedule where she went into the office Monday through Wednesday, when Sam and his daughter-in-law shared baby-sitting duties. Beth worked from home on Thursday and

Friday, and managed to satisfy her duties during baby Isabel's frequent naps and in the evening.

After delivering the veggies inside to Rachel, Sam offered to help, but was shooed outside again. He sat beside the long rows of beans and religiously pulled weeds until he spotted Maryellen's van rumbling up the gravel driveway.

Chapter Seven

Evan burst from the van and raced toward Sam; his grin stretched from ear to ear. "Gramps!" He threw his arms around Sam's middle and hugged him.

Sam ruffled his hair and hugged him back, swinging him from side to side. "Hey, pal. What's up?"

"I hit a home run, Gramps. Can you believe it?" The boy's eyes shone. At almost twelve years old, baseball had taken over his life. That is, baseball and keeping track of his father's movements in Baghdad via satellite phone and email. Andrew Moore was due home from the war in two weeks, and every day the event grew closer, the family's nerves grew more frazzled. He'd made it through two tours of duty, and if he could just keep safe for a couple more weeks, Evan and Timmy would finally have their father back.

"I'm so sorry I missed it, buddy. Your dad would be so proud. Wouldn't you know, the one game I don't make."

"It's okay. I'll try to do it again next time you come."

The boy was amazing. He was actually trying to make Sam feel better. "I know you will, champ. Today was just the first of many. Wait'll you make the major leagues." Sam was rewarded with a brilliant smile.

"You think so? You think I'm good enough?"

"You bet I do."

Sam wrapped his arm around his grandson's shoulders and headed toward the van. Timmy tumbled out with his mother close behind. He pumped his three-year-old legs as fast as he could.

"Papa!" The boy barreled into Sam, attaching himself to his leg. "I'm Spiderman!"

The boy released Sam and pointed to the front of his red tee shirt with Spiderman emblazoned across the front. "I gonna get da bad guys!"

Sam scooped up the child, surprised at how heavy he'd become. The kid was solid. When Andrew returned home, he'd be shocked at how much he'd grown.

"You are, are you?" Sam laughed.

Maryellen reached his side and ran her hands over Timmy's hair. "Look what your grandson did, Sam. He found my scissors and tried to give himself a haircut."

"I cut my hair!" Timmy shrieked. His eyes shone with pride.

Sam looked closer, and spotted three areas where the boy had almost scalped himself. He tried not to smile. "Oh, my. You sure did. Wait'll your daddy sees it."

Timmy beamed at him. "Daddy come home soon."

Sam kissed the boy's soft peaches 'n cream cheek. "I know, buddy. Isn't it great?"

Maryellen grimaced. "I don't know if I should buzz it, or just let it grow out."

Sam chuckled. "It's not that bad. I didn't even notice it at first. Why don't you just let it grow out?"

Beth's red Toyota Corolla turned into the driveway. All heads swiveled to watch her park.

"Here. Let me take him." Maryellen held out her arms for Timmy and they headed for Beth's car.

Evan trotted beside Sam, with an expectant expression. "Can I hold the baby again, Gramps?"

Sam smiled down at him and nodded. "Sure you can, champ." The boy had become a surprisingly attentive cousin, and Isabel adored him.

Beth had unbuckled Isabel from her car seat by the time they arrived at her side. Evan grabbed the baby bag and hoisted it to his shoulder, leaning in to make a silly face at Isabel.

"Thanks, Ev," Beth said. She sat Isabel on her hip as the baby gurgled and smiled at Evan.

"Where's your friend?" Sam asked, ducking down to look in the car and finding no one.

"Held up at work," Beth said, sounding disappointed. "But she might make it after dinner."

Sam shifted attention to his granddaughter, running the back of his hand along her soft cheek. "You're getting prettier every day."

Her eyes had morphed from muddy dark blue to bright cerulean. He almost said, "Where did she get that blond hair and blue eyes?" but stopped himself. He wondered again about the donor, and who he'd been. Was he one of the many medical students who needed extra cash? Would he end up being a doctor, like Sam? He knew the speculation was a waste of time, but he couldn't help but muse about Isabel's biological father.

Sam and Rachel both had dark hair. Rachel's brown eyes and his hazel eyes had somehow produced an olive green set for Beth. Her copper-colored hair had skipped a generation, inherited from Sam's mother. But there had been no blue eyes for several generations on either side of the family. Of course, Timmy had also inherited his red hair from Sam's mom, and his blue eyes from Maryellen. He shelved the trivial thoughts and held out his arms. There were more important issues at hand. "Give me my granddaughter."

"She's a little wet." Beth smiled ruefully at her father. "You sure you want her?"

Sam chuckled and took the baby in his arms. He shifted her so the wet spot wouldn't soak him, and kissed the top of her head, inhaling the scent of baby shampoo. "That never stopped me before. Come on inside, we'll get her changed."

Sam and Rachel kept a bureau full of baby girl clothes in the spare bedroom, next to the crib that Timmy had outgrown this year. All three grandkids stayed overnight frequently in the bedroom that used to be Beth's.

Beth pecked her father on the cheek. "I'm starving. What are we having?"

"Your mother's been cooking all afternoon. I'll let her tell you." Surrounded by the babble of comforting family chatter, Sam ambled with the family into the house.

Rachel sat across the dining room table from Sam. He watched her tired eyes crinkle with joy when Evan scraped the last of the scalloped ham and potatoes from the Pyrex dish.

"Gram. These are *so* good!"

They had demolished the meal, including the casserole, Harvard beets, Parmesan zucchini, tomato and cucumber salsa, and chocolate cake. Much to Maryellen's chagrin and Rachel's delight, after two pieces of cake, Evan had come back for more ham and potatoes.

Rachel sank into her wheelchair, as if all the energy she'd summoned for the feast had blown out of her body like air let out of a balloon. "Thank you, honey. They're made with your grandfather's potatoes. That's the secret." She winked at Sam and tried to smile, but the muscles in her face didn't quite cooperate.

Sam worried—he knew she'd pushed past her usual energy reserve. The multiple sclerosis was ruthless in the afternoons, when her body's natural steroid production was at its lowest level. Usually she lay down for a few hours before dinner, and retired shortly after they'd done the dishes together.

He caught Rachel's eyes and motioned upstairs, mouthing the words, *you ready to go up?*

She nodded and released a sigh, leaning over to grab hold of Isabel's pudgy hand. "Gramma's gonna say good night, baby girl."

Isabel sat in the antique wooden high chair that used to be Sam's. With her free hand, she grabbed the spoonful of applesauce Beth held and flung the contents skyward. Baby food spattered the wall on the opposite side of the room and dripped from Timmy's forehead.

Timmy reached up to smear the mess on his face, then broke into a huge smile. In a millisecond, he reached for leftover squash on his plate and shot it across the table. It landed on Evan's baseball shirt. With a horrified moan, Maryellen was after him in a flash. "No, Timmy. We don't throw food!"

The boy's smile cracked, and he began to howl. The sobs were more like shrieks, filling the entire room with sound. Isabel's face fell, and her mouth flew open as she prepared to join the fray. High-pitched screams punctuated Timmy's crying as he flung himself on the floor and began to pound it with his fists and feet. Evan wiped the zucchini from his shirt, trying to hide his disgust. "Geez, Timmy."

Beth whisked Isabel from her high chair just as the doorbell rang. Timmy and Isabel quieted suddenly, but started up again, louder than before. Beth looked from the door to Isabel to her parents with a horrified expression.

"Oh my God. She's here."

Rachel wheeled backwards, as if to head for the door.

"Hold on there, hon. I've got it." Sam jumped from his seat and hurried to the door, expecting to greet Beth's new girlfriend. His nerves jumped when he pulled open the door and looked into the apologetic eyes of Officer Ned Olsen.

"Sorry to trouble you, Sam. Hope this isn't a bad time?"

Ned stood tall and scrawny in a uniform that hung like a tent on his body. He looked toward the dining room, where baby wails continued to erupt, and held out one bony hand. Sam clasped it and ushered his old classmate inside.

"No, it's fine. Come on in. We're just finishing dinner. Sorry for the noise, but the grandkids sort of fell apart a minute ago."

Beth hurried to the door with the wailing Isabel in her arms, but her expression of anticipation faded quickly when she realized the visitor was Ned. "Oh. Hi, Mr. Olsen. Um. Sorry, I was expecting someone else." She colored and retreated into the dining room, bouncing and shushing her daughter.

Sam guided Ned to the living room, and motioned to one of the overstuffed chairs in the corner.

"Let me get Rachel upstairs first. I'll be back in a second. Want some cake and coffee?"

Ned's expression brightened. "Sure. That would be great. Thanks."

Sam hurried back to the noisy dining room and leaned down to whisper in Rachel's ear. "Come on. Let me get you upstairs. Ned's here. Probably wants to talk about Ginger. You ready?"

She nodded. Maryellen yelled over her wailing son. "Dad? We're gonna fly. Timmy's overtired, and..."

Sam motioned for her to go. "Don't worry about a thing, honey. Get the boys home and I'll clean up later. See you tomorrow?"

Maryellen repositioned Timmy under her arm like a football, grabbed her purse, and collared Evan on her way out. "Thanks, Dad. Mom. Love you guys."

By the time Sam had settled Rachel into the bedroom, Beth had quieted Isabel and sat discreetly nursing her in the dining room with her cell phone clamped to her ear. He flashed a tired smile in her direction on his way to the kitchen, and grabbed a piece of cake and two cups of coffee. On his way back, she wiggled her fingers in the air and laughed at the person on the other end of the line, her face alive with delight.

Must be the new girlfriend. Hope she's better than the last one. He tried not to think of the woman who looked like an Egyptian princess and who'd won their hearts, and subsequently almost annihilated the President of the United States when he'd visited their little town of Conaroga to celebrate the opening of a new arts center. Zafina had been a pro—she'd wooed and won Beth's heart, wormed her way into their family, and used their home as a launching pad for her own terrorist activities. The woman had been crafty and gorgeous. Her feline eyes and fluid movements had almost caught him in their snare. Thankfully, he'd resisted and stopped her cold.[1]

Sam shook off the unpleasant memories and eased into the living room, careful not to spill coffee on Rachel's new oriental rug.

"Okay, Ned. Here we go. Now tell me what brings you out to our neck of the woods."

---

[1] *Terror Comes Knocking* (February 2012)

Chapter Eight

Ned accepted the cake and coffee from Sam, his eyes bulging with desire. Sam knew the officer's appearance had something to do with a thyroid problem, but they seemed to pop even more when he caught sight of the fudge cake with the gooey frosting.

He accepted the plate and mug with a huge smile. "Damn, that looks good." He took a giant bite from the oversized wedge and crammed it in his mouth. "Mmm. Delicious. You were so freakin' lucky to marry a great cook."

Sam couldn't help but agree. Poor Ned had always looked like he needed a decent meal, even in elementary school. Although he married a girl the entire football team considered "a catch," his pretty cheerleader wife had been attractive, but hadn't had much in the brains department. Apparently they'd been compatible, though, since they were still married and had produced seven children and a tribe of grandkids. Ned also belonged to Sam's church choir, and sang in a smooth baritone voice.

Sam pulled himself back to the conversation. "Yeah. I was lucky in a lot of respects. Rachel's gorgeous, she cooks the best food in the county, she keeps me laughing, and she gave me two beautiful kids."

Ned mumbled through his cake. "Speaking of the kids, how are they doing?"

"Andy's in Iraq. Due to come home soon. For good. Of course his boys are dying to see him. It's been hard on them."

"And you?" Ned asked. He took a swig of coffee and attacked the cake again. "Isn't it hard on you?"

"Yeah. It's been tough. Rachel and I are praying he makes it through the last few weeks without incident. Every time we see film clips on the news about the latest suicide or roadside bomber, we're scared to death. It's especially rough on Rachel."

"I can bet. How about Beth? How're she and the baby doing?"

Sam didn't believe in keeping his daughter's preference for women a secret. He wanted to be able to talk to his friends about it without worrying who "knew" and who didn't. His daughter liked women better than men. Big deal. It was a simple fact of life. Ned already knew about last year's fiasco with the woman who broke Beth's heart. "She's a wonderful mother, Ned. We're real proud of her. And I'm in love with my little Isabel. She's so pretty, she looks like a little china doll. Except when she poops, then it's clear she's a real baby." He chuckled, realizing he shouldn't have mentioned bodily functions when Ned was enjoying a chocolate cake.

Ned didn't miss a beat and seemed not to care. "Ha. Yeah. I hear ya. My first few grandkids were real stinkers."

"How many do you have now?"

Ned wiped his mouth with a napkin, then counted on his fingers. "Let's see. There's little Ned, Annie, Sophie, Lucretia, Sylvie, and now we have little Gerald. So that makes six." Ned gobbled the rest of the cake and looked longingly at his empty plate.

Sam gestured toward the kitchen. "Want another?"

With a sigh of regret, the officer shook his head. "No. Better not. Cholesterol." He drained his coffee cup and assumed a more official expression. "So. How're things?"

Sam sighed. "Jeepers crow, Ned. Are you gonna tell me why the hell you're here tonight or do I have to drag it out of you?"

Ned set his plate and cup on the glass-topped coffee table and apologized. "Sorry. You probably know why I'm here."

Sam grunted and folded his arms across his chest. "Is this about Ginger Kennedy?"

Ned settled back in the chair and stretched his legs. "Yup. Lou told me you knew the victim."

Sam rolled his eyes. "A long time ago, Ned. A *lifetime* ago."

"She said you'd met on spring break or something like that?" Ned's expression was carefully neutral.

Sam suspected that Lou had spilled the beans about the nature of his relationship with Ginger. The whole thing was ridiculous.

He slammed a hand on the armrest. "God in Heaven! We had a fling. Forty damned years ago."

Ned didn't blink.

Sam leaned forward. "Did Lou tell you?"

Ned looked relieved that he wouldn't have to pretend not to know. "Sorry, Sam. She told me...everything." He pulled a notepad out of his pocket and began to scribble notes. "So. You haven't heard from Ms. Kennedy since then?"

"No." Sam closed his eyes and shook his head, wondering who else Lou told about his past.

Ned stopped scribbling. "Any idea why she'd come all the way up here to see you?"

Sam frowned. "All the way from where? And what makes you so sure she came here to see me?"

"From Utah. That's where she's lived for the past thirty years, I guess. And I just figured she *must've* come to see you, since your name was circled in the phone book."

Sam batted the air with a hand. "I'm not so sure, Ned. Maybe she just needed a doctor."

"Too coincidental, Sam. We think she came here to pay you a visit."

"We? Who's 'we'?"

Ned didn't answer.

Sam huffed and got up. "But, why? After all these years, why?"

The officer shrugged his shoulders. "Looks like she was broke. At the end of her rope. Lost her house and car, just claimed bankruptcy, according to the info we dug up today."

Sam sighed. What a sad ending for the vital woman from his past. "That's awful, Ned. But what's it got to do with me?"

Ned leaned forward. "Maybe she was going to ask you for a loan. You know, for old times' sake?"

Sam's patience wore thin. "Hell, Ned. I knew the woman for *three* lousy days. We didn't exactly have that kind of relationship. I was a kid, we rolled around in the hay for a few days in a drunken haze, and that was that. Fini. Over. Never heard from her again, and never wanted to."

Ned's eyes narrowed. "What about blackmail?"

Sam looked at Ned as if he'd just sprouted purple hair. "Blackmail? Are you nuts? What would she blackmail me over? The fact that we had a hot affair decades ago?"

The marble pulsed in Sam's pocket. He jumped and reached to cover the anticipated flash of green, hoping Ned didn't notice. What was Billy trying to tell him? *Was* this nutcase woman from his past intending to blackmail him?

"Maybe. Maybe she thought you'd kept the affair hidden from your wife and wouldn't want her to know."

"That's rubbish. I didn't even know Rachel then."

"Yeah, but maybe *she* didn't know that. Apparently she had a fiancé at the time. Maybe she figured you did, too. And she knew you were a medical student, so maybe she thought you'd be rich by now."

Sam snorted. "Right. Like being a country doctor would have made me rich. I would've been a plastic surgeon if I wanted yachts, castles in Spain, and a Ferrari. Today Rachel and I are lucky to pay all the bills and keep the Highlander going."

Ned's expression didn't change.

"Geez, Ned. There's a hell of a lot of speculation going on in your head. What's the matter; are you having trouble finding suspects?"

The officer sobered. He stuttered, and his face darkened to the color of old bricks. "Um. Well, er. We don't exactly have any leads at the moment. We were hoping you could give us something to go on."

"There's that 'we' again. Have you been discussing my sordid past as a med student with the whole damned department?"

"No, honest. Just me and the Chief. And Lou, of course."

Sam rubbed his fingers across his lips. *Damn Lou.* "Tell me the truth. Do you suspect me?"

Ned forced a laugh, but it didn't make Sam feel any better. "No! No, of course we don't." He'd lowered his eyes, but looked up at Sam again. "I take it you were probably home with Rachel all night?"

Nice way to lead into my alibi. "Of course I was. Just like every other night of my life for the past gazillion years. We ate dinner at five, did the dishes, let the cat out, went up to bed to watch a little TV. It was some God-awful Lifetime movie Rachel wanted to see. I was bored to tears. We turned it off at ten. Read for a while. And fell asleep around ten-thirty. Real exciting, huh? Wild night life of the rich, retired doctor."

"Sorry. I didn't mean to interrogate you, man. It's just we *are* getting kind of desperate. We've got nothing to go on. And the town supervisor's putting pressure on the Chief. And that means the Chief's on my back all day long. He's riding me hard, Sam."

Sam stood and rubbed his hands on his pants as if to rid himself of the subject. "Hey, I understand. Sorry I can't help you guys. But like I said, I haven't seen this woman since I was a med student. I'm as clueless as you are."

Ned took the hint and got up. He slid the notebook back into his pocket and headed for the door. Halfway there, he turned. "If you think of anything, will you give me a buzz?"

Sam followed him to the door and opened it. "Of course. But don't pin your hopes on it. I barely remember her," he lied.

No reason I should share my amorous memories with the whole Conaroga police department. Word would spread like wildfire, then be talked up by the cops' wives in the supermarket, and maybe even get back to Rachel. Even though she knew what happened with Ginger, she wouldn't want the gossips to stare at her every time they passed her on the sidewalk.

Ned smiled and touched his fingers to an imaginary cap. "Hey, thanks for the cake. And I'm real sorry to have bothered you at dinnertime. Maybe something will come up and we can put this one to bed."

Sam winced. The word "bed" made him see Ginger all over again in her youthful glory. He pushed the salacious thoughts from his mind and tried not to compare the images to the woman he'd seen dead on the pink and black bathroom floor. "I hope you do."

On his way to his cruiser, Ned called over his shoulder. "See you in choir practice, Sam."

Sam grimaced. "Yeah. Okay. 'Night." The last thing he wanted to think about now was standing beside Ned, singing "Rock of Ages," especially knowing Ned was well aware of his wild affair with the murdered woman. He needed to get his head straight, erase the image of Ginger from his memory banks, and get on with his life.

That is if Billy would let him.

Chapter Nine

DAD? WHAT'S WRONG?" BETH SNAPPED HER CELL PHONE SHUT AND BUTtoned her blouse when Sam entered the dining room. Isabel lay in the portable bassinette on the table, eyes closed and lips pursed in total satisfaction.

He brushed away his irritation and peered down at his granddaughter. "Nothing, honey. Ned just had to ask me about that woman who died at the Twin Sisters last night."

She rose, fidgeting with the baby's diaper bag. "Right. Mom mentioned it. An old girlfriend?" Her eyes avoided Sam's.

Sam sighed. "Oh, Beth. Not you, too."

"What?" Her eyes widened, but she couldn't hide her concern.

"Listen. This woman was part of my distant past. A very small part. It all happened three years before I even met your mother, and five years before you looked just like this." He stroked the blond fuzz on Isabel's head. "I only knew her for three days. She wasn't what you'd call a girlfriend, exactly."

"Oh?" Beth's guarded expression told Sam she wasn't convinced.

"For crying out loud, honey. We had a very brief relationship. On spring break."

Her eyebrows rose. "Spring break? Oh. *That* kind of relationship." She paused and shot a quizzical glance at him. "I'm sorry, Dad. I just can't picture you like that. You've always been the perfect example of...decency. So devoted to Mom."

Sam grimaced. Here he was, years after one indiscreet weekend, trying to explain his behavior to his grown daughter. It galled and burned him at the same time. "Honey, I was twenty-something then. A fool. I had no damned judgment. You know how men are at that age."

She chuckled. "I guess. Not first hand, though."

Sam smiled at her joke, then cupped her chin in his hands and looked directly in her eyes. "You *know* I'm devoted to your mother. I've never looked at another woman since I fell for her. Never wanted to, never did. She's the only one for me. And if I lost her, I wouldn't remarry. No one could take your mother's place. Nobody."

Beth tried on a smile, but it didn't quite fit. "I'm sorry, Dad. I know. It was just weird hearing about your past that way. I know you love Mom."

Sam held out his arms. She melted into his embrace and laid her head on his chest, while he stroked her deep copper hair, just like he had when she was a little girl. He remembered the tough times when she'd lost a swim meet as a teen or fallen from her horse in front of all her friends at a horse show. He'd always made her feel better, and afterwards they'd go for hot butterscotch sundaes at Friendly's.

Isabel stirred and whimpered in her sleep. The peepers began singing outside, their songs punctuated by a chorus of crickets in the background. The voile curtains in the window blew gently against the evening breeze.

Sam stepped back and held her at arm's length. "So, what happened to your friend tonight? When do we get to meet this mystery lady?"

Beth sighed. "I'm sorry about that. She was on call, and wouldn't you know it, they needed her."

"On call? What does she do?"

Beth giggled. "She's a doctor, Dad. An obstetrician. Her name's Penelope. I call her Nel. Or Nellie. She grew up in Maine."

Sam cocked an eyebrow. "Really? A doctor? Now why would you want to date one of those strange creatures?"

She laughed and ran the back of her hand against his bristly cheek. "I don't know. I guess I must've met a few doctors along the way I admire."

They hugged again, and finally separated when Isabel stirred and started to fuss. Before she picked up her daughter, Beth searched Sam's eyes with hers.

"I love you, Dad."

Sam answered with his usual response. "I know, honey. But I love you more."

ꟃ

It was after eight when Sam finally dried the last of the dishes. He filled two plastic tumblers with ice water and grabbed a cheese stick for Rachel. She loved the swirled variety made from yellow and white cheddar.

He shut off the porch light, turned the nightlight on under the kitchen cabinets, flicked off the overhead switch, and headed for the stairs. Lila had come back inside when Beth and the baby left, and streaked up the stairs ahead of him.

His legs felt wooden tonight, and he grunted with each step. "Getting old. Geez, I'm pathetic." When he made it to the top, he turned left down the hall, filled up the tumblers with water from the bathroom tap, and found Rachel lying down with her glasses on and a book propped on his pillow.

"Did you remember my—"

"Cheese stick?" Sam said, wiggling it in the air.

"Ha! Thank you, sweetums." Rachel sat up while Sam fluffed her pillows and discreetly moved his own back to his side of the bed.

She peeled back the plastic wrapper with anticipation, then slowly stripped skinny strings of cheese from the stick, making it last as long as possible. "Mmm. This is so good. Thanks, Sammy."

He grinned. "My pleasure, m'dear." He changed into his shorts and tee shirt and tossed his jeans and work shirt on a nearby chair. "So, what's on the tube tonight?"

Rachel dangled one of the curly cheese bits over her mouth and let it slowly descend. She mumbled, "*Love Comes Softly*. Remember we saw that a few years ago? It's a Michael Landon movie. About the young couple who travel by covered wagon, and the horse gets loose, and—"

Sam rubbed his hands together. "Right. I remember! That was a good one. I liked the frontier stuff. A lot more than those Lifetime movies."

She jabbed him in the ribs. "Sam!"

He reached for the remote and slid under the covers, wiggling his legs to get comfortable. "What channel?"

Before she could answer, the phone rang.

Sam rolled his eyes. "Holy Mother of God. What *now*?"

Rachel reached for the phone beside the bed and shushed him as she picked it up. "Hello?"

Sam watched her, hoping it wasn't her friend Emma. She had a tendency to call just as they were starting a movie, and liked to gab for hours. Or so it seemed to Sam, who usually waited, fuming in the bed beside his wife.

"Yes. He's here. Just a moment."

She covered the receiver. "It's Louise."

Sam blanched. Why the hell would she call him this late at night? He took the phone from Rachel, frowning. "Lou? What's up?"

She sounded strange. Croaky. Like she'd been crying. "Sam. Sorry to bother you so late. I just wanted to know if you had plans for breakfast. There's something I need to tell you, and I'd rather not do it over the phone."

Sam hesitated. "Is it about the murder?"

Lou didn't skip a beat. "No. It's personal. I owe you an apology, and I wanted to explain."

"You mean for spilling the beans to Ned about the nature of my relationship with Ginger?"

"Er. No. I mean, yes. That, too. I'm sorry, Sam. They just kept asking me a million questions and it kind of...slipped out."

Sam didn't hide his irritation. "It's probably all over town by now."

"I'm really sorry. But please, this has nothing to do with the murder. I just need a friend right now, and I thought maybe you'd have a few minutes to—"

"Hold on a second, Lou."

He covered the receiver and rolled his eyes. "She wants me to have breakfast with her tomorrow. Something she needs to tell me. Do you think I should—"

Rachel waved a hand at him as if shooing a fly. "Sure. Go. It's not like she's going to jump your bones or anything." She snorted and flashed a mischievous smile. "Go on. Go back to Clara's. There's not much can happen there."

Sam hesitated, then capitulated and uncovered the phone. "Okay. How about Clara's? Eight o'clock?"

Lou agreed in a rush. "Great. I'll see you at eight. And please tell Rachel I'm sorry for disturbing you at home."

"Okay. G'night." Sam couldn't hang up fast enough.

"Good night. And thanks, Sam. Thanks a lot."

Rachel took the phone from Sam and set it back on the base. "There."

He looked at her like a wounded puppy. "Rach?"

"Don't worry about it, honey. She'll probably tell you about Mel's betrayal, and that will be all. I'm sure she's embarrassed about how she acted today."

He snuggled close to her and put his head on her shoulder. The natural, familiar scent of her comforted him. He reached his arm over her chest and hugged her. "I'm one lucky man."

"Damn right you are, Doctor Moore. Now put that TV on HBO and find our program."

He aimed the clicker at the television and chuckled. "Yes, ma'am." When the program started, he lost himself in the world of hardship, loss, and love. And thanked God he'd never had to mourn the loss of his soul mate, like the woman in the show. He was lucky, all right. So lucky it scared him.

Chapter Ten

Sam settled himself into a booth at Clara's the next morning and waited for Lou. When she arrived, she walked toward him with a trembling smile. Her bedraggled hair looked as if she'd been stuck in a windstorm for hours.

She nervously raked her hands through it, tossed her purse onto the seat, and slid into the booth. "Sorry I'm late."

Purple smudges rimmed her reddened eyes. A spot of coffee stained her blouse, which wasn't tucked in all the way and bunched up on the side. The blouse looked familiar, and although he rarely noticed what people wore, Sam idly wondered if she'd slept in yesterday's clothes.

"Lou? What the hell happened to you?"

She grimaced and smoothed her sleeves with shaking hands. "That obvious, huh?"

He nodded. "Yeah. You look like you've been on a bender."

Lacey approached the table with order pad in hand. She smacked her gum, covered a huge yawn, and resumed chewing. Today she wore a brown silky uniform with a black apron.

"Sorry. Up late last night. What'll ya have?"

Sam answered first. "Just coffee, please."

"Me too." Lou said.

"No breakfast?" Lacey said. "We've got some killer blueberry muffins back there today."

Sam put up a hand. "Okay. Fine. We'll have two muffins."

"Good. You'll both need your strength today."

Sam did a double take. "What?"

Lacey smiled. "Just kidding. We all need a good breakfast to start the day, don't we, Doctor?" She swished away to another table before he could respond.

Her cavalier attitude bothered him. Yesterday she'd been sincere and scared of losing her job. Today she smacked gum and acted too casual. And she didn't even acknowledge the fact that they'd contributed to her hurting finances. "Weird," he mumbled, shaking his head. "How'd she know I was a doctor?"

Lou picked up a menu, but her eyes glazed over. "Everybody knows you around here, Sam. I'm sure Clara told her."

His tense shoulders fell a fraction of an inch. "Yeah. I guess. But before she comes back and interrupts again, tell me what *the hell* is going on."

Lou lowered her voice and glanced around to see if anyone was listening. "I guess I'd better just spit it out."

Sam resisted the impulse to tap his fingers on the tabletop.

She hesitated, dug in her purse for a tissue, and sat back in the booth like a sand-filled doll who'd just sprung a leak and was deflating fast. "Okay. Here goes." She dabbed at her eyes and took a deep breath. "Mel's leaving me."

Sam sat back and let his jaw drop. It wouldn't do to let her know he wasn't surprised, not one bit, and that the ladies in the grocery store had already been gossiping about her private hell. "No way in hell!"

Tears pooled in her eyes and she hiccupped. "I'm dead serious. He's got a little chippie on the side. A brunette. She's only thirty-three, Sam. Thirty-freakin-three years old." Bitterness crept into her words like poison spreading in a bowl of broth.

Sam sat still while Lacey slid the coffee and muffins onto the table. He waited until she was out of earshot. "Mel's an ass."

She sniffled and nodded. "Yeah."

"I hope you've kicked him out."

"I did. Last night. He packed his things and took off. Went to her place, I think."

"Damn."

"Yeah." She tried to collect herself, sniffled a few times, and finally drew in a deep breath. "Anyway, the reason I asked you here was to apologize. I knew about it yesterday, and I don't know why, but seeing you so solid and dependable…and remembering how you were in med school…I just got a little sentimental, I guess."

He stiffened. "Sentimental?"

She nodded. "Yeah. Stupid and sentimental. Like I said, I had a monster crush on you in med school. And I sort of started fantasizing about you after I found out about Mel. It made me feel less...rejected, I guess. In my own crazy mind. I kinda lost it."

The look she gave him made him nervous again. It contradicted her words and seemed to say, *couldn't we give it a try?* She seemed desperate, her eyes beseeched him.

He sat up straight and squared his shoulders. "You know I'm married, Lou. That's crazy talk." He didn't soften the blow and delivered it with a no-nonsense tone he wanted her to read loud and clear.

She barked a nervous laugh. "I know. I'm being ridiculous. I'm sorry. Stupid of me. I'm just not myself this morning." Her hands shook when she lifted a napkin to her lips.

"It's okay. You're under a lot of stress." He stared at the table. Anywhere was better than looking into her pleading eyes. After adding two creamers to his coffee, he poured in some sugar and stirred. "Muffins look pretty good."

She tried to smile and took a sip of black coffee. "I guess." Picking at her muffin, she barely dislodged a crumb. "You know, Sam. I appreciate your friendship. There aren't a lot of folks from our generation who haven't wimped out and moved to Florida." She reached over to cover Sam's hand with hers. "We tough, old birds have to stick together."

Lacey paused on her way back to the kitchen with a tray of dirty dishes on her shoulder. "You folks okay?"

Sam nodded, wrenching his hand away from Lou's to cradle his coffee cup with both hands. "We're good. Thanks, Lacey." But he wasn't fine. Far from it. Lou was driving him bonkers.

Lacey smiled and headed for the kitchen. "Be back with refills in a bit."

"Thanks," Sam called to her retreating back. He raised his eyes to Lou's and felt a pang of sympathy. Damn. She was such a wreck. "You really should eat."

She swiped at her eyes. "I guess you're right. I didn't eat anything last night, just paced around the house and smashed things. I didn't even notice what I had on this morning. Just slept in these smelly old clothes, and when I got up I headed over here..."

Sam's patience thinned. He hurried to finish his muffin and downed the last of his coffee. He wanted to get home to Rachel and the garden. And the marble had been pulsing against his thigh for the past few minutes. "Yeah, probably a good idea to get some food in your stomach and go home. Take a nice hot shower and maybe a nap, too. Better yet, call one of your daughters and have her come over." He stood abruptly, slapped a five on the table, then dug out seventy-five cents for the tip. "I've gotta run. If you need anything, feel free to call Rachel and me. Maybe you could stop by for dinner one of these nights? She's a great cook, you know." His mouth had just taken over and started blabbering. He really didn't want this woman at his dinner table.

Lou seemed to deflate a little. She shot him a half-smile. "Thanks, Sam. I'll let you know how things go. Maybe we can do dinner next week."

More nervous now than before, he tentatively patted her on the shoulder, pulled his hand away quickly, and pushed the money closer to his empty plate. "Sounds good. Hang in there." He squared his shoulders and made a beeline for the exit.

By the time Sam pulled into his driveway, swirls of green sparkled around his face, nearly obstructing his vision. The marble seared his thigh, urging him toward the other realm before he'd had a chance to throw it into park and step on the parking brake. He hurried to the barn and into the old horse stall that had been Cricket's. Before he could choose a comfortable spot, his vision blurred green and he collapsed on the straw-covered floor.

"Sam. Wake up."

Sam stretched his young legs and rolled over in bed. His throat burned, and he still smelled the ether they'd used to knock him out for his tonsillectomy. Billy's voice sounded funny, as if he were hearing it through water. He tried to open his eyes, but they wouldn't cooperate.

"Sammy. Come on. Wake up. I have a present for you."

Sam heard his mother shush Billy. "Leave him be, Billy. He's just come out of the recovery room."

His father's deep and gentle voice rumbled about the price of hospital parking. Someone sat on the edge of his bed. Billy, he thought.

"Are you okay?" his little brother asked. "I was worried about you."

Sam rolled over again, facing the shifting shape that had to be his brother. He struggled to open his eyes all the way, and finally managed to keep them open. The bright hospital light seared his brain and nausea overcame him.

"I'm gonna be sick," he mumbled, throwing his head over the side of the bed and retching.

"My stars and bananas," his mother said, eyeing the mess. "Go get the nurse, Billy. Tell her we need a sick bucket."

Billy backed toward the door. "Gross!"

Sam's head swam. The walls buckled, zooming in and out. He broke into a cold sweat, and started shaking. He moaned and lay back on the bed.

"It's okay, son. Just relax now. It's just the ether. Everyone gets sick afterwards."

Sam closed his eyes and tried to picture the images he'd cultivated before the operation. The wide open plains. A big pinto horse, trotting beneath him. In his vision, he wore the complete cowboy outfit, from the chaps and boots to the ten-gallon hat. Cattle lowed around him, pushing through the dust as the sun bore down on them. The image shifted and shimmied as his nausea returned.

Billy hurried into the room as his mother finished mopping the linoleum with brown paper towels from the bathroom. Sam noticed three other beds in the room, one in each corner. Kids in various stages of recovery occupied each one. He vaguely remembered talking to the freckle-faced boy across from him before surgery. His name was Toby. Or Tommy. Or Todd. Anyway, the kid was going to think about the circus before his operation. That was his plan. He seemed to be out cold, with one arm thrown over the side of the bed. His surgery had been scheduled just after Sam's. He wondered how much Toby-Tommy-Todd had thrown up.

Billy must've run down the length of the corridor. He panted and hung on the side of the bed, warily eyeing the wet patch on the floor. "Here you go. It's to throw up in."

"Thanks." Sam cradled the metal basin in his arms and swallowed to keep the bile down.

"I got you something." Billy's hazel eyes lit up with excitement and he waved a roughly wrapped package in front of Sam's face. "Open it."

"Can't. Too tired. Do it for me."

"Okay." He beamed at Sam and ripped into the package, brandishing a new baseball glove. "Here ya go. I even oiled it for you."

Sam reached a shaky hand toward the glove. The smell of the leather was intoxicating, and helped a little to push the ether smell out of his nostrils. "Wow. Thanks. It's really keen." The effort of talking wore him out, and he strained to keep his eyes open.

The back and forth experience was a wobbly mishmash between his sixty-two-year-old brain and his eight-year-old viewpoint. He watched from afar, yet felt curiously integrated into his boyhood body. Sam clearly remembered having his tonsils out. It had been rotten for a few days after the surgery, but the next week in bed was bliss. Unlimited ice cream and ginger ale. Heaven. They'd even rolled the television into his bedroom during the day. He'd watched *Howdy Doody, Father Knows Best, The Lone Ranger,* and *Rex Trailer* until his head ached.

Billy hopped onto the bed again and put one hand on his brother's arm. "Don't you worry, Sam. I'm gonna take care of ya. Whatever you want, I'll get it. Mom says you can eat ice cream and drink soda all day. Won't that be great?" He looked at his mother for confirmation. She nodded and smiled. "See? I'm gonna take real good care of you. Don't you worry, okay?"

The words reverberated in his head, over and over again, as if Billy meant them in a much deeper sense than they were originally intended.

Don't worry. I'll take care of you.

His brother's face wavered, with eyes and forehead bulging and receding, then disappearing all together. The hospital room faded, and Sam was propelled through steamy green fog back to the present. He awoke on the floor of the stall, with Billy's words ringing loudly in his head. He picked a strand of straw out of his hair and sat up.

Don't worry. I'll take care of you.

The words clanged over and over again. Worry about *what? And why in God's name will you need to take care of me, little brother?*

Chapter Eleven

In the living room, Rachel peered at Sam over her reading glasses and laid down her copy of *Hunted*, by S.W. Vaughn. Sam glanced at the unique cover that featured a girl with glowing eyes. He'd have to ask her about it later, but now the radio played Rachel's favorite show—a classical music program called "Noteworthy" with local music professor Gus LeGarde.

"How'd it go, sweetie?"

Sam slumped against the doorframe. "Pretty much like you said it would. But it's still damned uncomfortable."

"Oh, poor baby," she said, patting the sofa beside her. "Come listen with me. Japanese Melodies, by Camille Saint-Saëns. They're so pretty."

Reluctantly, he shuffled to the couch and dropped beside her. "Okay. Maybe for a little while." Sam's usual tastes ran to Ella Fitzgerald's crooning and Duke Ellington's band. But he tried to maintain an open mind as he slid close to her and slipped an arm around her shoulders. She snuggled into him and closed her eyes.

The cello and piano duet invaded the room, soothing and saddening Sam at the same time. The music glided into his heart, plucked at his emotions, and tantalized him. The piece Professor LeGarde analyzed was particularly evocative, with searing melodies that sounded mildly Japanese and Spanish at the same time. Sam imagined a Japanese tea garden with a flamenco dancer poised on an ornate bridge. The next time he saw Gus in Wegmans, he'd have to thank him.

When it was over, Rachel clicked off the radio with the remote and sighed, almost as if she were about to burst into tears. They sat for a few minutes in silence.

He finally broke the spell. "Wow. You were right."

"Thanks for letting me hear the rest of my program, honey." She sat up and smoothed back her hair. "Okay, tell me more. What exactly did Lou say?"

He laced her fingers in his. "She told me Mel was leaving her. She kicked him out last night."

She straightened and turned toward him. "I was right!"

"Yeah. And she was a wreck. Messy hair, eyes red from crying. She had on the same clothes as yesterday, wrinkled and stained."

"Not like your usual prim and polished county coroner, huh?"

Sam shook his head. "Far from it."

"So, you still felt awkward?" Her eyes asked the real question—*did she come on to you?*

"Oh, yeah. Plenty awkward. She said she was sorry for yesterday, that this whole thing brewing with Mel had set her off on a pretty nutty track. Said she was..."

"What?"

Sam flushed. "Fantasizing about getting together with me." His voice trailed off to a soft whisper, as if he was afraid someone might hear. "But then she turned right around and apologized again for the idiocy of it. But the problem was not what she said; it was how she looked at me."

Rachel closed her eyes and laid her head on his shoulder. "Tell me. I can take it."

"I'm hoping you can," he chuckled, "'cause I sure can't. Made me squirm in my seat. She kept looking at me like she was pleading for something. Touched my hand again, but talked about our 'friendship' being important to her."

"The poor woman. She's not only got it bad for you, she's lost her mind, too. She'd never have acted so unprofessional in the past, would she?"

"Hell, no. We always kidded around whenever we crossed paths in the business. You know, when I'd be called into court to testify about someone's health or on the rare occasion she needed a second opinion. Or at charity dinners. But it was always in good taste, and like she was just one of the guys. You know, like Garcia."

"Dr. Garcia is certainly not 'one of the guys', Sam. She's a beautiful woman. But I'm glad you saw her that way, since you spent two years training her before you handed over your practice to her."

He leaned closer. "It was *easy* with Garcia. She loves her husband and talked about him all the time."

"She's a peach."

"Yeah. But this morning, I couldn't get away fast enough, especially with that new waitress watching our every move as if we were having some kind of secret affair."

Rachel's mouth twisted. "Not very likely."

"As mad as I feel toward her, Rach, I'm a little worried. When I finally left her, I picked up on a sense of desperation. Like Lou was lost. Disconnected from reality." He took one of his wife's soft hands. "And I wondered—just for a split second—if she would hurt herself."

Rachel sat up and stared into Sam's eyes. "Sammy. You don't think she would, do you?"

"I don't know. But when I told her, in no uncertain terms, that I was a happily married man, and that she was talking crazy, she kind of...um...deflated."

Rachel frowned. "You didn't let her down too gently, then?"

Sam studied his fingernails. "Not exactly. She made me so nervous I just told her straight out."

Rachel's eyes shifted from pride to concern. "Maybe we'd better check on her, honey. Or call someone?"

Sam blanked. "What about her daughters?"

"Good idea. I think the oldest girl works at the nursing home. What was her name?" She looked off in the distance as if retrieving the memory. "Oh, right. Nancy. And she married that Morrison boy."

"Okay. I'll look up the number for you."

After several unsuccessful attempts to reach Nancy Morrison, they gave up.

Rachel set the phone on the coffee table and sighed. "Maybe you should call Lou in a little while. You know, check up on her."

Sam's insides slumped. He knew she was right, but dreaded another encounter. "I guess. Or *you* could call."

That one earned him a disapproving scowl. "Sammy. She's your friend. A call from me could upset her. She might think I was trying to protect my turf."

He snorted. "Your turf? Is that what I am?"

She chuckled and tickled his stomach. "Yes. With nice soft grass, right up here." She ran her hands through his thick gray hair, earning a smile from him. "Come on. Be a big boy now. I know this is hard for you, but it's the right thing to do."

Sam wrapped his arms around Rachel and hugged her close. "You are something else. Always reminding me why I married you in the first place."

"Why? My great sense of civic duty?" she mumbled against his chest.

He nuzzled her neck and lifted her chin to kiss her lips. "Well, yeah. That and your chocolate cake."

"Still no answer?" Rachel wheeled back from the dishwasher and closed the door. "How many times have you tried?"

Sam grimaced. "Five. Once every hour since lunch."

She glanced at the clock. "It's dinner time. Maybe she went out and will be home soon."

"She's got no one to cook for anymore, so she might be avoiding it. Maybe she's with one of her daughters?"

Rachel rolled to the phone. "Let me try Nancy again. She should be home soon."

She dialed and frowned, leaving a short message. "Darn."

Sam looked at her and at the stove, where a maple-glazed ham and a bubbling casserole of zucchini squash, tomatoes, onions, and cheese simmered.

"Okay. Let's eat first. Then I think we ought to take a drive over there."

"We?" Sam said.

"Sure. I'll wait in the car while you check on her."

His expression fell. "Oh. Okay. Well, that's better than going over alone. I'll just tell her you're waiting for me, and it won't be so bad."

Dinner was quiet as they both let their thoughts roam. Rachel surprised Sam with a pan of walnut brownies, smothered in vanilla ice cream and hot fudge sauce. He had two helpings, and wasn't sure if it was due to procrastination or gluttony.

"Let me do the dishes tonight, honey. You've cooked up a storm today."

Rachel's face was wan, her eyes tired. She hated to let Sam help in the kitchen. "Okay. I'll just sit here and keep you company."

Sam started to rinse the dinner plates and glasses. "You sure you're not too tired to come with me?"

"I'm beat, but I don't want you to face this alone. I can get comfortable in the car and bring my CDs. It'll be nice."

"How about your pillow and blanket? We can get you really comfy."

She laughed. "I'll probably pass out if you do that."

"Ha! Okay. Almost done here. Just one more pan. Want me to freeze the brownies or just keep them out?"

She thought about it for a minute. "Leave them out. They're Andy's favorite, and he'll be here in three days."

"I doubt if there will be any left, honey. You know how much I love them." He dried the last pan. "Okay. Done. Let's go."

Rachel used her cane to get to the car, with Sam's assistance. When he had her settled in the front with a quilt, pillow, and her favorite music, they set out for Lou's.

"Do you remember which one it is?" Sam asked. All the houses in Indian Meadows looked alike to him now. So many new homes had been added in the past twenty years. The newer models were high scale, with fancier fronts and walkways, bigger doors and windows than their simple ranch predecessors.

"It's that one, the one with the brick front."

Sam pulled into the driveway. "You sure?"

Rachel nodded. "I am. Remember they put in those giant skylights last year?"

"Right. But where's her car?" He put the Highlander in park and opened his door. "Maybe she's not home."

Rachel pointed to the garage. "Look in the window, honey. See if she parked it in there."

He did as she suggested, and saw nothing but junk inside. Boxes, camping gear, old toys, a boat—it was packed, and there was no room for another bicycle, never mind a vehicle.

He returned to the car and got in. "Nothing. She's not home."

"Darn. Can you think of anywhere else to look?"

"Her office? Maybe she's burying herself in work?"

Rachel nodded as if it were settled. "Good. Let's go."

Sam turned the car around and headed up to the village. They drove north on Goodland Road and then snaked over to Main Street. At the head of the road, they turned into the county offices.

"There!" Rachel said. "Isn't that her car?"

Sam drove slowly past the red Bronco. "Looks like it." He parked two slots down. "Should I go inside and bother her? Maybe she's doing fine, just caught up in a case."

"Just check on her, honey. If she's fine, then you can come right back out. Tell her I'm waiting. That we both were concerned."

He nodded. "Okay. Back in a flash." He left the engine running so Rachel could stay cool. The day's temperatures hadn't yet moderated, even though it was almost seven.

"See you soon, Sammy. Tell Lou I said I'm sorry about Mel. And if she needs anything, tell her to call me."

Sam looked into the honest brown eyes of his wife and felt his heart melt. After all Lou had done, she still had it in her heart to forgive and show empathy for the woman. He leaned over to brush her lips with his. "I love you, Rach. You just blow me away."

"Enough already," she laughed and pushed him toward the door. "Just get this over with, and we can go home to bed."

Chapter Twelve

SAM PASSED THE EMPTY RECEPTIONIST'S DESK AND HEADED FOR THE ELEVATORS. At this time of day, all of the DMV offices on the first floor were closed, as were the various county departments on all three levels. He checked his watch and was surprised to find it was already seven-fifteen.

He punched the button for the basement and waited, whistling a theme from the Japanese Melodies. After an inordinate wait, the car arrived and whooshed open. Sam nodded to the cleaning lady, who stepped off before him and stared at him like he'd grown horns and mooed.

"Everything's closed up, mista. It's after seven."

If Sam had worn a hat, he would have tipped it. "Evening, ma'am. I'm just going down to see my colleague, the coroner."

The tag on her uniform read "Berta". She shuffled closer to him, backing her cart out onto the floor. A wet mop, bottles of spray cleaners, rags, and an array of polishes clinked and clanked when she rolled it toward him. "Ain't nobody down there, mista."

Sam pressed the button to keep the door open for her. "My friend's car's still in the lot. Mind if I take a quick look?"

She peered at him through big black eyes and yawned. "Guess not." Buttoning up her blue smock, she glanced sideways at Sam. "I lock up in a half hour. So make it snappy."

Sam hurried onto the elevator before the doors shut again. "Yes, ma'am," he said, "I'll be fast."

He rode to the basement with questions rattling back and forth in his skull. Maybe Lou had just been in the restroom and the cleaning lady missed her. With determination, he strode to the coroner's offices and pushed inside. "Lou?"

Nothing.

Sam looked in her office. The light was on. Her coat hung on the rack. He called again, then quickly searched the desk. Her purse sat in the bottom right hand drawer.

She's here all right.

He turned and looked. Past the window in the back was a lab, and behind that, the morgue.

Sam pushed through the back door and called again.

"Lou? You in here?"

A body lay on the table, partially covered with a white sheet. He walked toward it and swallowed hard, his heart thumping a conga beat behind his ribs. He lifted the sheet. A long gray braid swung down below the steel table.

Ginger.

Sam blanched and backed up a step, letting the sheet drop. "Lou? Where the hell are you?"

Hurrying now, he walked past the body and approached the white-walled morgue. Stark and sterile, it smelled of disinfectant. The floor had been freshly mopped, presumably by Berta. Moist swirls dried on the gray linoleum.

"Lou? Where the hell are you?"

Sam moved into the room and tried not to think about what was in the human-sized drawers on the wall. He scanned the area, looked behind the tall row of file cabinets, and found nothing.

Where is she?

A macabre sense of curiosity made him look back at the wall of drawers. Coffins on wheels.

One drawer wasn't pushed in all the way. The marble pulsed against his leg when he walked toward it. It pulsed again when he wrapped his fingers around the handle. And seared his flesh when he hesitated.

Open it.

The voice sifted through his brain, unmistakably Billy's. Shaking now, Sam pulled and the drawer opened on well-oiled slides.

Lou lay on her back on the slab looking up with dulled eyes and a waxen complexion. No more pleading, no more beseeching. One hand fell off the table as he slid it farther out. He noticed her wedding band had been removed, and in its place, white skin echoed the symbol of her ruined marriage. Her hair had been combed, her clothes changed. And her neck wore a wreath of hideous blue-black welts.

Strangled. In her own morgue.

Sam stepped back and flew out of the room into the hallway, stabbing at the elevator button until it opened. By the time he reached the main floor, he'd calmed slightly. Berta looked up as he panted and ran toward the phone.

"You find her?" she asked with mild interest.

Sam took a deep breath and grabbed the phone on the receptionist's desk. "Unfortunately, I did." He dialed 911 and looked at Berta with sludge in his heart. "She's dead."

✿

The first to arrive was Ned Olsen. His cruiser screeched to a stop with lights flashing near Sam's Highlander, where Sam sat with Rachel.

"Here he is." She raised her head off her pillow, looking exhausted. "That was fast."

Sam nodded, his features impassive. The horror had turned him numb. He slowly opened the door and got out.

Ned hurried to his side. "You're sure she's dead, Sam?"

Sam looked nervously toward the building. "Oh, she's dead all right."

"Damn." Ned hitched up his belt and rested a hand on his gun. 'Did you see anyone else lurking around in there?"

"Just Berta. She cleans the place."

"I know her. She cleans the station, too." He took out his notebook and scribbled in it. "How long do you think Lou's been dead?"

The irony of it shook him. He was being asked to do the coroner's job, on the coroner's body. "Hell. I don't know. She was pretty cold." He kicked a stone. It skidded across the parking lot and hit Ned's tire. A rising sense of anxiety filled him. Lou was dead. Lou was cold. Lou had a muffin for breakfast. None of it made a lick of sense. "We had a breakfast meeting. She was fine this morning." *Except when I shattered her hopes and shot her down in not too nice a fashion*. He cringed inside. The guilt would linger for a long time.

Ned reached inside the car window to squeeze Rachel's hand. "Listen, he could still be hanging around. Lock yourselves in here and wait. Reinforcements are coming."

Sam grimaced. "Come on, Ned. I've gotta get Rachel home. She's a wreck."

Ned peered at him. "I'm sorry, Sam. I'd like to let you go, but we'll have to ask you some questions."

Sam's patience evaporated. He slammed his hand on the Highlander's hood. "Listen. I just found her; I didn't kill her!"

Ned stepped back with his hands up. "Whoa. Take it easy. I'm not accusing you of anything."

Sam opened the door and slid into the driver's seat. "Ask the cleaning lady. Berta. She just let me in—like ten minutes ago—and knows what happened. I'm not a coroner, but Lou's been dead for hours. Like I said, she was stone cold. So you really don't need to ask me squat."

Ned's hands flew into the air. "Okay, okay. I know where to find you if I need you. Take Rachel home. And..."

Sam eyed him with suspicion and slammed his door shut. He wound the window down. "What?"

Ned flushed. "Er...thanks."

Rachel closed her eyes and rested her head against the pillow on her shoulder. "Bye, Ned. Good luck."

Sam started the engine. "You know where to find us."

They drove out of the parking lot against a backdrop of lavender sky. The sun had begun to drop, submerged in pastels that swirled over the valley. The beauty of it almost gagged Sam. It seemed insane. Unfair. Ridiculous that the sky could be so delicate and alive when poor Lou lay strangled in her morgue with a purple necklace of ugly welts.

"God. I can't believe this." Sam braked as the Main Street light turned yellow. "I just spoke with her this morning. *This morning*."

Rachel rested a hand on his arm. "Honey. I know."

"If I'd just called her sooner. Or checked on her. Maybe she wouldn't be dead."

Rachel groaned. "How can you say that? We don't know who killed her or why. And it certainly wasn't because you didn't call her. Light's green, dear."

"How can you seem so calm?"

She closed her eyes again. "It's a ruse. Just trying to help you cope, Sammy. Tell you the truth, I think I might throw up."

"I'm sorry, babe." His face lost some of its tight anger. "She went home to change like I told her to. She was all fixed up when he killed her."

"What?"

"I told her to go home, take a nice bath, and change her clothes. She must've listened, because she was in a new outfit and her hair was combed nice and neat."

"Oh." Rachel watched out the window for a few seconds, staring at the color-streaked horizon. "The police will probably want to know that, right? So they can track her movements before she was killed?"

Sam frowned as he wound his way along Goodland Road. "I guess." The Highlander dipped and rose over the hilly terrain, climbing the hills with a powerful growl. "I still feel kind of responsible."

"You're *not* responsible. Some monster is—not you. You just feel guilty because you rejected her. You *had* to. You couldn't lead her on." She kneaded his shoulder with her hand. "But you didn't kill her, Sam."

He nodded. "I know."

Rachel softened her expression. "I'm so sorry. Poor Lou. She didn't deserve this. Not after Mel dumped her like that. It's just not fair."

A sense of righteous anger washed over Sam. It wasn't fair. It wasn't right. And who the hell would have killed Lou in such a brutal fashion?

He quickly dismissed Mel as a suspect. He might be a philandering idiot, but he wasn't a killer. Sam had played gin with him a few times, had laughed with him. The next time he saw him, he'd be exchanging somber looks of sorrow at the funeral.

"It must be something she witnessed. Something only she knew. Don't you think?" He turned to Rachel with desperation. "And how did they get to her in her own office?"

Rachel gently tried to shush him. "Honey. Please. Let the police do their job. It's not up to you to solve her murder."

He ignored her. "I know, but the murderer must've been caught on videotape. There's a camera in the entrance."

Rachel sat back and sighed. "I'm sure the police know that. And I know you'd like to help them, but right now it's best to sit back and stay out of their hair. Don't you think?" She tried a sweet smile this time.

He pulled into the driveway and turned off the engine. "I guess. It's just such a shock."

"I know, Sammy. But now you need to help me inside. I'm really beat."

Sam shook off all thoughts of Lou. Rachel's eyes glistened, weary with tears. "I'm sorry, Rach. Come on, let's get you to bed."

Chapter Thirteen

SAM SAT IN THE NEARLY EMPTY WEGMANS' PARKING LOT. HE RESTED HIS hands on the wheel, stared at the pink light of the sun coming over the horizon, and listened to the engine ping as it cooled. He'd spent the past three days reviewing the last moments he spent with Lou, the unkind words he chose to rebuff her, the tone of his voice. The coldness of his uncomfortable dash for escape when he couldn't take it anymore. He was a heel. A spineless heel.

Rachel helped by talking him through each moment, reminding him—incessantly—that what he said or didn't say wouldn't have changed the murderer's intentions. He knew she was right, but couldn't help gnawing on the bone of guilt.

He'd run like a scared little boy when the situation grew uncomfortable, and would probably regret it for the rest of his life. Lou had been a wreck. She'd needed his help. He should have been kinder, gentler. Shoulda. Coulda. Woulda. None of his self-torment would make any difference, anyway. He'd just have to learn to live with it.

He finally unbuckled his seatbelt, locked the Highlander, and pushed the grocery cart along the bumpy parking lot to enter the cool, quiet early morning world of Wegmans. Few customers dotted the store. It was the best time to shop. The fresh produce had just been restocked and the aisles were blessedly empty. Lush tropical fruit perfumed the aisle he navigated, studying Rachel's list. Mangoes, starfruit, papayas, avocados, and pineapples were piled in the bins before him.

He checked the list. What the hell is a kumquat? He scrutinized the paper in his hands as if the answer would jump out at him.

"Need some help?"

The voice was familiar, but it was in the wrong setting. Sam turned to find Dr. Andrea Garcia smiling beneath a sweep of dark bangs and thick black lashes.

"Garcia. What are you doing here?"

She laughed and put one hand on her hip. "What? You think my husband does the food shopping? Hell, no. If I want any food in the house, I have to drag my butt out at the crack of dawn before my practice opens. Ridiculous, but the man just can't get it right. Doesn't know a mango from a papaya." She pointed to the fruit on the shelf and then eyed Sam warily. "Do you, Dr. Moore?"

He chuckled. "Sure I do. But I'm having a little trouble finding the kumquats."

She snorted. "Sam. You kill me. Look, they're right here." She reached over him and pointed.

"What? Those little baby oranges?" He squinted at one and rolled it on his palm. It wasn't much bigger than a grape. "What do you do with them?"

"You can eat them with skins and all. At least I do."

Sam wrinkled his nose. "Really? Well, Rachel needs a dozen. Who am I to argue?"

Garcia stared at him for a minute, as if she wanted to say something, but was holding back.

He peered at her. "What?"

She touched his hand. "Sam, are you okay?" She dropped her eyes, then met his again. "I mean, about Lou and all?"

He smiled halfway. "Hell, Garcia. Rachel and I knew Lou for years. And of course, since she was one 'of us'. You know what I mean."

Garcia nodded. "I do. You mean because she was a physician. Somehow it seems like these things aren't supposed to happen to us. We're here to heal, to help, to solve medical mysteries."

He knew she'd get it without a lot of explanation. "Yeah. We're not supposed to be murdered in our own office. Or morgue. As the case may be."

She grimaced and looked down at her shoes. "So I hear they think it might have something to do with that case she took in the city last year. The drug dealer."

It had been all over the news, probably leaked by someone on the force. Lou had been called up to Monroe County the year before, when the coroner had taken ill, and the case she'd dealt with had been a bad one. Because of her acumen, however, she'd helped the detectives link the victims to a local drug dealer who'd been arrested, sewing up the case. The trial was pending, and theories of the killer's gang wanting to silence Lou as a witness had been splashed over the front page and incited local talk show callers.

"I guess that's the theory right now. If you can believe the—" He was interrupted by a touch on his sleeve.

"Dr. Moore?"

He turned to find Lacey poised behind her shopping cart.

"Lacey," Sam said. "How are you? This is Dr. Garcia. She took over my practice. Garcia, this is Lacey. She works at Clara's."

The ladies shook hands and exchanged a few pleasantries. After a few minutes of chit-chat, Garcia checked her watch.

"Nice to meet you, Lacey. But I have to run. The office opens soon, and I've got a whole shopping list to run through." With a smile, she took off toward the Mediterranean bar.

"She's a doctor?" Lacey asked.

"Yeah, and a damned good one. If you're looking for a primary care physician, you couldn't do better than Garcia."

"Uh huh." She seemed distracted. "So, what are you shopping for? Looks pretty exotic."

Was that a twinge of jealousy in her eyes? Sam looked at her cart. Chips. Macaroni and cheese. Soda. Maybe she couldn't afford the pricier fresh produce. He knew how much it cost to eat healthy. It was a hell of a lot more than the crap diet most college students lived on.

"My son is coming home from Iraq," he said. "I'm picking him up tomorrow morning, and Rachel's going to cook up a storm."

She fingered one of the mangoes with longing. "These are so expensive. Are they any good?"

Sam shrugged. "They're like fruit of the gods, especially if they're ripe. But you pay through the nose for that pleasure, don't you?"

"I guess." She put the fruit back and raised her eyes to him. "Sam. You seem so…normal this morning." She studied his face as if looking for evidence of the abnormal.

"What are you talking about? Don't I usually seem 'normal'?"

"I mean considering everything that's happened. You know." She lowered her voice. "Lou's murder."

Eyes narrowed, he stared at her. She ran her hand through her glossy, short black hair and smiled nervously.

"Well, of course I'm upset about Lou." Irritated, he counted out a dozen kumquats and bagged them. "How do you think I should act?"

"I don't know. But since you and she were so close. I mean, weren't you two..." she wiggled two fingers together as if to imply something decidedly non-platonic.

Sam pushed the fury down. It welled in his throat, made him see red. But it wouldn't do to lose it in the supermarket. "No. We weren't."

She looked askance at him, confused. "But I saw you holding hands."

He bristled, counted to ten, and managed to keep it together. "You saw her put her hand on mine. Then you walked away. What you didn't see was me pulling my hand away."

She fell silent, then blanched as if something horrible dawned on her. "Oh."

Sam continued. "Lacey, I realize it's easy to get the wrong impression when you're flitting past people in the diner. Lou and I saw each other twice this week. Once to discuss a case, and then again because she was going through a personal crisis and needed a friend. That's it. I'm married to a wonderful woman named Rachel. She's the love of my life, and I don't have eyes for anyone else. Period."

She studied her fingernails. "Oh. Then I might've made a little boo-boo."

Sam sighed, unable to hide his exasperation any longer. "What *are* you talking about?"

She looked contrite. "When the cops asked about her, I sort of let it slip that you two were in the diner a lot. And I guess I might've said you were an item."

Sam's body turned to cement. Defeat drained him of the reaction he wanted to let loose. Anger. Indignation. Irritation. But he just stood there. And wondered. There was something in Lacey's eyes that didn't quite fit her words. A flicker of vicarious pleasure. Or was it spite?

Impossible. And ridiculous. She hardly knew him. He let the crazy thoughts slide over him like rain on a blade of grass. It gushed away and left him feeling empty. "So," he said. "I guess I'll expect another visit from the police."

She laid her hand on his arm and leaned in, her eyes big now, flickering with empathy. "I'm so sorry. I really screwed up."

He brushed her off and threw a bunch of bananas in the cart. "Don't sweat it. It's just a misunderstanding. I'll clear it up." Turning the cart away, he rolled away from Lacey and headed for the bread aisle.

ഗ്ര

When Sam reached home, Ned Olsen's cruiser was already parked in the driveway. Prepared for the worst, he trudged inside with the groceries and set them on the kitchen table.

"Sam? Honey, is that you?"

He grimaced, dreading the interrogation that lay footsteps away in the living room.

"It's me. Just putting away the groceries."

"Okay. Come on in when you're done. Ned's here."

He frowned and slowly dipped into the bags, stuffing the fruit in the crisper drawers and the pasta and canned goods in the cabinet. Rachel laughed in the next room, one of her almost-flirty laughs. Sam's brows pinched together.

What the hell?

He finished the job, squashed the plastic bags into a small ball, pushed them into the recycling container, and steeled his nerves.

When he entered the living room, Ned barely looked up. He waved half-heartedly and turned his rapt attention back to Rachel, who was halfway through a funny story about the little field mouse she found in the kitchen the week before. She had charmed Ned into submission—and now entertained a cop-turned-puppy dog.

Sam approached, received a blinding smile from his wife, settled on the couch next to Ned, and waited.

When Rachel wrapped up the story, Ned roared with laughter, slapping his thigh with his notebook and rocking in place. Sam's jaw dropped. He recovered quickly when Rachel shot him a wink.

"And that poor little mouse ran outside as if his life depended on it. Which it did."

Ned guffawed again.

Rachel turned to Sam. "Ned stopped by because of a misunderstanding, sweetie. But I cleared it all up."

Ned actually looked embarrassed. He flushed and shifted beside Sam, avoiding his eyes.

Sam brought it up first. "I ran into Lacey in the supermarket. She told me what she said about Lou and me."

Rachel laughed, this time a nervous titter. "So ridiculous. The poor girl really got the wrong impression."

Ned shook his head and started to rise. "Again. I'm so sorry, Rachel. And Sam..." He still couldn't meet Sam's gaze. "I, er...I apologize for listening to that tripe. This Lacey-woman is new in town, and I don't know why she took such pleasure in reporting your supposed tryst with Lou. I should have known. I knew Lou. And I know you." He looked down and slowly shook his head. "I just should have known."

Sam followed him to the door. "It's okay, Ned. How were you to know? Lou had started to melt down the last time I saw her. Maybe the desperation in her eyes was easy to misread. She did grab my hand a few times. She was telling me about Mel."

Ned put his hand on the doorknob and hesitated. "Right. I heard about that. The bastard."

Sam nodded. "Yeah. And the day after he dumped her someone strangled her." His voice cracked a little. "God, life is unfair."

Ned opened the door and turned. "I know. We're working to link that drug case to her murder, but so far nothing's gelling. Not on the videotape from the camera, or the physical evidence. It's driving me nuts. This should be an easy one to crack, you know?"

Sam shot him an empathetic glance. "It's gotta be tough, especially since you all worked with her for so many years. Hey, what about having her coworkers look at the tapes? Or maybe folks in the DA's office?"

"It's in the works. But there's a four-hour window to view. Takes a lot of time. Do you know how many people go in and out of that building in four hours?"

Sam shuffled in the doorway, anxious now for it to be over. "No. That's a lot of video."

"A lot, Sam. A helluva lot. We'll be in touch." A new thought struck him and he touched Sam's sleeve. "Will I see you in church Sunday?"

Sam groaned inside. He'd been avoiding church for a while. But he knew the choir needed his bass voice—he was one of the few men in the group who could actually harmonize without going off-key. "I've gotta see how Rachel's doing," he lied. The choir could wait. "And Andy's coming home tomorrow, so she might want to just hang out with him for a while."

Ned covered a yawn. "Sorry, been up almost all night." He rubbed his eyes. "I forgot about Andy coming home. Well, we'll pray for a safe flight home for him."

He waved and headed to the patrol car. Sam leaned against the doorjamb, suddenly exhausted. He watched until the taillights disappeared down the driveway, then headed back inside to Rachel.

Chapter Fourteen

THE MARBLE WARMED AND THRUMMED AGAINST SAM'S THIGH THROUGH-out dinner and during the movie he and Rachel watched in bed that night. Contrary to the usual stereotypes, he loved *Pride and Prejudice*, but Rachel barely tolerated it.

"I can't understand what they're saying, Sammy. Their accents are too thick." She blew her bangs up in frustration with her usual complaint whenever they watched a British movie. Sam chuckled, squeezed her hand, translated when need be, and couldn't take his eyes off the screen—even to visit the bathroom.

"I want to buy this one. God...I could watch it a million times over." There was something so alluring about the music, the sumptuous scenery, the gardens, the dinner scenes, the lofty ideals of the time that grabbed him by the heart and wouldn't let go. Even the backgrounds mesmerized him. In the final scene, the pastel pink sunrise and gray foggy field where the two lovers finally admitted their affection for each other tore his heart apart. He grabbed Rachel's hand and squeezed. "Just like us. Huh?"

She laughed and rolled her eyes. "You can watch it again while I'm asleep if you want, you big romantic fool." She yawned and stretched as the credits rolled, making rustling sounds with her pink flannel gown. "I'm falling asleep, anyway."

He was tempted to watch it again, but the marble had been insistent all evening. He knew he couldn't ignore Billy much longer. "Want me to read downstairs? I can turn out the lights for you."

She nodded, sleepy and already halfway to her dreams. "That would be nice. Thanks."

Sam grabbed his copy of *The Lonely Silver Rain*, by John D. MacDonald and slipped down to the living room. The marble heated up in his pocket. He looked at the book with longing, then tossed it aside and settled onto the couch with a pillow and quilt. With deliberation, he turned off the lamp and took out the marble.

The cat's eye glowed in the open palm of his hand, misting green fog in widening spirals. Sam's eyes reflected in the strange light, and his body grew into the mist that surrounded him, tucking around his arms and legs, elevating him to the other realm. As he was rushed into the past, Billy's voice echoed in the background.

I'll take care of you, Sam.

ജ

It was always a tossup whether Billy would propel him into his own childhood body, or float him near the ceiling, suspended by a ghostly green mesh over some significant scene from their past.

There he was. On the beach with Ginger Kennedy. Spring break. Florida.

He floated closer, watching the scene below. Remembering. Almost tasting the sea salt on her skin as he slowly sank into the strong, young body of his youth.

Soft blackness sparkled with stars. The seagulls huddled together on rocks along the breakfront and waves lapped softly against pearly sand. No crabs scuttled on the beach, no children raced past with pails clanging, and no bodies marred the beach, except Sam and Ginger, who moved rhythmically on a soft white blanket hidden from shore by a cluster of massive boulders. Sam, on top, increased his movements at her soft insistence. "Faster."

With a final thrust, Sam exploded inside her. She screamed with pleasure, arching her back and bucking beneath him.

When their breathing slowed, Ginger stroked his back and flopped her head to the side. "Sam. You're killing me." A sleepy cat smile crept onto her lips and spread over her face, glistening with perspiration. She loosened her long legs from their tight wrap around him, then stretched one leg and pointed her toes toward the sky. "I'm tingling all over."

Sam collapsed on top of her, laying his head on one breast and tracing his fingers along her sandy skin, once again almost moved to tears by the pure physical joy of the coupling. "I'm killing you? You're dehydrating me."

She touched her pouty lips to his and sighed. "Sorry, Doctor. Do you want me to leave you alone now?"

He rolled off and lay on his back, facing the stars. The cool air tickled the perspiration on his arms and legs. Every muscle in his body quivered with delight. "Hell, no. I wish it could last forever. And I'm not a doctor. Not yet, anyway."

"You will be, soon." She sat up slowly and blew the sand from his arms, legs, and other parts, lingering over his throbbing, sensitive areas. He rolled his eyes and begged for mercy. "Geez, Ginger. Aren't you hungry? How about a burger at the grill?"

She kissed him on his inner thigh and let loose a throaty chuckle. "Okay. I guess could use more fuel." She twisted her chunky topaz ring around her forefinger, stood, and wrapped a bright orange sarong around her body. The wet fabric illuminated her rounded hips and full breasts, sending another shudder of desire through him.

He pulled on his swim trunks and tee shirt, shook out the blanket, and followed his willowy lover with her swinging, long red braid up the hill. He'd never experience anything like this. The primal mating has unleashed a luscious lurid part of him he'd never met before. It was freeing; yet his desire took him prisoner. He already wanted more.

They settled outdoors in a café with round metal tables and chairs. From afar, his older self remembered the feeling of the cool seat beneath his legs, the fireflies that winked in the parking lot, and the red and white Coke sign that chattered in the breeze on the side of the burger shack.

After they ordered at the window, they sat down to wait. Sam stared at Ginger with longing. He snaked his fingers through hers and played with the ring on her finger. "Ginger, I'm really starting to fall for you."

She pulled back and pouted. "No, Sam. You can't do that. You hear? I have someone at home and this is just a lark. One last fling before I get hitched."

His jaw dropped. He'd been trying to figure out how he could get her up to Rochester so they could get married. He'd imagined his little studio apartment as a love nest. He'd pictured giving her half of the closet space, a few drawers in his bureau. His damn brain had been going wild in overdrive, thinking she must want him the way he wanted her.

Stupid, stupid! She just wants to screw you, you dumb jerk.

She kissed her finger and pressed it against his lips. "Oh, honey. Don't be sad. Didn't you know that's what spring break is for?" She touched his foot with hers and rubbed it up his calf, pushing him to a heightened state of arousal. "People don't expect to get all serious here. It's part of the deal."

Sam looked at his hands. "I've never been on spring break. I thought…"

"Listen. We can still have fun. But first of all, I gotta give my fiancé a call to keep him off my back. Back in a jiffy."

His face fell. "Fiancé?"

She sashayed to the phone booth, swinging her hips and tossing her braid.

Sam's shame burned his cheeks. How could he let himself get like this? He'd only known her a few days. Sure, they'd been plastered to each other almost continually since they met, but it was only days. Nobody fell in love in two days, did they? Had he completely deluded himself?

Was it because he'd kept himself from women for the most part? Was he so ripe, so ready, so primed for love that the first woman who rocked his world made him swoon, too? Was he that vulnerable?

Ginger plopped some coins in the phone. This time, Billy amplified the memory. Sam could hear both sides of the conversation as if he were inside Ginger's head.

She turned her back to Sam, but each word was crystal clear.

"Honey? It's me. Just calling to check in."

A rough voice answered. "Where the hell've you been? You were supposed to call at eight."

Ginger laughed it off. "Oh, a few of the girls and I went to the beach. Sorry, Raoul."

His tone softened. "Yeah? Well, I guess it's good you're having fun." His words ran faster, as if he'd been impatient to get the small talk out of the way. "But I need you back here soon. I found a great spot for the next ceremony. And I recruited more members. Do you think we should wear black or purple robes?"

Her face tightened, then relaxed. "Oh, I don't know. Do you really think we need more people? You can't fit too many people around a Ouija board, you know?"

Raoul grunted. "There's more to ceremonies than just the Ouija board. We might have to do a sacrifice one of these days."

Ginger frowned. "Not a live animal? I couldn't stand that, honey. Too gross."

His voice growled with pleasure, as if enjoying her discomfort. "Okay. Maybe we'll use a grasshopper or something little to start. But you know," his voice turned low and spooky, "the gods will want us to give them something."

She snorted a laugh. "Oh, Raoul. Be serious. I'll call you tomorrow. Remember, we're getting married in three months. We've got a helluva lot more to plan than black robes and sacrifices, silly."

Raoul huffed. "I guess. Call me tomorrow?"

She giggled and turned to wave to Sam. "Maybe. But it's our last night. We might be out partying kinda late. Why don't I just call you when we land?"

After some more small talk, they hung up. Ginger swished toward him, the orange sarong blowing in the breeze, lifting to show her long, lean legs and giving him brief glimpses of more private areas. He should have looked away, but didn't.

"Hey, cutie. You okay over here?" She twirled his hair around her fingers at his temples, then pushed him back in his seat to straddle him. Their mouths almost touched. He felt her warm and moist and squirming on his body. He nearly lost it.

She whispered in his ear, tickling him with her soft breath. "I'm sorry about the misunderstanding, babe. How 'bout after we eat I try to make it up to you?"

Sam's shattered heart gave way to a growing primal desire. But he couldn't yet articulate.

"Oh, hell, Sam. When I take you back to the room, you can ask for anything. And I'll do it right, too."

His mouth opened, but no sound came out.

Ginger lifted it with one well-manicured finger. "I'll take that as a yes?"

The burgers arrived just in time to save him embarrassment. When she swung off him, he covered his lap with a big cloth napkin and hoped he'd recover in time to walk back to the hotel.

With a snap of the cola sign in the warm breeze, the scene blinked out, fizzling in a green silk screen. Sam plummeted into his sixty-two-year-old body on his comfortable couch and in minutes, fell into a deep sleep.

Chapter Fifteen

Rachel clamped the phone to her ear and grinned. "Okay honey, Dad will pick you up in an hour just outside the gate. Can't wait to see you, Andy. Love you."

Sam grabbed his keys from the counter. "So, he actually made it without a hitch. It's a miracle." A smile crept onto his lips. "Maryellen and the kids will be thrilled."

She rolled beside him, pushing him toward the door. "I know. She said the boys are so excited they've been bouncing off the walls. They'll meet us here as soon as Evan's game is over. Should be about the time you get back, Sammy. Now, hurry! Well, don't *hurry*. I don't want anything to happen to you. But get going."

He leaned down to brush her lips with his. "You're not excited, are you, hon?"

She chastised him with a playful swat. "You know how excited I am! You got everything you need?"

"Got my keys." He patted his pocket. "My wallet." He pretended to search for his head. "Oh, right. There it is. Got my brain."

"Oh, Sam." She covered her mouth when she laughed. "I *do* love you. But get yourself over to that airport and bring our boy back to me."

He straightened, and saluted. "Yes, ma'am. Back in a flash."

ꕥ

Sam waited at the Greater Rochester International Airport, glad he lived near a city that offered the convenience of an airport without the crushing crowds like Boston or New York. He loved their little airport, with its two short runways, easy parking, and plenty of room to stretch. He stood outside the glass doors near the security guard, watching for his son's face to appear in the crowd that streamed through the exit.

After what seemed like forever, he finally caught sight of him. With a goofy smile plastered on his face and his heart jack hammering, Sam studied his son who waited patiently for the people ahead of him to filter through the doorway. Andy's camouflage uniform was wrinkled, his hair shorn close to his scalp. His eyes screamed exhaustion, tired lines framed his mouth, and even from twenty feet away, Sam could tell he needed sleep. Lots of sleep. Sam's heart swelled with pride as he neared, and he reached for his boy, trying to stem the tears that welled in his own eyes.

Andy wrapped him in a crushing embrace. "Dad. God, it's good to see you."

"You too, son." The words came out in a choke. He continued to hug his son, never wanting to let go and not caring if anyone thought he was an old softy.

"Dad?" Andy pulled back a few inches. "Can we head over to baggage claim?"

Sam snorted a laugh. "Sorry. I just don't want to let you go. It's been too long. Way too long."

"I know. It's good to see your face, too, Dad."

Snatching the small carry-on bag, Sam linked arms with Andy and headed toward the baggage claim area as his son reported on the rigors of the trip.

"I almost missed my connection in Athens. It was so close. Luckily the plane was delayed, and here I am. Only twenty minutes late."

Sam couldn't stop grinning. "Thank God. Maryellen and the boys are going to be so glad to see you. And your mother's going bonkers. She's been cooking all week." They boarded the escalator and grabbed the handrail. "Wait until you see your niece. She's such a beautiful baby."

"Isabel, right?" Andy asked. "Nice name."

They reached the baggage claim area and located the carousel matching Andy's flight.

"Back in a sec, Dad." Andy slid sideways through the jostling crowd to grab his duffel bag from the belt.

Sam flipped open his phone and dialed home. The weak signal crackled, and he finally gave up after trying twice. Rachel would want to know they were on their way, but he'd have to try again when they got out in the parking lot.

The marble had been pulsing and burning his leg since he left home an hour ago, but he hadn't had time to deal with it. Annoyed, he plucked it out of his pants pocket and slid it into the outer pocket of Andy's bag. As much as he adored his little brother, he wished he'd let him live his life for a while before he whisked him off again for another romp through the past. And for what? So far, none of the excursions had lent him any comfort or given him anything to go on. Why was Billy so damned insistent today? Didn't he know Andy was coming home?

For a moment, green flashed before him, almost catching him in the mist, but when he dropped it, the sensation abated. Billy had something to say, but Sam willed him to wait.

"Okay. Let's get out of here." Andy tried to keep his bloodshot eyes open. His shoulders slumped, and he almost buckled against Sam. "Whoa. Dizzy. Gotta sit for a minute."

Sam handed him the bottle of water he'd stashed in his coat pocket. "Here you go. Drink this."

Andy drained the water, wiped his forehead, and smiled. "Thanks."

Sam watched the color come back to his son's face. "Better?"

"Yeah. I'm good."

"Come on, then. There's a nice meal waiting for you at home. And you can catch a little nap on the drive home if you need it."

Andy looked sideways at him. "Can't hide anything from you, can I, Dad?"

Sam slung the carry-on to his shoulder and swept an arm around Andy's shoulders. "No way, my boy. No way. You never could."

When he turned south on Route 390 toward East Goodland, Sam tried to call Rachel again. After the second failed attempt, he hung up and shrugged. More to himself than his sleeping son, he mumbled, "Cat must've knocked the receiver off the hook."

Andy smiled with his eyes closed. He'd snuggled down into the seat five minutes after they left. "Mmmmhmmm. Try her cell."

"Right." Rachel kept it in her wheelchair pocket for emergencies. Sam rarely called that number, but had it stored in his own phone.

He scrolled down to find it and pressed send. He let it ring ten times. Nothing.

"Maybe she didn't turn that one on this morning. Or didn't charge it."

Andy's snores answered. After five unsuccessful attempts from Rochester to Avon, Sam's stomach knotted and churned. He turned left on Route 20A after exiting the highway, then swung right on Goodland Hill Road. Eight minutes later they rolled into the driveway. He'd tried to call three more times, to no avail.

Were the lines down? Had someone hit a pole?

He tried to drive around the ruts in the gravel road, but in spite of his care, Andy stirred.

Where was she? Had Maryellen changed her plans and picked her up to do some last minute shopping?

Unlikely. Very unlikely.

Maybe she'd taken a bath? Sam preferred that she didn't try to do it alone, but she could still stand for a few minutes well enough to get in and out of the tub if necessary.

That's probably it. She must be in the bathroom.

Andy's head slumped sideways on the door, jostling as Sam drove over an unavoidable bump. His eyes opened to slits and welcomed the scene before him. "Home."

"We're here, son. Looks like we beat Maryellen and the boys, but they'll probably be here any second."

Andy flashed a broad sleep-muddy smile and unfolded his long legs from the car. He stretched and looked toward the house. "The place looks good, Dad." He scanned the gardens out back. "Is the corn ready?"

Sam snorted. "Ready? Of course it's ready. We've been eating the early varieties since mid-July."

Andy elbowed his dad and laughed. "Just kidding, Dad. I know you better than that. First to plant. First to harvest. That's your motto." He hefted his bags from the car and allowed his father to take one. Together, they strode toward the porch. "Smells good. Is that pot roast?"

Sam opened the kitchen door for him. "Yup. And fresh dug Yukon Gold potatoes. Nantes carrots. And Lutz beets. I picked some Purple Cherokee tomatoes this morning, too. The ones you used to like so much."

Andy smiled. "Now all we need is apple pie, and my life is complete."

"Change that to peach cobbler and you've hit the nail on the head," Sam chuckled as they edged inside. "Rachel? We're here."

The empty kitchen surprised him. He'd expected Rachel to be perched by the door, waiting anxiously for her boy.

"Honey? We're home."

They dropped Andy's bags on the floor and headed into the living room. Sam's heart skipped a beat when he scanned the room. "Rach? Where are you?"

He trotted to the stairs and called. "Honey? You upstairs?"

Heavy silence answered. They exchanged worried glances.

"I'll check down here, you check upstairs," Andy said.

Sam was halfway up the stairs before Andy finished his sentence. He hurried down the corridor and skidded around the corner to the bedroom. Empty. Bed made, room tidied. All as usual. He ducked into the hall and checked the bathroom. The boys' room. Both empty.

Andy called to him from downstairs, his voice thick and strangled. Four words. Four words that changed Sam's life forever.

"Dad. I found her."

Chapter Sixteen

SAM RACED TOWARD THE LAUNDRY ROOM IN A PANIC. RACHEL'S WHEELchair sat abandoned in the hall, and Andy froze in the doorway, hands clenching and unclenching at his side.

Andy's voice thickened. "Maybe you shouldn't come in here." He spun and held out both hands to keep Sam out of the room.

One of Rachel's shoes lay beside the doorjamb. The brown clogs. Slip on. With lambs' wool lining. She loved them so much she even wore them in the summer.

Sam drifted closer, terror pooling in his stomach. As if in anaphylactic shock, his throat tightened and threatened to close off his air. His heart beat wildly now, in his throat, ears, chest. He barreled past his son and stumbled into the room, his voice hoarse. "What happened?"

As soon as the words left his mouth, he saw her. She lay on a basket of laundry, her eyes wide open, looking with blank surprise at the ceiling. Sam's garden shears protruded from her heart. The image danced before him like heat waves on tar, shimmering with unreality. Blood ran from Rachel's floral print blouse to the sheets stained red in the basket, pooling on the white linoleum floor.

The room tilted. A series of screams of *No No No No No* resonated in his head. Or maybe he yelled it aloud. He couldn't tell as he shoved Andy aside and collapsed beside her, checking for the pulse that evaded him like a cruel tormentor. Neck. Wrist. Ankles. No beating met his probing fingers.

"NO!" He drew the shears from her chest, sickened by the soft sucking sound it made, then wadded up a compress of pillowcases and held it over the wound to stem the flow. More blood dribbled from the wound and curled around her pearl buttons. He realized with a start that she was still warm.

He looked wildly about the room, as if a solution lay beneath the neatly folded piles of towels and linen. "Call 911. Hurry!" He cradled Rachel in his arms, smearing the blood between them, and feeling her arms dangle away from him, as if she didn't have the strength to return his embrace.

Andy cried out, anguish pinging across the small room. He squeezed between his mother's body and the washing machine, holding his hand out to his father. "Dad. It's too late. She has no pulse. I checked, too."

"NO!" Sam's mind reeled, his vision clouded, and the scent of blood tasted metallic on his tongue. "Who did this? Is he still here? She's still warm, Andy. *Find the bastard!*" He stiffened when his brain repeated a phrase he'd heard during some of Rachel's favorite shows.

Don't disturb the evidence.

Panic slewed over him, boiling inside his head, freezing his arms and legs.

My garden shears. The killer took them from the barn. Used them on my Rachel. And my prints are all over them.

A great gulping scream filled his throat, tearing out of him like a primal scream. "RACHEL!"

Her head slumped sideways when he moved away, as if she was rejecting him. He checked her pulse again, muttering under his breath. "No way. No. No." In a sudden manic thrust, he stood and reached for the marble, searching his pockets, patting madly at his pants and shirt. "My God. Where *is* it? What did I *do* with it?" Sam shouted, "Billy! Why didn't you warn me?"

Inside the double-stuffed world that batted him between reality and nightmare, he remembered the marble's insistent throbbing all morning. Billy *had* tried to warn him, had tried hard.

"Dad, come on. You can't help her now." In spite of Andy's two tours of duty in the heat of battle in Iraq, the bodies he had seen and possibly created, and his soldier-toughened soul, he wept. Loud and strong, he wept and choked on his words. "*Dad. Please.* Leave her be. It's over."

Andy pulled him to his feet. Sam stared at his son as if he'd never seen him before. His eyes widened, trying to piece together a puzzle. *Who is this nice young man? And why does he look so familiar?*

Andy took him by the elbow and started to shuffle him toward the living room.

"Come on, Dad. Let's go sit down."

"No. Please. My wife needs me. She has multiple sclerosis, you know."

Andy's eyes popped open. Tears still streamed from them, and he shook his father's shoulders as if he could not only snap him out of it, but maybe bring back his mother, too. "Dad! Come on. Hold it together. Don't do this."

Sam stopped and stared at his bloodied hands. His legs weakened to jelly. He stumbled, then braced himself against the wall as sobs wracked him in waves of increasing amplitude. He slid to the floor and buried his face in his hands.

Rachel.

Dear God.

Not Rachel.

The police had left hours ago, taking Rachel's body with them. Strange bedfellows of thoughts stabbed Sam as he sat on the couch between Beth and Andy, trying to ignore their questions and attempts at consolation.

"Dad? Can't I get you something? Andy says you haven't eaten since breakfast?" Beth's hand brushed Sam's face as if she could remove the cobwebs that kept him apart from her.

He idly wondered whom the county had collared as coroner, since Lou was dead. Who would examine the next body on the cold steel tables in the room whose air raised goose bumps on his skin? But not on the skin of the dead. No goose bumps there. They were dead, dead, dead.

Dead. Red. Red blood. Blood spatter.

Had they noticed the blood spatter in the laundry room? Where had that come from?

Billy's dead. But he died in the water. No one had stabbed him with garden shears.

Ginger.

Lou.

And someone else.

But who?

A trickle of alarm ran down his spine as he avoided the last thought and tried to concentrate on his list of gardening chores. Weed the strawberries. Pick and freeze tomatoes. Dig more potatoes. Blue ones. Not red ones.

Red. *Blood spatter.*

He shook his head. His stomach rumbled, sick with hunger and dread.

Where am I? Where's Rachel? And why won't Andy and Beth leave me alone?

Andy stood and put his hands in his pockets, staring out the window. Beth followed him, then embraced him and sobbed against his shoulder. Sam wanted to help them, but his feet and hands were bound by an unearthly force.

It wasn't green. It was red. And tight. And unforgiving.

I shouldn't have left her alone.

He shook off the thoughts again.

Left who alone?

Where's Billy? Where's the marble? I need to see him. I need to go home. Now.

Spying Andy's carry-on bag in the kitchen, he rose slowly, scurried to it, and unzipped the side pocket while the kids were occupied with their grief. Over something. Someone.

Had someone died?

Before they noticed, Sam slid into the bathroom, locked the door, slumped to the cold floor, and traveled to Billy's side in a rush of green.

ꕥ

Sam slid into his ten-year-old body and pressed his hands and face against the window, staring out at the street. The farmer across the way had just visited, mumbling something about a dead dog at the end of the road. He'd held his battered cap in his hand and stared at his dusty shoes.

"Sorry to bother you folks, but I thought it might be your beagle."

Billy sniffled beside him, watching the driveway. "Is that them? Do they have Sugar?"

Sam's heart fluttered in fear as two figures approached in the distance. When the farmer had turned to leave, his parents had hurried outside, and he and Billy waited in the house with hearts hammering.

No No No No NO!

Between them, his parents carried the dead body of his beloved Sugar.

NO!

His heart fell from his body and crashed to the floor. His mouth opened in denial, a wide howl of disbelief.

NO!

Billy collapsed against him, weeping tears of horror.

"Not Sugar. Oh, Sammy. It *can't* be."

The scenes flashed like lightning now. Fast. Blinding. Spinning out of control.

They held each other as Sugar's body was tactfully deposited out of sight. Mrs. Moore hurried to them, cradling both boys in her shaking arms as she cried with them. The tears had lasted all afternoon and night.

Mr. Moore offered to buy a new dog for the boys, and Sam had screamed at him as he tore away from the dinner table.

"I don't *want* another dog! *I want Sugar!*"

His mother had come to their room that night, as both boys wept softly into their pillows. Sam remembered her rubbing his back, trying to make it better. She tried awfully hard, but nothing soothed the raw hole that gaped in his heart.

After she left, Billy had whispered to him in the dark. "Sammy? Will Sugar come back?"

Sam had tried to stifle the sobs and bite back the bile that rose in his throat. "No, Billy. When they're dead, they don't come back."

Chapter Seventeen

BILLY HOVERED IN SAM'S MIND, COMFORTING AND CONSOLING HIM WHILE he stood under the umbrella at the open grave. Slate gray rain misted sideways, blowing black skirts and coattails in the morbid breeze.

It's okay, Sammy. Just a little longer. I'm here for you.

He'd been holding cryptic and mysterious conversations with his little brother's spirit for the past three days, while people buzzed around him with incessant, annoying sincerity, pressing his palms and embracing him with apparent sorrow. Five casseroles took up room in the refrigerator, something Rachel wouldn't tolerate when she got back. She took pride in her cooking, and all this unnecessary charity from neighbors would bother her. Besides, Sam didn't feel the need to eat any more. He felt sated inside his mind. With an inward grin, he thought *Maybe I've become a breatharian. Don't need food, water, or people. Just air. Just let me be outside by myself, with Billy to keep me company. That's all I need.*

When Rachel returned—Sam couldn't quite remember where she'd gone, whether she was visiting friends or helping to organize another MS walk—she'd make him go out into the garden to pick until his baskets overflowed, and she'd whip up something fresh and delicious. When she returned. He hoped it was soon. He missed her already, and maybe she could help him understand all the fuss being made around him. He just wanted them all to go away so he could drop down into his glider and let Billy take him home, back to their childhood.

Something bad had happened; it was obvious from all the crying and carrying on. But he couldn't quite put his mind to it. Lou had died. He knew that much. That was bad enough. He hadn't seen Mel to tell him how sorry he was, although he really didn't *want* to see him. He'd cheated on Lou and broken her heart, hours before someone stomped right into her morgue and stopped her heart for good. He was a disloyal bastard, and Sam knew he'd have a hard time saying, "So sorry for your loss," when the prick had cheated on her just days before. It was just so wrong, on so many levels.

Maybe he could avoid him. It might work.

But who lay in the coffin before him? Had the killer struck again? Had some other poor victim been strangled by the bastard?

Andy and Beth had forced him to this funeral. He stood miserable in the rain and fog, shoulder to shoulder with his children. The umbrella over his head darkened the view of the gravesite, the coffin, and the people with bowed heads under their own umbrellas. His neck chafed from the tight collar on his new white shirt. His hands felt clammy, in spite of the chill in the air. Why had they made him come here?

Does it always rain at funerals? Sam asked.

Seems like it, Billy said. *Don't worry. I'm right here.*

I'm fine, Billy. No need to worry about me.

Sam's face ran wet with tears mingled with rain, but his shoulders and body were trapped in a vice. Not shaking. Not moving. Not convulsing. The strange combination made the physician in him curious.

How can one weep without shaking shoulders?

Trails of moisture squeezed from his unblinking eyes. Dozens of black umbrellas fluttered in a sudden gust of wind.

Something awful must have happened. They all look so devastated.

His brows knit together, and he swiped the tears from his cheeks with one soil-roughened hand. *Why the hell am I crying?*

No! Don't think about it. He pushed the thought away again and glanced around the gravesite.

Reverend Hardina stood at the head of the coffin, holding his damp bible pages in the whipping wind. He spoke, but the words were snatched away before Sam computed them. They floated and twisted on the wind, words he didn't want to hear and hoped would never reach his ears.

His family and friends were all in attendance, heads bent under their sodden umbrellas, wearing various shades of gray and black. Andy, looking drained and pale. Beth, eyes swollen red. She nuzzled and kissed Isabel, who rested her head on her shoulder, wrapped up in blankets so only her eyes peeked out. Maryellen, with lips held tight so she wouldn't cry. Evan, looking lost and confused. And even little Timmy, who squirmed in his mother's arms and reached for the soggy pink daisies near the head of the casket.

There was Garcia. What the hell was she doing here? Did she close the clinic for this? What about all the kids with running noses and bronchitis? Someone should be tending them.

On the far side stood Officer Ned Olsen. That doesn't help much. He comes to all the funerals.

Beside him, Clara, owner of the diner. And was that Lacey huddled beside her? Her black dress matched her wet black bangs. She wore a raincoat with the hood pulled over her head.

But not Lou. She wasn't in attendance. *Lou's dead,* his brain said as he pictured the swollen necklace of flesh she'd worn in the morgue. He pushed that thought away, too. Too many disturbing thoughts to ruin his day.

There was his childhood pal, Senator Bruce MacDonald. Soon to be President of the United States of America. Maybe. If all went as expected. Secret Service agents hung back along the tree line, trying to blend into tombstones, their postures stiff and their eyes watchful. Were they on guard for a murderer? Someone with strong hands who wielded garden shears as his weapon?

Ridiculous, Sam thought. *And why does Bruce look so sad? So empathetic? Sort of like how he looked at Billy's funeral last year.* Sam shrugged inwardly and listened for Billy's response. It took a few seconds, delayed.

He cares about you.

Sam paled and swayed when he looked at the casket again. Beth cradled Isabel in one arm and reached out to steady her father. "Dad? Are you okay?"

He stared at the coffin. Pale pink with red Victorian flowers around the edges.

Rachel would have liked that design.

He looked around for her wheelchair, troubled when he couldn't see it, worried she was getting drenched. Did she have an umbrella?

Where is she?

Billy didn't answer.

Andy grabbed Sam's other elbow when he faltered and lost his balance, nearly dropping to the muddy ground below.

I just want to go home. Please.

Billy's face floated before him, wide hazel eyes probing and full of sadness. Sam lowered his umbrella and looked up at him as the image rose slowly to the heavens. Rain streamed down his cheeks. Light freckles scattered across Billy's nose, and his lips stretched in a smile. His skin looked dry—untouched by the moisture in the air.

It's okay, Sam. I'll take care of you.

The trees popped in and out of focus. The ground shuddered. A black donut circled Sam's vision, and he slowly slipped to the ground.

ꙮ

Beth gasped. "Is he okay?"

Sam felt hands probing him, feeling for a pulse, listening at his chest. His eyes wouldn't open, but the words he heard were amplified with crystal clarity.

Garcia's voice. "I'm worried. I think he needs to be admitted."

Andy's croaking response. "Isn't there another option? When Billy died, they locked him up for three months. He still can't talk about it, and that was fifty years ago."

The minister's voice continued to drone in the background, repeating the psalm with the backdrop of rain pattering on the mud and coffin.

Garcia said quietly, almost whispering, "It wouldn't be for long. Just enough time for the therapists to help him face the truth. To deal with his loss. Right now he's totally disconnected from reality, Andy. And that's probably what happened to him when Billy died."

Beth's voice caught, but the sound of Isabel gurgling nearby almost made Sam smile. "We have to do what's best for him, Andy. Dr. Garcia is right."

An ambulance wailed in the background. He shuddered inside and realized, somewhere, in a very muted and distant part of his brain that it was coming for him.

Chapter Eighteen

Sam opened his eyes. His cheek rested on a rough pillowcase scented with bleach. He lay still and trailed his eyes along the blue linoleum floor. Scuff marks. A ding near the wall. A single line of cement blocks joined the floor and walls, painted sickly ochre. Beige walls climbed to the ceiling, paint peeling on cement did a poor job hiding profanity scratched into the surface. The wall over his head showed hash marks denoting days and weeks. Someone had recorded fourteen weeks and three days in captivity. Sam's stomach twinged. *How long have I been here?*

The frosted window let in some light, but its heavy metal casing said *locked, don't even try to open me.* It was too high in the wall to see through, and too narrow to escape through. So why did they frost it and put it up so high?

Idiots. Didn't they know depriving someone of fresh air and sunshine would drive a person crazy?

He stirred and flipped to his back. Cool air encircled his bare legs. The wimpy excuse for a pillow couldn't compete with the down pillow Rachel found him at Linen's 'n Things. That one fit his head just right.

He sat up with a start. *Wait a minute. Where am I?*

"Rachel?"

No answer.

This place feels familiar. Too familiar.

Oh my God. I'm in the nut house. Again.

The taste of cotton batting filled his mouth. His tongue swished thick and dry against his teeth. A sense of dread coursed through his veins. *I'm doped.*

Sounds of heels tapping along the floor outside the room merged with a crow cawing muted beyond the window. The world spun when he swung his legs over the side. He steadied himself momentarily. The back of his hospital gown had come undone, allowing a blast from the overhead AC vent to chill his spine.

He slid sideways on the high cot and lowered his feet to the cold floor. The room twisted again, briefly. A plastic vase of flowers sat on the table beneath the window, surrounded by cards. He didn't want to know what they said inside, and looked away.

A covered tumbler of water with a bendy straw sat on a scarred table beside a flat box of cheap tissues. He grabbed it, tossed the straw, and gulped it down. Two photographs perched beside it—one of the family last April when Isabel was born, minus Andrew, who'd still been in Iraq. Rachel, Beth, Isabel, Maryellen, Evan, and even rambunctious little Timmy had stood still long enough in the maternity ward hospital for a family picture. And Sam stood proudly in the back, behind Rachel's wheelchair. He remembered the nurse who'd taken the picture, a skinny little blonde in pink scrubs who had chattered nonstop.

The second snapshot—black and white—came from his childhood. Billy and he, arms draped over each other's shoulders, smiling into the camera. Billy's front tooth had fallen out that week, and he loved showing off the gap by poking his tongue through it. It was taken in front of their barn, near the elderberry bushes. Sugar sat beside Sam's feet, looking up at him with adoration on his beagle face.

Billy.

Sam's head cleared a little, but memories of the last and only time he'd been hospitalized in this facility flooded his brain. He'd been twelve, whisked away to the children's ward of the psychiatric hospital after Billy rode off on his new birthday bike and never came back. Billy had simply vanished.

When he was hospitalized, he'd been grilled hours a day by the gray and wizened Dr. Prendergast, until he forced himself to pretend everything was okay just to get the hell out of that horrible place. But it *hadn't* been okay, because his brother and best friend had been taken from him, with no explanation.

Sam had been sure at the time God was punishing him for *something,* and he had a long list of possible transgressions. He'd stolen a Milky Way bar at the age of five. Slid it into his pocket and stuffed it in his face out behind the grocery store. And he'd lied to his father about playing around with matches the day he set the incinerator on fire by himself. He'd also allowed Fletcher Biddle to copy his math homework one time on the bus, in exchange for a pack of Twinkies. They had tasted devilishly good compared to the usual raisins and apples his mother packed for dessert. But the sticky sweetness faded as the guilt plagued him for a whole year, constantly afraid of discovery.

He shook himself and scanned the room again, returning to the table. Water. Kleenex. Two photos.

Were they framed with glass? Did they trust him not to shatter it and slice himself into oblivion?

He startled himself with the thought.

Why did I say that? I don't want to die.

His heart pounded briefly.

Do I?

Pausing, he looked at the locked door and window. Panic began to set in.

Without warning, Billy's voice entered his head, and a green glow rose from the table.

It's okay, Sam. I'm here.

A small plastic dish, tucked behind the tissues, held a comb, a washcloth, some small change, and Billy's marble. With a lunge that generated a wave of nausea, he reached for the marble and squeezed it tight in his hand.

"Billy," he said.

I'm here.

"Get me out of here."

A sense of strength washed through him as the marble warmed not only his fingers, but flowed through his body. His head cleared and vision sharpened.

With marble in hand, he rose and walked unsteadily to the small bathroom tucked behind the door to the hallway. A bare bulb hung high over ancient porcelain fixtures. Clean, but old. He set the marble carefully in a soap dish and splashed water on his face, running his hands through his hair. He dried his hands and face with a rough brown paper towel, then picked up the marble again and looked in the mirror.

Black smudges floated beneath his eyes. At least a week's worth of gray beard crept around his chin and climbed toward his ears. He scratched it and tried hard to focus.

How long have I been here?

Billy's face appeared in the mirror, wavering and translucent, yet clearly recognizable. The sandy hair. Wide hazel eyes. The light spray of freckles on his nose. Beside him, another image formed as the marble heated in Sam's fingers.

Gray hair. Brown eyes. Summer sweet smile.

Rachel.

Sam's heart drummed hard beneath his ribs. He reached toward the double image.

This time, Rachel's voice came through, clear and musical. The marble hummed against his skin.

Sam. Her eyes pleaded behind the glass, rippled with green. *Fix this, Sam. Take me home.*

He collapsed onto the cold grouted tile, sliding along porcelain until he came to a rest against the shower stall. Slowly, he nudged the bathroom door around and closed it.

His breathing came hard now as the events from the past few weeks slammed into his brain.

Ginger…

Dead.

Lou...

Dead.

Rachel…

Dead.

Some bastard had killed his wife.

He took a deep breath and held tight to the marble, willing its strength into his fevered brain.

Some bastard had killed all three of them.

He waited for the thoughts to settle, swallowing bile. A few hot sobs escaped him, but he collared them and shoved them away.

Okay. I'm okay. I can do this.

He brushed at his too-long hair, pushing it out of his eyes.

Some sick bastard killed my wife. And I'm the only one who can go back in time to figure out who did it.

He took a deep, shuddering breath.

And fix it.

His own words floated back to him.

No, Billy. When they're dead, they don't come back.

He slammed his fist repeatedly against the wall, loosening a white tile and shooting pains up to his elbow.

Screw that.

He pulled himself up, leaning on the sink, and searched the mirror for the images that had dissipated, leaving only a faint ripple of green. He touched the glass, feeling a slight vibration and a hint of warmth in the silvered surface.

Screw it all.

I'm bringing her back.

Chapter Nineteen

A FLASH OF UNDERSTANDING FLOODED SAM IN AN INSTANT OF CLARITY, and his brain kicked into gear. Staring at the mirror, he began to plan, focused on one goal.

I need to know who killed them, and why. And Billy's gonna help me.

Maybe he already had?

What had Billy been trying to tell him by bringing him back to the scene with Ginger on the beach? Or with that poor little girl locked in the dark room?

Was the child Ginger? Had she been abused as a little girl, locked alone in a rustic cabin with a tattered blanket, while her mother danced around a demonic campfire with wild-eyed lunatics?

Sam shuddered, then turned on the tap and splashed cold water on his face, drying it with a paper towel.

If so, how could the abuse have led to her death, and the subsequent deaths of Lou and Rachel?

Or was Lou's murder totally unrelated? Had some drug-crazed buddy of the guy on trial in the city actually sneaked into the morgue and done her in?

He steeled himself, trying hard to think about the next part without actually seeing it in his mind.

And why the swift violence toward Rachel? Who—if they wanted her dead—would go all the way to the barn to get his garden shears, bring them into the house, and chase a nearly crippled woman down the hall into the laundry room? There were plenty of kitchen knives or other weapons in the house that would have done the same job. If they'd been bent on robbery, they could've just left her in the chair and taken whatever they wanted. Had it been an execution—born of some mysterious vendetta—they could've just shot her, or knocked her out, or...

He leaned against the sink with both hands and stopped for a minute to collect himself. The whole idea of his wife being gone was unthinkable. Monstrous. Unacceptable. He needed to remain detached, if he was going to get through it. Just like he had when Billy had disappeared so long ago.

But, why?

Why kill Rachel?

He clamped down on the emotions that threatened to sabotage his logic, pinched his nose, and took a deep breath.

Rachel's past was an open book. He'd known every intimate detail of her life.

Hadn't he?

Could there be some ex-beau from high school who'd come back to haunt her? Some nut case she'd jilted long ago? Or cut off on the highway? Or a door-to-door salesman whose wares she'd rejected?

Do people kill you when you don't buy their Avon products?

Sam rubbed his fingers over his eyes and shook his head. It was all so unlikely. And the obvious explanation stared him in the face. His face, the one that still looked back at him through the now clear mirror on the bathroom wall.

It's all linked to me. Someone was trying to set me up. My garden shears. My wife. My name circled in the phone book. My old girlfriend. My colleague, recently seen with me in the restaurant.

Ginger.

Lou.

Rachel.

There has to be a connection.

Sam pulled open the bathroom door and reentered his room, nearly colliding with a clipboard-carrying doctor wearing a starched white coat.

The man stared at him with slightly widened eyes over bifocals sitting low on his nose. He looked at the chart one more time, then back to Sam.

"Well, good morning, Dr. Moore."

Sam nodded and walked to the closet in the corner, rummaging for his clothes. "Morning."

"I'm Dr. Prendergast. I've been following your case for the past few weeks."

The past few weeks? Sam's hand trembled as he pulled his blue denim work shirt from the hanger. He turned with the shirt in hand and stared at the doctor.

"Wait a minute, did you say Prendergast?" Sam studied the man's face. High forehead. Piercing eyes nested in crinkly skin. Hollow cheeks. Sallow complexion. "You sure haven't aged much in fifty years."

The doctor emitted a bark and ran a hand through his thinning hair. "You must've known my father. Abe Prendergast. He practiced here, many years ago. He passed away a few years ago."

Sam grabbed his jeans and the rest of his clothes. The doctor followed his movements without a word. With his clothes bundled in his arms, Sam faced Prendergast and swept a hand toward the door. "Do you mind? I'd like some privacy."

"Certainly. In just a moment. I wanted to say I'm glad to see you're up and alert. You've been unresponsive for the past fourteen days, Dr. Moore." He dragged out the words, "fourteen days."

"I know. And you drugged me into oblivion. What'd you give me?"

Prendergast smiled slightly and tapped the chart. "A pretty heavy cocktail. Standard stuff. You were rather…er…distraught."

Sam grimaced. "Imagine that. My wife is murdered in our home, immediately following the killings of two other friends, and I was… er…distraught."

He mimicked the doctor's tone, then instantly regretted his sarcasm. "Look. Of course I was upset. I just lost the love of my life to a senseless act of violence."

The doctor stared at him.

Sam paled. "Wait a minute. They don't still suspect *me* of these killings, do they?"

The doctor averted his eyes. "Not officially. But there were rumblings in town before you were admitted for observation. And Ned Olsen has been in a few times to see if he could talk to you."

Sam relaxed. "Good. I need to talk to him, too. And I need to see my family. They must be going insane…" He paused, realizing the irony of using that word when he was the one locked in the psych ward. "I mean, they must have their hands full, dealing with Rachel's death and then me going off the deep end."

"Did you?"

Sam eyed him. "Did I what?"

"Go off the deep end?"

Frustrated now, Sam slammed his clothes onto the bed and looked the doctor square in the eye. "Are we in a session now, Doctor? Because if so, I'm afraid I haven't time for this. I need to get out of here. Now."

The doctor gestured toward the bed, pulling up a metal folding chair beside it. "Have a seat for a second, Dr. Moore."

Sam leaned against the wall and folded his arms. "I'd prefer to stand, if you don't mind."

"Fine." Prendergast turned toward him. "But just slow down for a minute and listen." He took a breath. "Your family signed you in because you suffered a severe emotional trauma. You needed help. Serious help. And even though you feel better now, it's up to us to determine if and when you're ready to return to society without being a danger to yourself or anyone else. *We* will make that decision." His lips pressed together in a tight line. "So it would behoove you to cooperate."

Sam spoke through gritted teeth. "I want to speak to your head administrator, my colleague Dr. Andrea Garcia, my lawyer, and my son. In that order. Would you please arrange a meeting today with whoever's in charge? And remind them that I'm a physician with some pull in this community."

Prendergast sat back under the onslaught and pocketed his pencil. His left eye ticked. "Okay, okay. I'll see what I can do. You do appear to have spontaneously returned to a stable state. I just want to be sure it's sustained."

Sam tried to reason with him. "If it doesn't last, you can drag me back in here, can't you? You know my children will do the right thing. And send Ned Olsen in as well, if you can reach him. He'll assure you I'm no risk to society."

Prendergast pursed his lips and stood. "I'll see what I can do."

He smoothed his crisp white coat and moved toward the door. "If you'd like breakfast, the nurse will be by soon to take you to the morning room."

Sam's stomach grumbled. "Thanks. But please, tell her no more meds. I need a clear head."

Prendergast didn't agree, but murmured something about possibly changing orders as he slid out the door.

ꟷ

Sam intended to wait until after breakfast to take out the marble, but as soon as the door shut after Prendergast, a glow shone from the bathroom. Fingers of wispy green light snaked across the floor, beckoning him.

He poked his head into the hall. Deserted and quiet. Nobody to bother him for a little while.

"Okay, Billy. I'm coming." He shut the bathroom door, grabbed the marble from the soap dish, and slid to the floor with his back wedged against the door.

The transition was abrupt this time. No lazy swirls of green fog gently deposited him into another realm, suspending him above a scene. This time Billy plunked him live in the middle of a dark night. Woodland grass wetted his sneakers. Peepers chirped from the trees. A shooting star blazed over his head, partially hidden by the swaying black tree limbs.

He looked at his hands. *How old am I?* The skin was well-worn, with stained creases lining his index fingers, indicative of years of weeding. Jeans and a flannel shirt protected him from the night chill.

At least Billy didn't transport me in my hospital gown.

A stirring caught his attention to the left, a pheasant squawked at him and trotted away as if insulted. Beyond the startled bird, yellow-purple sparks of a bonfire roared. Drumming shattered the silence, followed by soft chanting.

Sam pushed his way through the brush, ignoring searing scratches from briars. He lay on the ground and stared through a honeysuckle bush at the scene before him.

Bodies swayed in the firelight, dressed in scant clothing reminiscent of animal hides worn by cave men.

What was Billy up to this time? This looked like the same scene he showed him before, but this time there were no monkish robes on the dancers.

The stereo system whisked what seemed like a medieval witching ceremony to the twentieth century. A gas-powered generator hummed from a rough-hewn table of wooden planks and saw horses, powering the system. Someone cranked the volume, blasting the primal beat through the forest, shattering the would-be calm.

He crept closer, focused on the figures gyrating around the flames.

"Hail Satan!" The scream chilled Sam's blood. The man's voice, vaguely familiar, resonated through the ferns and birches, shaking branches and leaves. Lean and dark-haired, he spun and raised his arms to the sky, repeatedly crouching and thrusting upward. An owl hooted overhead, as if offended by the raucous behavior. Six other bodies danced around the fire. Sam studied them.

Three bearded men, probably in their twenties. Four lithe young women, all with long hair that streamed down their backs. One overweight, spectacled youth; he seemed no older than eighteen. He watched them circle the fire. The last figure came into view: a pregnant woman, her rotund belly naked in the light of the fire. Sam drew back. The vision of a woman with child dancing to the devil drove a cold spiral of horror through him.

On his stomach, Sam eased forward on a carpet of moist leaves, the fecund scent rising from the path he made as he squirmed forward. The drums beat faster, and a heightened sense of dread washed over him. Fury thrummed through the woods, echoed in the words spewed by the leader.

"We beseech thee, O mighty One. Favor us with a sign."

The man ripped his loincloth from his body and flung it into the fire, facing the flames as if in supplication. Quickly following his lead, the others cast off their odd collection of furry ragged garments, circling the fire with arms stretched to the sky. Fire reflected on young tight flesh; muscles rippled in the orange-red light; legs and arms flashed.

The dancers began to slowly rotate, their eyes closed as they mumbled strange words Sam didn't understand. The pregnant woman, slender except for the roundness of her belly, shook out her hair pinned in a chignon at the base of her neck. Red-gold locks flew and spun around her body, wrapping her shoulders, arms, and distended abdomen in a flurry of spun copper.

Sam froze. His jaw dropped. He blinked and refocused.

Oh my God. It's Ginger.

He woke to the sound of someone calling his name.

"Dr. Moore? You okay in there?"

Sam answered in a thick voice, pulling himself up by the sink. "I'm fine. Just give me a second." He leaned over to flush the toilet, then splashed water on his face again.

"Okay. I'm your nurse. I'm here to take you to the morning room for breakfast. And you have visitors arriving at eight-thirty, so you'd best hurry."

He dried his face and hands and opened the door.

The nurse, a gray-haired matron with kind eyes and dark purple lipstick, smiled at him. She looked vaguely familiar, but he couldn't place her. "Dr. Moore. My name's Doris. It's nice to see you up. Would you like to dress this morning?"

He headed for the clothes on his bed, holding the gap in his gown closed with one hand. "You bet I would."

Chapter Twenty

Doris waited outside the bathroom while Sam dressed. When he was sure he'd buttoned his shirt correctly—he'd been paranoid that any "off" behavior would signal him worthy of lifetime incarceration—he double-checked his fly and his sneakers. Assured that he looked much more normal than he felt, he opened the door and joined Doris. "I'm starving. I don't suppose you could roust me up some eggs Benedict and sourdough toast?"

She chuckled and patted his arm. "Oh, Dr. Moore. It's so nice to see you back among the living."

Sam cocked his head and stared at her for a moment. "Doris? Do I know you?"

She clucked at him like a mother hen. "Oh my goodness. I don't expect you'd remember me. I worked as a nurse at your children's school for two years back in '92. I don't think we ever met officially, but I used to see you picking up your children after school quite often."

"That's it! We had to walk past your office to get to the principal's domain, didn't we?"

She tittered and covered her mouth with her hand. "Indeed you did. Your Beth got in more trouble than Andy, didn't he?"

Sam smiled. "She was a rebel, all right. Until we got her into swimming. That straightened her out."

"Oh, my. I remember your Bethie winning quite a few meets."

Sam brightened. "Yes. She was a real fish in water, that girl."

They'd been edging toward the corridor step by step, when Sam finally put up his hands. "Enough of memory lane. I really need some food."

"Of course, dear. Let me give you the royal tour." Doris walked him down a long corridor lined with painted cement bricks and various patients' doors. Sam didn't see any people inside and assumed they'd all be in the cafeteria. They reached the end of the T and turned left.

Doris fluttered a hand to the right. "Down there are the treatment rooms, doctors' offices, and a gym."

"A gym?" Sam's eyebrow raised. "They didn't have that when I was here before."

"It's new." Doris looked at her feet. "I heard about your stay here when you were a boy. I'm sorry you had to come back, Dr. Moore. It must be a very difficult time for you."

Sam paced evenly beside her toward the noisy end of the corridor. "I won't lie to you, Doris. It's been rough."

"I can't imagine losing a brother and a spouse. You're a very strong man."

Her sympathy threatened to shatter his control. But he couldn't lose it in front of her. She might tell Prendergast, and he might never get out of the place. "Sometimes I don't feel so strong, Doris."

She tossed him a sympathetic smile and motioned to a room just ahead of the noisy room on their right. "There's the visitors' center. And here we are. Our private dining facility. It's not fancy, but there's plenty of food."

He brushed his hair back from his forehead and straightened his shoulders. "Okay. Let's do this."

Doris walked him to the long buffet filled with hot dishes, cereal, coffee, tea, and juice. He couldn't see the eating area from the alcove they entered, but could hear the voices and clinking of silverware. "Here's where you pick up your tray and silverware."

Sam grabbed a tray, napkin, and utensils.

Doris opened the cover on the first hot dish. "We have eggs every day, and some sort of meat. Today, I think it's ham." They shuffled down the line, and he loaded up his plate. "Here are your usual assortment of cold cereals, and three types of bread you can put in that toaster over there." They walked farther. "Coffee?"

Sam nodded. "Yes. Please. Lots of coffee."

Doris poured it for him, added cream and sugar at his request, and walked with him around the corner. She stopped short of the eating area. "I'd recommend that table on the far end. Those folks are usually pretty quiet. I don't think you'll have any trouble with them."

Sam looked at the crowded room and steeled himself. "Okay. Thanks, Doris. I appreciate the help."

She touched the buttons at the top of her uniform and produced a wan smile. "Of course, Dr. Moore. I want to help however I can. I was a great admirer of your practice. You helped so many of my friends and their families over the years. You're a good man. You deserve better than this."

He took a few steps toward the tables, then called over his shoulder. "Thanks. But don't worry. I'll be out of here soon."

A man in a blue bathrobe at the closest table burst into laughter. "Sure you will, buddy! We're all getting out this afternoon." He chuckled into his cereal bowl and peeked at Sam beneath bushy black eyebrows. Two women at his table snickered and stared at Sam.

He closed his eyes briefly, opened them, and forged toward the far wall.

Sam devoured two plates of scrambled eggs and ham, and four pieces of whole wheat toast. He refilled his coffee three times, drawing strength from its sweet warmth.

At least fifty patients crowded around the cafeteria tables. Some ate with vacant stares, others required urging by nursing assistants who spoke in very loud voices with patronizing overtones.

One man with a long braided beard swatted flies that no one could see while a patient, white-coated woman fed him bites of oatmeal. Another refused food and rocked in the corner, humming "Amazing Grace." A few fights broke out on the far side of the room. Doris had steered him right. His table was relatively quiet, with three men focused solely on their plates and a half dozen women who talked to each other and ignored him. It was just as well.

The frazzled young woman to Sam's left darted a nervous glance at him and nervously straightened her pile of ten pieces of toast. She drew the salt, pepper, jam bucket, and as many utensils as she could reach into a pile before her, guarding it as if it were a fortune.

Working on his last piece of toast, Sam slowly reached for a small rectangular packet of strawberry jam. She eyed him with ferocity and yanked it back to her place when he was done.

"Hope it's okay," he mumbled. "I'm really hungry."

Her shoulders relaxed a fraction of an inch and she released a long breath. She pushed back greasy blond bangs and nodded. "'S okay. I like the grape, anyway."

He piled on the last teaspoon of strawberry jam, popped the crust in his mouth, and pushed back from the table.

God in Heaven. I don't belong here.

The clock on the wall read eight-twenty-eight. With a polite nod at his hoarding neighbor, he brought his tray up to the moving belt at the exit and headed for the visitors' center.

Chapter Twenty-One

Ned Olsen sat at a table, tapping his pencil on his notebook and trying to avoid conversation with an elderly Indian man with bulging eyes and grabby fingers.

"Sorry. I'll need that." He pulled the pencil out of his reach and stood when Sam entered. Relief flooded his features. "Sam. Good to see you up and about."

They migrated to a quiet section of the room where two shabby stuffed chairs squeezed into a corner.

"Ned." Sam took his hand and held it, almost reluctant to release it. Although Ned had troubled him in the past, the familiar sense of being in the presence of someone he knew, or rather, *someone who knew him,* was overwhelming.

Ned cast his eyes down and away, then back to Sam's. "I told them to call me the minute you, er, came to. I'm really sorry about your loss."

Pain stabbed at him, but he pushed it away. *No time for grieving. I need to figure out what happened and undo it.* For a moment he wondered if he'd said it aloud, but Ned continued to look at him with empathy.

"Thank you." Sam waited a beat, then looked directly in Ned's eyes. "Have you got any leads?"

Ned shook his head. "Sorry, no. I've been on the case solid for the past two weeks, and haven't got too far. That's why I wanted to talk to you. We need to go over a few things."

Sam swallowed hard. He'd have to talk about Rachel, and wasn't sure if he could trust himself. Steeling himself, he gave his assent. "Go ahead. Ask away."

Ned took out his notebook, frowned, then scribbled in it. "We have no motive, Sam. No robbery. Nothing was missing, according to your daughter. No forced entry."

Sam shook his head. "There wouldn't be a forced entry. We don't lock our doors."

Ned frowned. "Not wise, Sam." He hesitated, then rushed the next few words. "I'm going to be honest with you. My boss is pushing me to arrest you. He's going with a 'crime of passion.'"

Sam rolled his eyes. "That's insane. You know how much I love… loved Rachel. That's pure nonsense."

Ned twirled the pencil in his fingers. "So, what do you think happened?"

Sam folded his hands on the table and looked down. "Christ. I don't know. But I've had a lot of time to think about it, and I'm betting all three murders are linked."

Ned stared at him, unblinking. "Uh huh."

"And…I think they're linked through me."

"How so?"

Sam shifted in his seat. "I'm not sure. But it's too coincidental. Ginger. Lou. And Rachel. All within days." He blew out a long breath. "I knew *every little thing* about my wife and her history. I can't summon one single memory of a person who held a grudge against her, or felt persecuted by her, or simply disliked her. There's *nothing* in her past that would remotely motivate such a…brutal killing." Sam's voice shook, but he kept going. "So it has to be either something she witnessed or something even more bizarre. Something that links the three murders."

Ned's tight brow relaxed. "I thought the same thing. And I've been doing some research on Ginger Kennedy. I've learned a little more about her."

Sam raised one eyebrow. "And?"

"She had quite a past. Was involved in some weird goings-on in the sixties with the guy she partnered up with. Raoul Mercedes."

Sam looked up with interest. "Raoul?"

"Right. He died last month. You know him?"

Sam didn't hesitate. "No." He waited a minute before asking the obvious. "So, how'd he die?"

"Mugged coming out of a convenience store. Stabbed in the back. The guy got his wallet and disappeared."

"Wow."

"Yeah. Well, he was a real piece of work, that one. Accused, but not convicted, of killing two young women as part of a satanic cult. Sacrifices, they speculated. But they couldn't make it stick. Suspected there were many more victims, but he was a slippery bastard. Covered his tracks very well."

"Ginger was actually with this guy?" Sam slowly shook his head. "Wow. She seemed so...normal back then."

"Yeah. Well, you never know. Guess they'd been together since before that. There was one weird thing, though."

"Weirder than human sacrifices?"

Ned shot him a half-smile. "Well, no. But I thought you might like to know about it. It could explain her visit here."

"Really?"

"Yeah. Nine months after you had your...er...relationship with Ginger, she had a baby."

Sam pictured Ginger dancing around the fire, her belly round with child. She'd been young, very young. Probably about the same age as when he'd... He shook himself and turned to Ned. "How do we know it wasn't Raoul's?"

"We don't. But the birth certificate said differently."

Sam sat up. *"What?"*

"Yeah. She named the father."

"And?"

"She named you."

Sam felt numb. "Wait one minute, here. Are you *sure*? I never heard squat from her."

"I know. But I think maybe she came up here to tell you. After Raoul died, maybe she felt she should clear the air, set things right."

Sam stared into the distance. "Unbelievable. Boy or girl?"

"Girl. Susan. Ginger kept her maiden name. Susan Kennedy."

"Susan." He looked off into the distance. "I have another daughter?"

"If Ginger told the truth, of course."

Sam let out a long sigh. "We could do a paternity test."

"You could, but we can't find a trace of her. We're trying to get a snapshot from school, but they moved a lot, so there are spotty records. We're not even sure the child was properly schooled, for that matter. There were a few mentions of home schooling, and one record of a very long psychiatric stay."

Sam's eyes widened. "Really?"

Ned nodded, trying to avoid the truth that stared them in the face.

"Guess it runs in the family, huh?" Sam almost laughed, but held it in. It sounded too nutty.

Ned put out a hand in protest. "Don't say that. You had a really good reason to lose it."

He grimaced. "Yeah. I did. But maybe Susan did, too. Who knows what she witnessed as a child? Especially if she was raised with Satanism."

Ned pursed his lips. "Not a pretty picture."

Sam's face fell. "Poor kid."

"She's not a kid any longer, Sam. She'd be around forty."

The marble heated up in Sam's pocket. He reached down and quickly covered it. "It's a lot to digest. Do you mind if I rest now? I'm suddenly feeling whipped."

Ned pocketed his notebook and slid the pencil behind his ear. "Not a problem." He pushed up from the chair with a grunt. "How 'bout I stop back tomorrow?"

Sam walked Ned to the door. "If I'm still here. If not, I'll call you from home." His face darkened with suppressed rage. "I mean to find out who killed my wife, Ned. And I'll be honest, I want revenge. Real bad."

Ned sighed and rubbed his fingers over his eyes. "I understand. I want him almost as bad as you do. But promise me you won't do anything on your own. You're under suspicion as it is."

The marble vibrated again. Sam abruptly turned to leave. "I promise. See you tomorrow."

Chapter Twenty-Two

SAM STUMBLED INTO HIS ROOM AND WEDGED HIMSELF INTO THE BATHROOM before he collapsed in the green fog licking his ankles.

The marble propelled him back to the damp woods in a flash, but this time crispy bronze leaves layered the path where he crouched. A full moon filtered silver light through overhead branches, splotchy and wavering on the ground at his feet. Cold air rustled beneath his collar and up his shirtsleeves. He shivered and listened against the sound of his own breathing.

In the distance, drumming and chanting pulsed against the rhythm of the night. Just like before.

Why was Billy showing him this scene again? He already knew that Ginger was pregnant. That she was involved in this cult. What more could he learn tonight? And why was it autumn this time?

He rose and pressed forward on the narrow path flattened by deer hooves, flanked by bracken woven into the ferns and brambles. Lights flickered in the distance again. A bonfire—three times the size of the last one—wavered against the velvet night.

A circle of one hundred black-hooded beings surged around the fire and wove among each other in a serpentine. All arms shot to the sky in supplication, shrieking words in Olde English, or a perversion of Latin. Sam couldn't be sure. One thing that was sure, the coven, or whatever it was called, had expanded its ranks. The fire leapt high in the clearing as if to second his thoughts.

Sam treaded lightly, but stopped in his tracks when he spied a young girl standing on the edge of the forest. Dark hair. Undernourished pale limbs. A thin cape of ragged pink cotton, dusky in the moonlight. She gasped and held a hand to her mouth in horror, gazing toward the ceremony. Sam followed her line of sight and froze.

An upright coffin stood near the fire, its cover closed. Sam watched as a hooded man opened the cover with great ceremony, exposing a bound and gagged woman inside. He jerked her from the enclosure by the ropes that tied her wrists together, but she fought him hard, struggling and kicking with her unbound legs. The hackles on Sam's back rose when shrieks of terror escaped beneath the gag on the young woman's mouth.

Four figures raced forward to stop the captive's struggle. Like a rock star being propelled on a wave of human arms, she was passed over the circle of gyrating worshippers, bouncing up and down on the crest of their mania.

When she'd been passed around the circle, two of them held her on a rough fashioned table, made with boards and sawhorses like the one that held the sound system. They quickly tied her down, in spite of her twisting and turning.

The whole scene had struck Sam as unreal, as if he were watching a bad horror movie on television. But when a knife flashed upward, glinting white in the moonlight, he jumped. Before he could stop himself, he let loose with a wild cry. "STOP!"

The girl at the edge of the clearing, sobbing now, suddenly turned and stared at Sam in horror. Her mouth dropped open; her hands fell to her sides. At first Sam thought she'd welcome his help, but in seconds her eyes narrowed and her lips curled. "Intruder!" She pointed at him as if she were accusing him of witchcraft. Something about her eyes made Sam hesitate. Familiar, yet not. He couldn't move; his legs were stuck to the ground as if he'd grown roots like the ancient trees that waved their branches overhead.

Can she actually see me? Am I truly integrated into this time?

The murderer with the weapon stopped before slashing his victim and turned his head in their direction. Raoul's twisted features emerged when the hood slipped back. "After him!"

Raoul's primal scream sent coils of fear through Sam and his stomach tightened. Vindictive cries filled the air. The horde of robed cult members streamed up the hill toward him, roaring obscenities and moving as one like the black hand of the devil. The girl collapsed sobbing against a tree when Raoul and his followers crested the hill. "He's over there! He's watching us!"

Wait a minute. Just wait a minute. I've gotta get the hell out of here. Jesus Christ, this is for real.

Sam turned and ran as fast as his sixty-two-year-old legs could carry him. Stumbling over roots and branches, he flew through the underbrush, heart walloping in his chest and legs burning.

The frenzied crowd grew louder; closer. He heard their ragged breathing over his own. In one panicked moment of clarity, he realized his only hope lay with his brother's control of this place and time.

Out loud, he screamed. *"BILLY! Get me out of here!"*

Arms reached for him, fingers brushed his back. He stumbled on a tree root and flew sideways, hitting his head against a tree trunk. Darkness threatened as he was smothered by the frenzied mob.

ꙮ

Sam woke on the floor of his bathroom, hands grimy and cold. He stood slowly, stretching his bruised and aching legs. His head hurt like hell. When he reached up to feel the bump, he saw the scratches under his shirtsleeve that crisscrossed his arms. He looked in the mirror and plucked a twig from his hair.

My God.

He felt himself grow unsteady, but continued to stare at his reflection.

I can do it. I can actively *be* in the past.

They saw me. I felt their hands on my back.

His brain grew fevered, searching for possibilities. But nothing emerged.

He cleaned himself up, dabbing at the scratches on his arm and a deeper one on the palm of his hand. When the bleeding stopped, he headed back into the hospital room for a clean long-sleeved shirt to cover his arms. Someone had brought several changes of clothing from his closet at home. He guessed Beth, but it could have been Andy. He rolled the bloody shirt into a tight ball and wedged it down under the trashcan in the corner of the room. Buttoning the clean shirt, he began to pace.

I've got to find out who did it.

He perched for a moment on the edge of the bed, then strode toward the window.

Billy. Why can't you just tell me?

He removed the marble from his pocket and turned it in his fingers. The cat's eye gleamed cold; its jade glass sparkled in the muted light that filtered through the dusty window.

Come on. Can't you show me more?

The sphere remained unresponsive, smooth and cool in his hand. Before Sam could try again to summon his brother, a brisk knock on the door was followed by the appearance of Doris.

"Someone else to see you, Dr. Moore. She's waiting in the visitors' center. Her name is…" She looked down to check her clipboard. "Dr. Garcia." Atop an easy smile, Doris's eyes twinkled. "You're quite the popular patient today."

"Thank you, Doris." He eased past her matronly figure and hurried out into the long corridor. At the end of the hall, he swung left and burst into the visitors' center. Garcia stood on the far side of the room, holding back a curtain and gazing out the window.

"Garcia."

She spun around to face him. The deep creases in her brow relaxed slightly when she took in his appearance. Hair combed. Clean-shaven. Dressed in street clothes. No bloody scratches showing from his out of time and body experience.

"Sam." She extended both hands to him. "You look better. Much better. Are you?" Her Latin eyes studied him intently.

He squeezed her hands, then pulled out a chair for her and one for himself. "Yes. I'm fine." Poised on the edge of the seat, he drummed his fingers on the table. "And I need to get the hell out of here. Today."

She averted her eyes momentarily, then leaned forward and touched his sleeve. "Sam. You know you don't want to rush these things."

His expression hardened. "I've been here for two weeks, Garcia. *Two freakin' weeks!* Look at me. I'm dressed. Clean. Alert." He regulated his breathing, forcing himself to sound calm. "Don't I seem okay to you?"

She nodded hesitantly. "You seem great, today, Sam. But it's the first day you've really felt better, isn't it? The first day you've actually been able to converse and walk and…"

His hair puffed up when he expelled a frustrated burst of air. He paused and steadied himself. It wouldn't help to show his impatience. "You're right. But I feel like I'll go crazy again if I'm stuck here for another minute. I need to be home, Garcia. With my kids. My grandkids. I need to grieve with them, to cry over Rachel's grave. I need my family."

Her eyes softened, filled with empathy. "Oh, Sam. I'm so sorry. I still can't believe she's gone."

His mouth tightened, and he worked hard to check his emotions. "I know. It's insane."

She surprised him by twisting in her seat and hitting the table with a clenched fist. "Why would anyone kill her? It makes no sense."

He leaned back, shoulders slumped. He tried to push the vision of Rachel's dead body from his mind. "Murder never makes sense."

She blinked her eyes and wiped away a tear.

"How's the practice?" In spite of his concern for his own dilemma, he couldn't help asking. He'd spent his life building that practice and worried about his patients. Former patients, he reminded himself.

"It's crazy busy. I might have to hire a second doctor to help me handle the workload. With all the school physicals for sports, the vaccines needed, and the summer accidents, I've been doing extended hours and still not seeing everyone."

Sam touched her arm and tried a winsome smile. "If you hire someone, make sure they're as good as you were for me."

They chatted for another fifteen minutes about patients and the office, about new legislations that hampered the actual doctoring Garcia wished she could focus on, and finally came around to Sam's family again.

"Andy's holding up pretty well, but Beth's a wreck. I saw her last night at Wegmans. It's going to take some time, Sam. For all of you."

He tightened his jaw to control the wave of sadness that threatened. "I know. That's why I need to be back with them, Garcia. They need me as much as I need them."

Scraping back her chair, she stood and smoothed back the loose strands of hair that escaped her ponytail, tucking them behind her ear. "I know, Sam." She flashed a half smile and leaned down to give him a hug. "Listen. I'll see what I can do. Let me talk to Prendergast."

Sam stayed at the table long after she left, ignoring the persistent buzz of a fly that repeatedly landed on the back of his hand.

Would she do it? Would she push for his release?

He fingered the marble, thinking through the events of the past month.

Ginger Kennedy. Murdered the day she arrived in Conaroga. Apparently about to contact him. Was she planning to reveal the existence of his daughter, Susan? If he could believe the reports and her testimony on the birth certificate. And if he really did have a daughter born of those few moments of youthful lust, who would try to stop Ginger from telling him? Who would care? Raoul was dead. He was the only one who might object. The only possible monetary angle Sam could think of would be if Ginger sued him for paternity. Of course, his daughter was forty, so that theory was crazy. And Ginger's death pretty much eliminated that scenario.

Could her death have been completely unrelated?

Unlikely. Billy had been showing him far too many bizarre scenes to ignore the aspects of the cult-laden past. The poor little girl, helpless and locked in a room while her mother participated in sacrificial rituals. The confused brainwashed preteen, standing watch at the edge of the forest. Had she been Susan? The child had been badly abused. And if the reports of her psychiatric stays were correct, she'd been hospitalized as a result.

And what about Lou?

Poor Lou. Devastated over the impending end of her marriage, she'd fallen apart just before she was strangled. But according to Ned Olsen, nobody of any consequence was caught on the videotape going in or out of the public offices.

So why was she murdered?

Was it coincidence that she died days after Ginger, just before Rachel?

Abruptly, Sam stood and walked toward the nurse's station at the far corner of the empty room. "May I please make a local call?" He used his most charming voice and tossed the young woman a warm, fatherly smile.

"Why of course, Dr. Moore." Sam dialed Ned Olsen's number; surprised he remembered it after all that had happened.

"Olsen here."

Sam sat in the chair beside the nurse and turned his back to her, speaking in low tones.

"Ned? Sam. Listen, I think it might help if you let me view that video tape."

"To look for Lou's murderer?" He answered as if it were the most natural request in the world.

"Yeah."

"It's evidence, Sam."

"I know. But you said no one stood out as a suspect, right? And have you gotten any further since we talked?"

Silence.

"Have you?" Sam repeated.

"No. I haven't. I suppose I could order a copy of the tape."

Sam relaxed. "Good." He lowered his voice further. "Listen, I'll let you know if they spring me from the nut house today. But if you don't hear from me, bring the tape here."

Ned answered quickly. "Will do, Sam. I'll get it to you as soon as I can."

Chapter Twenty-Three

At two in the afternoon, Sam sat in Prendergast's office, one ankle resting over his opposite thigh with hands clasped on his lap. He'd purposely arranged himself in the seat to look confident and comfortable. Every action and response had to scream "sane". Otherwise, he might not ever get out of this goddamned place.

The lunacy of his own rehearsed actions and doublethink almost made him laugh. *For crying out loud, I am sane! I just have to act like myself and not let anything like the marble creep into my conversation.*

Prendergast scratched his pencil across a yellow legal-sized tablet. "So, Dr. Moore. Is that how you want me to address you? Or would you prefer Sam?"

Sam smiled. *I'm just an easy, affable guy sitting for a chat with another doctor. Don't get pissed. Don't show him how anxious you are to get out of here.* "Call me Sam."

"Okay, then. Sam it is." He uncrossed his legs and leaned forward with a knowing smile. "How was your day? Are you exhausted yet? You've had quite a lot going, considering this is the first day you've been out of bed in weeks."

Sam waited a beat, as if he were carefully weighing the question. "I'm feeling pretty darned good, Doc. A little tired, I guess."

"How did your visits with Olsen and Dr. Garcia go?"

"Great. It was good to see them."

"How are you feeling about your loss? Have you accepted what happened, Sam?"

My loss? "Doctor, since I woke up this morning, I realized who I am and what happened. Right now, I just want to get home to my family to grieve with them. I need them, and they need me." He closed his eyes and slowly opened them again. "Can you understand that?"

Dr. Prendergast looked over the top of his glasses at Sam as if he weren't used to being asked questions in session. "Er. Yes. Of course I can, Sam."

"Can you imagine losing your wife on what should have been a supremely happy occasion, the homecoming of your son from the war? Can you imagine finding her laying dead in your laundry room with pruning shears sticking out of her chest? Can you, Doc?" Sam's voice cracked, and he didn't try to hide it. It was supposed to be healthy to let out the emotions, right? Good therapy. His eyes welled with unshed tears which he roughly brushed away. "It was just too much for me. My brain couldn't handle the pain, so I went where it wouldn't hurt for a while."

Prendergast stared at his tablet, swirling the pencil in small circles. "Like you did with Billy?"

Sam looked him square in the eyes. "Exactly. But I came out of that, and I've come out of it again, this time."

"Your Doctor Garcia thinks you'd do okay at home."

Sam tented his fingers and waited.

Prendergast tapped his pencil on the pad of paper. "What do you think?"

"I agree. I'm back to myself. I'm cogent, clear in the head, and functioning normally. I'll need lots of support, and therapy, to get over this. But I can do that as an outpatient." He had no plans to go through with it, or to come back for counseling. If he needed to talk, he'd seek out Garcia or other friends. But the idea that he embraced therapy might buy him some points.

Pendergast liked it. Although an eye still twitched, a faint smile crossed his lips. "Yes. I think you could manage from home quite nicely. You'll just need to promise to make your appointments here so we can track your progress."

Sam waited some more.

"Would you be willing to do that?"

"Of course."

Prendergast leaned back. "Okay, good. Well, why don't we start by talking about how you feel about being a widower? How will you cope when you see friends and family on the street? In the market? What will you say to people who haven't heard, or who want to know more about the murder case?"

Sam's insides jarred, shaken by the questions. He hadn't considered any of these, and didn't really want to think about it. "I, um...I guess I need to think about some pat answers for them in advance. I sure as heck don't want to start sobbing if they bring it up."

"I understand. Now how would that make you feel?"

"If I lost it in front of someone in Wegmans?"

"Yes."

"It would make me feel like a fool. Like a man who can't control his emotions, like a weakling."

Prendergast glanced up at him. "You think having emotions makes you less of a man?"

Sam flashed a half-smile, trying to add some humility to the mix. "Well, no. Everyone has emotions. But there's a time and place to break down crying. It's generally not thought well of in public. Is it?"

"I suppose you're right. As long as you're not suppressing those feelings all the time. You need to face them, accept and own them, and embrace them in order to get through this."

"I know."

The psychiatrist raised an eyebrow. "Good. Now, let's talk about your children."

"Beth and Andy?"

"Yes. For the past few weeks, they've had to play the parental role for you. They cared for you, brought you here to get help, took care of your home and cat, and things like that. How will you feel when they drive you home?"

"It's odd thinking of my kids having to take that role. I'm going to want to fix it and start taking care of them. After all, their mother was just taken from them. They have to be in agony."

Prendergast frowned and shook his head. "That's all well and good, but Andy and Beth are adults. It might behoove you to treat them as equals. Let them help you as you help them. Shared responsibility for each other's wellness might be the way to go." He put his pencil down.

Sam leaned forward and touched the doctor's knee. "You must know what kind of pain my kids are going through. How did your father die?"

Prendergast's head shot up, and his confident mask shattered. "Parkinson's. Three years ago. Horrible way to go." He rubbed his eyes and put his glasses back on. "It was hell for him, and it took a huge toll on my mother and me. I still miss him every day." He set his pad down and looked out the window to a manicured lawn with walkways and benches. "But I can't imagine losing a loved one to violence. You'd have no warning. No time to say goodbye. I honestly have no idea how you're handling this."

"Well, you saw how I handled it. By not handling it, I guess."

"Hmm. Seems like it worked for you." Prendergast checked his watch. "Your children are coming to see you tonight around dinnertime. Did anyone tell you?"

Sam smiled. "Doris has kept me up to date. I can't wait to see them. Will they be able to take me home tonight?"

"I'm thinking tomorrow afternoon would be more suitable, Sam. I've got a lot of paperwork to get started for you. You know the drill."

Sam stood and shook Prendergast's hand. "I do. And that'll work just fine, Doc. Thank you."

ᘓᘐ

After his session, Sam actually felt better. He hoped he'd seemed normal. Composed. Sane. He'd allowed his true emotions to play their course when they talked about Rachel, and his discovery of her body, but he'd pulled back sufficiently to maintain a semblance of control.

At least that's how he *thought* he'd behaved.

He sat in the yellow plastic chair beneath the window in his room, checking the clock again. Andy and Beth were due after dinner. Andy had called from work and made a date for six-thirty. He'd been overcome with emotion, choked up. And it had done Sam good to comfort his son. He needed to be there for his children. He needed to be the strong one, the one in control.

He brushed back a lock of hair and sighed. He watched the clock click from four-fifty to four-fifty-one.

He braced his fingers in a teepee.

Come on.

At four-fifty-five, a bell rang in the hallway.

Dinner.

Sam lunged to his feet and strode toward the dining hall, brushing shoulders with a few lethargic walkers who shuffled along the hallway on nurses' arms. The aroma of institutional food greeted his rumbling stomach. He'd missed lunch and was ready for more sustenance.

When he reached the cart, he found ground beef floating in gravy, white rice, canned green beans, and applesauce.

Not exactly a gourmet banquet. But decidedly edible.

He filled a plate, grabbed some plastic ware and a fistful of paper napkins, and found a seat on the far side of the room, away from the huddled group that rocked and mumbled nearby. The food needed seasoning, but the only choices were salt and pepper. He liberally sprinkled both on the food, then forked it into his mouth.

He tried hard not to picture Rachel's beef stroganoff, rich with wine sauce and savory herbs. Or the nutty brown rice over which she'd served it. The crisp romaine salad that always accompanied it, filled with black olives, shredded cheese, and yellow peppers. Her deep brown eyes floated in front of him, smiling. He imagined her pushing a piece of cherry pie toward him and refilling his coffee.

Hang on, baby. I'm coming back for you. Soon. Real soon.

He deposited his tray on the conveyor belt in the back of the room and grabbed two sugar cookies from the serving cart. Five thirty. Another hour to kill.

The marble heated against his leg, sending a shiver of anticipation up his spine.

Do I have time?

He decided to take a chance, hurried back to his room, and shut himself in the bathroom.

Chapter Twenty-Four

The marble sparked to life the minute Sam took it from his pocket and cupped it between both hands. In seconds, he was thrust back in time, landing in a large, dark closet that smelled of wet mop and Lysol. Voices and a crack of light drew his attention to the door. He shuffled slowly toward it and put his eye to the slit.

With a start, he recognized Ginger. She sat in her kitchen with Raoul and her baby. His baby. Little Susan.

This time, the sensation was different—like he was inside an inflated green balloon, pushing against a taut rubbery substance that vibrated when he breathed in and out. He touched it, and it rippled and stretched, but didn't burst.

Is this Billy's way of telling me not to interfere?

Raoul slouched at the table, dressed in a ratty tee shirt and undershorts, with his bare feet splayed out on the linoleum. His hair, tangled and greasy, hung over bloodshot eyes. Susan sat in a high chair to his left, rapping the wooden tray with a spoon.

Raoul massaged his temples and closed his eyes. "Jesus. Can't you shut the brat up?" A patch of sweat darkened the back of his shirt.

Ginger turned from the stove, a plate of eggs in her hands. Her face remained neutral, but stress showed in the tight lines around her eyes and mouth. "Here, honey. Try these. Sunny side up. Not too wet, not too dry. Just the way you like them."

The rapping turned to banging, followed by a piercing shriek when the baby's bottle fell to the floor. "Baba!"

"Get the kid her bottle or I'll..." Raoul slapped both of his hands on the table and glared at the child. A blue vein snaked down his temple, throbbing.

Ginger's eyes narrowed. With flushed cheeks and a frown, she bent down to pick up the bottle and rinsed it under hot water. Stiff-legged, she walked it to the baby who immediately popped it in her mouth.

She leaned both hands on the table and glowered, inches from Raoul's face. Her eyes spit fire. "You'll what, big man? Hit me again?" She lifted her nightgown to reveal a large purple bruise on one thigh.

"Does it make you feel like a real man? Or will you sink even lower and hit our daughter, too?"

Sam involuntarily sucked in his breath, hoping he hadn't made an audible sound. The discoloration on Ginger's thigh matched the size and shape of Raoul's meaty hands.

Raoul glanced at the black-and-blue mark as if it were a stain on the wallpaper, and took a bite of eggs. "Needs salt."

She flounced back to the stove and moved the fry pan off the burner, then turned to hiss at him, tossing her long red braid over her shoulder. "Get it yourself, you lazy oaf."

His face darkened, growing blacker as the seconds ticked by. With a roar, he thumped the table with his fists, rattling his coffee cup. "You get it, bitch! I bring in the money around here. Your job is to serve me. Now do as you're told."

The baby started to cry. Ginger ran to the counter, grabbed the saltshaker, and threw it at Raoul, who caught it mid-air. His expression changed from rage to shock, then withered to cold fury. She hurried to the child and picked her up.

"It's okay, Susie. Mommy's here. I won't let the big, bad man hurt you." She clamped the child to her chest and glared at him.

Raoul pushed back from the table, knocking over his chair. Coffee sloshed over the rim of his cup. Wrath transformed his face to a grotesque mask. He stomped toward Ginger and grabbed her arm, squeezing hard until she moaned and sank to the floor with her child. When he released her, red welts appeared where he'd pinched her soft skin in the vice of his cruel fingers. He cupped her chin and jerked her face toward him. "You listen and you listen good. I demand respect in this house. From both you and that little wretch you claim is mine. Every day her goddamn skin gets lighter, and I'm starting to think there's no Latino blood in her veins. If that's true, and you cheated on me, you friggin' whore…" He shoved her chin away. "Then you'll both pay. And one of these days, you two will end up in the sacrificial coffin. I think the gods would like that." He towered above her, leering into her face. He pulled back with a tight fist. Trembling, he held it in position.

"Go ahead. You coward! Hit the mother of your child!"

Sam pushed out of the green barrier. He opened the closet door, ready to defend Ginger and Susan from Raoul's next move. Ginger's eyes flared in terror when she first noticed Sam staring at her from the closet, then softened to a quizzical recognition. He put his finger to his lips, motioning to Raoul, who would likely erupt in a murderous frenzy if he found another man in their closet. Never mind that he was sixty-two years old. Instinct told him Raoul would flip out, no matter how old he was.

Ginger caught herself, sent him a slight understanding nod. She put the baby on the floor, stood, and turned Raoul toward her, away from Sam. "Honey. I'm sorry. Listen, why don't you take some of my pin money and go down to the diner for breakfast today? Treat yourself?"

Raoul relaxed and slumped into his seat just as Sam gently pulled the door closed and slipped back into the darkness.

"Nah. I don't feel like getting dressed. I'll eat your crap. But make me some more. These are cold." He shoved the plate halfway across the Formica tabletop, where it shuddered to a stop inches from the edge. Ginger scooped it from the table and carried it past the closet, to the sink. She chanced a look at Sam when Raoul bent to pick at his toenail. She flashed an alluring smile, still tinged with mystery. Her eyes asked *Why?* and *How?*

Susan crawled along the not-too-clean floor toward Sam, reaching toward the closet with a giggle. His daughter, his poor, little baby girl grew closer, ready to open the door with chubby fingers. He wanted to pick her up and love her, carry her off to a decent life, get her away from the monster who'd been told he was the child's father.

Instead, he felt himself being drawn back to the present as if sucked in the air stream of the deflating balloon. Whooshed through a green haze, he ended up on his bathroom floor, his back to the door and his feet splayed out in front of him. The aroma of fried eggs followed him, infused with a lingering sadness for the child he'd never known.

Sam brushed himself off and checked his watch. Another half hour until Andy and Beth's visit. He washed his face, brushed his teeth, and ran a wet comb through his wavy gray hair. He stared at himself in the mirror, wishing he had a razor. Maybe Doris would get him one in the morning? She might have to watch him shave, but at least he could get rid of the itchy half-inch of beard that made him look ragged and almost barbaric. He stared for a few more seconds. The beard began to look better. In a way, he liked his savage appearance. It matched how he felt when he thought about the relentless hunt he'd embark on to bring Rachel back. There was no doubt in his mind. He *would* bring her back. He couldn't accept any other outcome. He smiled and stroked his ragged stubble.

Maybe I'll keep the beard.

Sam picked out a clean gray long-sleeved shirt and rolled on some Old Spice. He tucked in his shirttails, straightened his shoulders, and headed to the visitors' room.

Andy and Beth sat by the window, away from other patients and their families. They rose as one, pain etching their features. Their forlorn eyes searched his. Sam couldn't let them suffer any longer. He opened his arms and drew them both to him. "I'm back, guys. Everything's going to be okay."

Beth sobbed against his chest. Andy squeezed his hand so hard it hurt. And for the next half hour, they emptied their buckets of sorrow onto his shoulders. He comforted, he kissed, he explained, and he apologized.

"Beth. Andy. Listen to me. I'm sorry this happened. I'm so sorry."

Beth almost lost it again, but managed to get her words out. "Dad. It was like we lost both of you on the same day."

Andy nodded. "It was horrible."

"I know, kids. But listen. It was out of my control until this morning."

Andy sat down and motioned for Sam and Beth to do the same. They settled close together on the stuffed chairs. Beth still held her father's hand. "What made you snap out of it?"

Sam looked into the distance. "I'll never know. I just woke up this morning, took in the surroundings, shook myself clear in the head, and was back to myself. I felt tired and a little woozy."

Tears streamed down Beth's cheeks. Andy leaned over to rub his sister's shoulder. "We're glad you're back, Dad. We both need you. And the boys are going crazy, missing you so much."

"I'll bet." Sam searched his children's eyes. "But you've both got to promise me something."

They sat forward with eager expressions. Andy whispered, "Anything, Dad."

Sam looked from one to the other. "You've got to start taking care of yourselves. You both look like hell." He cracked a grin and gripped their hands.

Beth snorted a laugh and Andy chuckled. They met each other's widened eyes, wailed with laughter, and completely lost it for several minutes, gulping and laughing so hard that the entire room turned to look at them. Sam wiped the tears of laughter from his cheeks. "Damn. I needed that."

Beth sniffled and smoothed her hair and pushed a dark copper lock behind one ear. "Dad! You're so bad. Do we really look that awful?"

He leaned forward and kissed them both on the forehead. "Hell, no. You look fine, considering what you've been through. God, I missed you two."

Sam returned to his room for one more night of breathing clinical air and sleeping on rough white sheets. Just as he was preparing for bed, Doris appeared in his doorway. "Doris, don't you ever get a break? You've been here since this morning."

She smiled, surprised he'd noticed. "Thirteen hours and counting, Dr. Moore. My replacement didn't show. It's gonna be a very long night."

Sam took out a pair of shorts and a tee shirt. He closed the drawer with his hip and turned to her. "Sorry to hear that. So what's up? Final rounds?"

She shook her head and looked behind her. "It's past visiting hours, but since it's the police and all, we agreed to let him in."

Ned Olsen squeezed past her into the room with a laptop in his hands. "Thanks for letting us use the room, Doris. This is sensitive evidence, and it wouldn't do to have just anyone passing by."

She ran her fingers through her short white hair and looked nervously behind her. The magenta lipstick from the morning had worn away, leaving just a trace on each lip. "Not a problem, officer. Just stop by my station when you want to be buzzed out." She slipped into the hallway and closed the door behind her.

Sam hurried to Ned's side. "The video?"

"Yeah. Got it burned on a DVD. Where's the power?"

They dragged Sam's night table in front of the cot, found an outlet behind the bed, and booted up the computer.

"I'm fast forwarding to the hour or two before we think Lou was killed. Ridiculous to view the whole damned day," Ned said.

"Right." Sam sat up straight, staring at the screen as it came to life. "Unless someone came in early and hid in the restrooms all day. Something like that?"

Ned launched the video. "Possible. But let's check this out first. I'll mute the sound," Ned said, playing with the touch pad.

"Wait a minute. Maybe something important was said. Isn't this camera mounted near the receptionist's desk?"

Ned squinted his eyes at Sam and grinned. "Guess you're right. Okay. I'll leave the sound on."

For the next hour, Sam's eyes grew weary as he stared at face after face in a constant stream of fuzzy images. The quality was poor, but good enough to recognize people

Most visitors headed straight for the DMV, their steps hurried, their faces frozen in sour expressions, as if they anticipated a long wait. They clutched forms and license plates, and sometimes the hands of their little ones. A small contingent streamed toward the elevators. Sam focused on them.

"There's Lisa Marie, from the salon," Sam said.

Ned looked at him with raised eyebrows. "Huh?"

Sam explained. "She cuts my hair. Does a great job. "

The officer nodded and yawned. "Uh huh."

Another twenty minutes passed. They pointed out a half-dozen familiar faces, all upstanding members of the community. A grocer.

A gas station owner. Ned's cousin.

Ned shifted in boredom. He'd done this already, and the circles beneath his eyes belied his claim that he wasn't tired.

"You can leave this with me, if you want. I've got nothing to do 'til they release me tomorrow."

Ned shook his head and stretched his legs. "It's okay. I'll stay. We're almost done, anyway."

Sam's attention was drawn to a familiar-sounding woman's voice. He stared at the screen. A hooded figure shielded her face with her hand, as if massaging her temple while she spoke to the receptionist.

"Wait. Go back," Sam said.

Ned bolted upright and clicked the mouse. The scene froze, then rewound. "Did you see something?"

Sam held up a hand to shush him. "Turn up the volume."

"Right."

They stared at the screen and listened.

"Which way is the morgue?" a woman's voice asked.

The receptionist glanced briefly at the woman standing before her and pointed to the elevators. "Take the elevators to the basement. You can't miss it."

She turned her back to the cameras and slid behind several people queued for the elevator, once again hiding her face.

"One more time, please," Sam said.

"You think you know who it is?"

"Shhh. Just do it."

Ned rewound the DVD. Sam closed his eyes and listened hard. The marble burned his leg, pulsing wildly in his pocket. "I know the voice. I know it." He pressed his fingers to his temples, rubbing them in circles. "I just have to think. Let me think."

Ned turned to him. "Try it again." He rewound the DVD and played it again, louder this time.

"Which way is the morgue?"

This time Sam saw the truth with Billy's help. The words emerged from lips pursed in a sour expression. Short black hair. Watery brown eyes. Pale complexion.

"Oh my God." Sam caught Ned's stare. "It's Lacey! From the diner."

Ned rolled his eyes. "Big whoop, Sam. She's just a waitress."

Sam shot him a steely expression. "She's not 'just a waitress.' She showed up in town right around the time Ginger died. And she's acted strange toward me. Said some bizarre things I just blew off. And why would *she* want the morgue? I think…" The marble pulsed again, insistent.

"What?"

"I think this is really important. You've gotta check her out."

Ned threw a doubtful glance at Sam and shut down his laptop.

"Okay. If you say so. I'll run a check on her. But it seems pretty far-fetched. I've been looking for a male suspect. Someone strong enough to—"

"I know. But it's possible a woman did it, isn't it?"

"Possible, not probable. She'd have to be pretty angry."

"Right," Sam said. "When someone's really angry or scared, their strength can be herculean."

Ned stood to leave. "Why don't you call me when you get out tomorrow? I'll tell you what I've learned."

"Will do. Now all we have to do is figure out why Lacey's so angry. And how she's connected to me."

Something inside Sam told him he already knew the truth. Deep down, a part of him collapsed when he faced it.

Lacey. *Forty years old.*

Lacey, banging on the steering wheel of her car in wild fury after getting yelled at for breaking the dishes in the diner.

Lacey, showing up in town when Ginger did.

Did she follow Ginger here? Or maybe Ginger followed her, hoping to forestall whatever rage-filled vengeance she had planned.

The truth settled in his gut like cold grease.

Lacey.

Susan.

His daughter.

Chapter Twenty-Five

Sam couldn't walk fast enough to Andy's car the next afternoon. Beth followed behind the men, trotting to keep up. "Dad! Slow down! I can't keep up."

He turned to her with a chuckle, catching the looming gray asylum in his peripheral vision. He shuddered, glad to be putting distance between it and him. "Sorry, baby. Just can't get out of here fast enough." He slid into the passenger side of Andy's sedan. The trunk thumped when Andy tossed his bag inside.

Beth slipped into the back. "Buckle up, Dad."

Sam laughed and pulled the belt tight, snapping it into the buckle. "You sound like me." He patted his pocket for the millionth time to be sure his marble was there. It rested cool against his leg.

Beth beamed at him. Tears glistened in the corners of her eyes. "I had a good teacher."

Andy started the car and pulled out onto the exit road. "Here we go." He wound down the hill toward Route 256, then headed north in the direction of East Goodland. The car wove around corners, up and down hills, and past oat and wheat fields ready to harvest.

"How are my tomatoes doing?"

Andy glanced in the rearview mirror toward his sister and smirked. "Don't worry, Dad. We've been taking good care of the garden. Haven't we, Sis?"

Beth groaned. "God. I hate gardening. I don't know how you do it, Dad."

Sam snorted. "You hate it? Come on!"

"I do. All you do is walk around in the dirt, lugging heavy hoses, sweating to death, swatting flies, and pulling those infernal weeds. And all for the same kind of produce you can pick up really cheap at the Farmer's Market."

Sam bristled. "Mine's better. It's fresher. Sweeter. And it's all organic."

Beth rolled her eyes. "But is it worth all that labor? You must spend six hours a day keeping up with the property, Dad. I can't see the point of it. Mowing. Mulching. Weeding. Picking. Peeling. Cooking. God, it makes me exhausted just thinking of it."

Before Sam could answer, Andy pulled into the driveway. Sam's heart beat faster, nerves spinning in his chest. As much as he missed his gardens, the house, and his cat, he worried about returning to the house where his sweet Rachel was murdered.

Beth reached up and squeezed his shoulder. "It's okay, Dad. We'll be with you."

Sam searched her eyes. "How did you know?"

A sad smile spread across her lips. "How could I not know? It's your first time back in weeks. You're bound to feel upset, Daddy."

He pressed her fingers. "It's been a long time since you called me Daddy."

Andy got out and tossed Sam's bag onto the porch. "I've got to get home to Maryellen and the kids. It's pizza night. Will you two be okay here?"

Sam opened his door and swung his legs out. Beth came around and pulled him to his feet. "Why do I feel so tired?" He grunted when he got up, walked beside Beth toward the house, then stopped short, throwing his arm out in front of her. "Wait a minute. Where's Isabel?"

Beth took his arm in hers and urged him up the stairs. "No worries, Dad. Maryellen's got her for the night. The boys are so excited about her staying over they almost forgot to bug us about when they'll see you again. I'm spending the night here, so you won't be alone."

Sam pecked her cheek. "Thanks, honey." He went up the stairs and picked up his bag. "Damn. I miss those kids so much. I need to see them."

Andy trotted up the stairs to hug him. "Don't worry. We're coming to get you tomorrow. You're having dinner with all of us."

"I am?"

"You are. That okay with you?" Andy winked at Beth.

Sam leaned against the door. "I'll look forward to it, son."

Andy backed around and headed down the driveway. They watched until his car disappeared.

Sam pulled open the screen door. If he hadn't already determined that he was going to fix things, to bring Rachel home again, just picturing her sitting in their kitchen would have thrown him to the floor in a fit of sorrow. But he knew Billy would help him get her back, and held fast to the thought. "Come on. Let's get this over with."

"I put a casserole in the oven. It's nothing fancy, Dad. Not like—"

Sam froze, then forced himself to relax for Beth's sake. "Not like Mom's. It's okay to talk about her. I think it's healthy to remember all the good things. And it's okay to be sad. That's what my shrink told me, anyway." Beth dropped into one of the kitchen chairs. "It doesn't feel okay, Dad. It feels wretched." Her voice cracked.

Sam kneaded her shoulders while she cried. He spoke softly, telling her everything would be okay. His idea of okay was likely not in her mental vocabulary. He'd get Rachel back and make his family whole again. And if things worked right, Beth and Andy wouldn't have to go through this pain much longer. He'd change history. He'd fix things all right. Fix 'em good.

ꟈ

Sam pushed back from the table. "You know, that was a pretty darned good homemade mac and cheese. You really made it from scratch, Bethie?"

Beth blushed. "I just followed the directions on the back of the macaroni box, Daddy."

Sam picked up his plate and brought it to the sink. "Maybe there's hope for you yet. Have you cooked for your new friend yet?"

"Nel?" Beth joined him at the sink. "She's the cook. She makes things like shrimp diavalo and mango chutney and homemade ice cream."

"I hope she doesn't serve them all at the same time."

Beth chuckled. "No, silly."

"So, she's more than just a great doctor, huh?"

"Yeah. She's more like superwoman. Sometimes I wonder what she sees in me."

"She probably just wants you for your pretty face. Oh, and maybe that gorgeous baby of yours."

Beth jabbed him in the side. "Dad!"

"Okay, listen. I want to meet her soon. And I want you to get some sleep tonight. You look so tired, baby. Let's turn in early."

"You wanna read in the living room for a while, like you did with Mom every night?"

He yawned. "Not tonight. I just want to get into my own bed and watch a little mindless TV."

"That actually sounds really good. I feel like I could sleep for weeks."

The phone rang and Sam reached for it. "Hello?"

"Sam, Ned here. You settled in okay?"

Sam covered the receiver and waved Beth toward the stairs. "Go on up, honey. I'll finish up here." He uncovered the phone. "Sorry, Ned. Just wanted to send Beth up to bed. She's a wreck. And yeah, I just had a good meal at my own table with my dear daughter, and I'm feeling better already."

"Think I could stop by tomorrow morning?"

"Of course. But listen. I'm pretty convinced Lacey is Susan."

"Already beat you there, Sam. She's your daughter all right. We finally got a snapshot of her. Matches Lacey to a tee."

"Damn. I was almost hoping I was wrong."

"I know. But listen, I have an idea I'd like to run by you. Maybe it'd be good to have your kids in on the conversation, too, if they're available." His voice grew more serious. "Lacey, or Susan, was spotted in your yard this afternoon by one of my deputies who's been following her. She parked behind your barn and just sat in the car." Ned sighed. "For three hours."

"What the hell was she doing here?"

"I don't know. Watching. Waiting. Thinking. Your guess is as good as mine."

"Damn. So it's really her. She's Susan? No doubt about it?"

"Yeah. Kinda confirms what we were theorizing last night. She's back at her apartment now. But I've got two men on her, so don't worry. You'll be safe tonight."

Sam frowned. "How are we gonna nail her?"

"That's what I want to talk about tomorrow. Try to get a good night's sleep, and we'll go over it in the morning. I'll be there around ten, if that's okay?"

"Sure. I'll have the coffee on, Ned. See you then." He hung up and headed up the stairs, dreading the bedroom more than he'd admitted to Beth. Each step was agony. The nearer he got to the dark empty room, the worse it got. As he stood in the doorway and tried to get up his courage to enter, the marble pulsed.

"Okay, okay. I'm going." Sam switched on the light and took in the scene. The bed was made. He forced himself to imagine Rachel already in bed, softly snoring. "Honey. I'm here. Everything's gonna be okay. Just hang tight."

Sam lay on top of the comforter in his clothes. He shut his eyes, turned out the light, and held the marble in his hand for comfort. After an hour of tossing and turning, he tucked the marble safely into his bedside drawer and fell into a dreamless sleep.

Chapter Twenty-Six

BETH PUSHED BACK FROM THE KITCHEN TABLE AND GLARED AT NED OLSEN. "You want him to *what?*"

Ned held out a hand. "It'll be perfectly safe. We'll have men stationed all over the place. We just need to get her to talk about what she's done."

Sam poured himself more coffee and rejoined them at the kitchen table. "It's not like she's gonna attack me in broad daylight, honey. There will be people everywhere."

Andy looked pensive. "What's to stop her coming at you with a steak knife, Dad? Especially if she knows you're trying to flush her out?"

Sam sat between his children and sighed. "Listen. If anyone can get this poor woman to confess, it's me. I'm her father."

"Dad!" Beth almost sobbed. "She killed Mom. She's not a poor woman."

He held out his hands as if to stem the tide of judgment. "I know, I know. I hate her and pity her at the same time. But she had a horrible upbringing, kids. We have to try to show a little understanding."

Andy frowned. "It's hard to do, Dad. Real hard."

Sam got up and hugged them both. "I know." He turned to Ned. "But I'm ready to do this. I have to do something. And what if she's planning another murder? What if she's planning to kill me while I sleep? I can't just lie around and let it happen." He knew the idea would frighten Beth. By the look in her eyes, he'd guessed right. But it worked.

"Okay. Ned, you promise he won't be in any danger?"

Ned added some half and half to his coffee and stirred. "No more than he's in right now, Beth."

It was decided.

The next morning, Sam headed for Clara's diner, preparing to trap his own daughter, his own flesh and blood. Guilt flooded him almost as much as the anger that boiled within him, but not nearly as much as his near rabid desire for vengeance. Red-hot anger flared every time he imagined his Rachel being murdered.

Sam entered Clara's diner when it opened at six-thirty, wearing a wire and breathing deeply to calm his frayed nerves. Two farmers hunched together in a far booth, warming their beefy hands on coffee mugs. Other than the two early birds, the place was practically empty. Three nurses sat in a booth five seats down from Sam, looking like they'd come off a tough shift. The school superintendent read a paper and attacked his eggs with gusto. One of Ned's officers hid in the storeroom, ready to burst into the diner if Susan became violent. Ned and his crew hunkered in the battered white electrician's van in front of the window where Sam sat. And two officers dressed in plain clothes sat at the counter sipping their coffee and supposedly reading the paper.

It hadn't taken the police long to connect Lacey to Susan by tracing her license plates and checking the non-existent restaurant records. She'd persuaded Clara to temporarily pay her in cash under the table with some wild story about losing her wallet to a mugger. Susan became Lacey, with one fragile lie and thanks to the benevolence of a kindly, yet misguided citizen.

"Can you hear me?" Sam whispered into his lapel. He flipped the menu for the twentieth time.

A soft buzzing filled his ear. "Just fine. Listen, Susan just pulled in around back and is heading inside. Don't let her see you talking to us, Sam. Try to act natural." Ned sounded worried, as if Sam would leap in the air and announce his intentions.

He nodded so Ned could see him through the diner window and turned the menu over one last time. Clara peered at him over her bifocals behind the counter, trying to hide her worry. Sam saw another officer pull into the back lot, idling in his patrol car around the corner after Susan disappeared inside.

He took a deep breath and tried to relax. Susan appeared, tying an apron around her waist. She blanched when she saw him. He waved and nodded hello, as if it were the most natural thing in the world. His heart thumped wildly.

She grabbed an order pad and approached him. He studied the menu without looking up; afraid his eyes would betray him.

"Morning, Lacey."

Her voice seemed strangled. "Sam. You're out."

He glanced at her and smiled. "Surprised?"

She caught herself and backed up a step. "Er. No. Glad to see you're feeling better, is all."

"Who told you I was in that awful place?"

She glanced sideways at Clara, who busily wiped down the counter for the third time in as many minutes. "Uh. It sort of traveled through the diner. News like that is hard to keep down in a small town, you know."

Sam motioned to the seat across from him, raising his voice so Clara could hear. "Why don't you sit for a minute? I haven't quite decided what to have yet."

Susan looked at Clara for approval. Clara waved a rag and nodded. The two farmers remained deep in conversation over eggs and coffee, and the rest of the patrons seemed content.

He studied the menu. She stared at him over the top of it, her eyes searching his.

"So, you're feeling better?"

He nodded. "Much."

She played with the string on her apron, her eyes transforming from wary to coy. "Any leads on your wife's murderer?"

Sam laid down the menu and looked into Susan's watery brown eyes. Insecurity blended with absurd pride, intertwining in a cyclic bubbling that turned his insides cold.

"Actually, yes. We have a suspect for all three murders, Susan."

It took a minute for her to react. At first she glanced sideways at him, unsure she'd heard him correctly. Sam covered her hand in an attempt to calm her. She pulled it back and stiffened. "What did you say?" Her eyes shrank to slits.

"I called you Susan, honey. Your real name."

She slumped against the back of the booth and her hands dropped into her lap. "So, how'd you find out?"

"My brother told me."

She eyed him with suspicion. "Your brother? I thought he was dead."

Sam nodded. "Yeah. He is. Just like Rachel. Lou. And your mother."

Lava erupted in her eyes. She braced her hands on the table and shot forward, her nose an inch from his. Her voice hissed with quiet venom. "You freaking deserted me! You chose a nice normal wife, and had more kids. And you let me rot with my weak mother and her psycho boyfriend." She dropped back in her seat. Her eyes burned and her chest heaved. "Why?"

Sam summoned every ounce of control, trying to soothe her. "I'm so sorry. I didn't know you existed. Your mother never told me."

She ran her hands rapidly through her short black hair and shook her head violently. "I don't believe you! She must've told you. Your name is on my birth certificate. She showed it to me after Raoul died."

Sam offered sounds of condolence. "No, Susan. She didn't tell me. She told Raoul he was your father. If I'd known, I would've taken care of you. I swear to God."

Tears streamed down her face, bathing her hot cheeks. Rage and disbelief flooded her eyes. "You never knew about me?"

Sam shook his head. "I haven't spoken with your mother in forty years. If I had known, I would have helped. I would have taken you out of that hellhole."

She slammed her fists onto the table, then laid her head down, screaming words that made no sense. Clara moved to the farmers, who quietly slipped into the back room with her. A deputy peered through the crack in the swinging door, ready to jump to action. The van door slid partially open.

"I did it all for nothing."

Sam murmured solace. "You did. It was you, wasn't it? You killed Ginger. Lou. And my Rachel."

The answer was garbled. She lifted her tear-stained face to his. "Mom tried to stop me. She was afraid I'd lose it around you. She wanted to try to get money from you, but I just wanted to see you.

To ask you why you never came to see me." Her shoulders shook as she wept. "We fought. And I got really mad."

Sam reached a hand toward her. She pulled back. "I would have come, had I known," he repeated.

She sniffled and glanced sideways at him, as if unsure of his intentions. "What about Lou?" Sam asked. "Why Lou? She was just a friend."

A bitter laugh escaped her lips. "I thought she was your lover. The way she looked at you. The way you guys had lunch together. Didn't find out until it was too late."

Sam sighed, his mouth turned down. "So when you discovered your mistake, you got angry again?"

Rage erupted in her eyes. "You bet. I took a huge risk going into that morgue. And she fought like hell. When Lou told me she wasn't with you, I freaked out. Of course I had to kill her."

Sam went cold. "And then you went after Rachel."

A veil of burnt emotion dropped over Susan's face, as if all feeling drained from her. "Of course. She was the one you chose over me and my mother. She didn't deserve to have you."

Sam bristled, trying hard to hold in his own anger. "Why didn't you just kill me, Susan? Why everyone around me?"

She glanced around, as if sensing the net was closing in. "I wanted you for myself, Sam. I was going to visit you in the asylum today."

"So that would have been it? You and I would have had visitations a few times a week?"

She dropped her eyes to her hands that tapped on the table in a spastic rhythm. "No. I planned to get rid of Beth and Andy, too. They would've been in the way. After they were gone, we could've started over. Like a real family. And when you were released, we could have moved into your farmhouse together. I would cook and clean for you. And you could take care of that big garden. It's real pretty out there."

Susan's voice took on a sing-song quality, rising and falling as if she were telling a fairy tale. Sam felt himself slump inside, as if all reason fluttered and fell to the floor. "You were going to murder my children?"

Susan nodded. "Eventually."

The sympathy he'd summoned vanished. Ned's forces descended, surrounding her. She seemed unaffected now, listless and almost dreamy. As they cuffed her and walked her out, she turned to Sam. "It would have been a great life, Dad. Just you and me."

Sam sat at the counter while the tech unbuttoned his shirt and removed the wire. Clara came by and offered him coffee. He didn't remember what he said, but felt his hands gripping the warm cup minutes later. He watched the van and patrol cars pull away until all that remained was a dust cloud on the horizon. After Clara stopped by to refill the coffee he didn't remember drinking, he took the marble from his pocket and held it up. Sunlight blinked on it and reflected green on the table.

Okay, Billy. Now help me get my Rachel back.

Chapter Twenty-Seven

SAM SAT AT THE KITCHEN TABLE, A CUP OF HOT CHOCOLATE COOLING beneath his fingers. He stared at the pile of news clippings. Selecting one, he stuck a few pieces of double-sided tape to it before pressing it in the photo album.

"Satan Worshippers Raise Murderer." The article, written by a top journalist in the Rochester Democrat & Chronicle, laid out the details of Susan's past and Raoul's Satanic entanglements. Susan's life events were listed in a neat timeline, aligning her age with the arrests of Raoul and the exploding growth of his cult. The reporter had done his homework.

A close-up of Ginger's pentagram and rose tattoo, probably finagled from the police files, spread across the next page. Sam felt his stomach twist as he remembered the ugly scene in the pink and black bathroom. Poor Ginger, she hadn't aged well under the care of the devil worshipper who called himself her husband. Sam tried to wash the image out of his head.

According to the article, "The Cloven Rose" logo had been permanently tattooed on the willing bodies of Raoul's cult members since 1971. Photos of ex-members had been taken at subsequent interviews last week, revealing a similar design on their arms and legs, and lending detail to the story behind the story. Some had tried to have the marks removed, but had been unsuccessful. For some reason, per the journalist, they'd resisted the usual laser treatment. Sam tossed the idea aside. They were probably just trying to stir up the readers by putting fear of the devil in them. *Stupid ploy.*

He picked up the rest of the article and pressed it onto the next page in the album. At the top of the page, a photo showed Susan looking bedraggled and confused, wearing an orange jumpsuit and handcuffs when she was brought into the Mann Psych Center in Rochester. The caption below read, "Local doctor's love child sent to forensic psych unit."

A blurry picture of him and Rachel, obviously taken from the photo journal files of one of the fundraisers they'd supported over the years, appeared below. Sam wore the tux he'd always hated, and Rachel stood beside him in a chicory blue crepe dress, leaning on her cane. The photo had been taken before the wheelchair had become a necessary nuisance. She wore white pearls and a sweet smile. Sam ran his fingers over her face, as if he could feel the soft skin beneath the grainy pixels. He closed his eyes and sighed deeply, trying to will it all away. He wanted to picture her here, beside him, sipping her coffee and warming his life with her presence, like she always did.

The sound of someone clomping across the porch floorboards forced him to open his eyes and refocus. Andy burst through the kitchen door and wordlessly hugged his father, then gestured at the pile of news clippings on the table. "What are you doing with all this, Dad?"

Sam raised weary eyes to his son. "Just trying to make sense out of it, I guess." Andy grabbed a mug from the dishwasher and poured a cup of coffee. He dropped into a chair and stared at him. "Pretty morbid."

Sam nodded and closed the album. "I know."

"Does it help? It seems like it would just upset you."

Sam shuffled the papers on the table and put them in a neat pile, sliding them into the front cover of the album.

"I don't know, son. I'm just trying to understand Susan better. I feel conflicted. The woman is my flesh and blood. My *daughter.* Who killed *my wife.* Who plotted the murder of my two children. It's just so...bizarre. I hate her. I want revenge. And...I feel sorry for her at the same time."

Andy released a burst of air through pursed lips. His eyes hardened. "Damn it, Dad. How can you feel sorry for her? Even if she is my half-sister, she's a murderer, and I don't care what kind of liberal sob story they dig up. She should have known better."

Sam covered Andy's hand with his. "I know, son. But she's sick. Really sick."

Andy pushed back, frowning. "That may be so. Or it might be a convenient excuse. I hope they lock her up for good this time."

Sam stared at his son, empathy flooding through him. It would be so much easier to hate Rachel's killer. Give in to the rage. Forget about Susan's circumstances. But in time, it seemed the feelings would diminish him as a human being, would eat away at his ability to survive. "Maybe we can both find a way to move on. Eventually. To let go of the anger," Sam said.

"You sound like my shrink."

Sam looked up in surprise. "Shrink?"

Andy's face softened, and he took a sip of coffee. "Yeah. Been seeing one since Mom died. Maryellen made me go."

Sam laughed in spite of himself. "Maryellen's a good woman, Andy. I'm glad you listened to her."

Andy flashed a wry smile at his father. "It's helping a little, so I guess Maryellen was right. As usual. She's always right."

Father and son exchanged knowing smiles.

"Do you think she'd like to get away for a while?" Sam asked.

Andy looked up with interest. "Get away? Where?"

"Garcia called and offered us their house on Honeoye Lake. Four bedrooms. Two baths. Right on the water. Nice sunny screened in porch. I've been there. It's really comfortable."

"Think Bethie would come, too?" Andy asked.

Sam nodded. "Already asked her. She's up for it, at least for a little while."

Andy nodded. "It would be good for all of us." He stretched and stood. "Yeah. Let's do it."

"Garcia already dropped off the keys. I'm packing tonight. I can get the place all set up for you tomorrow, do some food shopping and the like. How about we go really crazy and buy some fresh swordfish for grilling?"

"At eighteen dollars a pound?" Andy's eyes shone with anticipation. "Whoa."

"It's on me. I'll buy enough for the whole crowd. And we can invite Beth's new friend, too. Penelope, right?"

"I'd like to meet this famous doctor who never makes it to our get-togethers. She must be pretty special. Beth seems dazzled."

Sam smiled. At least something was going right in their lives. "She sure does."

Andy suddenly rose, rinsed his cup out, and set it in the drainer. "I'm out of here. Better get home to tell Maryellen about the cabin. She'll want to organize us all into a neat traveling machine. That's her way." He kissed his father on the top of his head. "I'll call you tonight for the details."

Sam stood and watched him back around the driveway and head out to the road. It would be good to have the whole family together in a new place. And he'd be sure to get away in the woods by himself with the marble.

He had plenty of work ahead of him and needed to come up with a clever plan to gently tweak the past. Billy would be there to help. And Rachel was depending on him.

He closed the door and called to Lila, who followed him toward the stairs and wrapped around his legs as he hesitated at the bottom with his hand on the railing. "Come on, girl. We're going on vacation."

Chapter Twenty-Eight

Sam packed the last of the garden produce in the Highlander, arranged the cooler and Lila's carrier so they wouldn't slide around, and headed for the road.

The drive to Honeoye Lake from East Goodland took just over a half hour. He headed east on Route 20A, through Lakeville and Livonia, and wound through Hemlock to cut east over the hills that dipped and rose, nestling Cayuga and Honeoye Lakes.

Turning south at the only stoplight in town, Sam drove the final three miles along West Lake Road to the tiny one-lane road leading to Garcia's place in Sunset Cove. She called it a cottage, but actually it was a full-sized house, big enough to hold his whole family. Four bedrooms featured queen or king beds, and two sleep sofas were placed back to back in the living room and sunroom, separated by a wall of sliding glass doors.

Lila mewed when he pulled into the parking lot.

"Okay, girl. Just hold on a minute."

The cottages flanking Garcia's property seemed to be empty, which suited Sam just fine. Socializing wasn't on his agenda, and the more privacy he had, the better.

He grabbed a duffle bag and the cat carrier, and wrestled the keys out of his pockets. The door opened on the first try, and he stepped inside, greeted by brilliant sun shining through the large windows and eighty-three degrees of August heat.

"Here you go, girl. Come on now, let's get you settled. Where's the blasted AC switch?" he mumbled, searching the room with his eyes.

He let Lila out, set a dish of cold water on the kitchen floor, and finally found the AC, mounted high on the living room wall near the door. After switching it to high, he made three more trips from the SUV to bring in the groceries and linens.

Lila followed him up and down the stairs to the bedroom that looked over the lake with large picture windows. "I claim this one," he said to no one, aching more than ever for Rachel's company. The bed—big enough for three people—was covered with a clean black and white comforter. Six fluffy pillows were propped against the headboard, more than enough to try to fill the empty space on the bed where Rachel should have slept. He unpacked his clothes and chastised himself for his morbid thoughts. He needed to stay focused, positive, and look to the future when he'd get Rachel back. Ignoring the niggling doubt that swelled in his gut, he pushed the feelings aside and turned to Lila.

"How about a swim, girl?" Lila mewed as if she understood, then hopped onto the windowsill, her long, skinny tail hanging in a question mark. "Not in the mood?"

He stroked her soft fur and let her repeatedly butt her head against his palm, rubbing her whiskers hard against his skin. "You're good company. I'm glad you came."

After changing into his swimsuit, Sam grabbed a towel and padded along the carpeted floor toward the sunroom. He opened the shades and whistled at the view.

The lake met three rounded hills at the southern end, their color bluish under the haze of distant mist hovering overhead. He stared at the peaceful scene for a long time.

Two ducks swam near the dock, creating wakes in the placid water that glistened turquoise and silver. The male, with his sparkly green-feathered neckband, seemed to be showing off. Both repeatedly ducked under the surface to catch whatever tidbits they could, their orange webbed feet flailing in the air as they tipped head first into the water.

Fisherman dotted the lake, disturbed occasionally by one loud Jet Ski that zoomed and crisscrossed around them, rocking the bass boats and creating a minor surf at Sam's feet.

The shore sparkled with wet round stones, and a few stray waterweeds lay in perfect still-life scenes at Sam's feet. He draped his towel on a green plastic Adirondack chair, and stepped onto the dock.

Garcia's boat rocked on its mooring beneath a canopy alongside the dock. He passed it, feeling the vibrations of the dock boards, and headed to the end, where a ladder was attached to posts.

The sun beat down on Sam's head, coaxing him into the cool green water. He placed one foot on the metal rung and slipped on the slime that had grown underwater. More careful now, he slowly lowered himself into the lake and pushed away, floating on his back. Weeds tickled his legs and the sun blasted his face. The sounds of motorboats hummed in the distance in soft counterpoint with a few Canada geese that honked overhead, getting an early start on fall.

An involuntary sigh of contentment slipped out as Sam relaxed for the first time since Rachel's death. He lifted his head after twenty minutes of floating, paddled back toward the dock, and pulled himself up the ladder. Stretching out on his stomach, he lay on the warm dock, hidden by the boat on one side and the trees in the cove on the other. A breeze whispered overhead in a huge cottonwood tree, rustling the leaves with the familiar tinkling sound, just like his cottonwoods at home.

He opened his eyes and gazed into the water below. Sunfish, bass, and perch sashayed below him in his own personal aquarium. He watched them for a long time, then went in for one more dip, sending the fish scattering.

Afterwards, he sat on the edge of the dock, mesmerized by the water. Finally, hunger borne of swimming in the fresh air drove him inside, where he prepared garlic chicken, paste tomatoes, and fresh peapods sautéed in olive oil. It was one of the meals he'd learned from Rachel. Simple and delicious.

Andy and Beth called, both planning to arrive in the morning. Sam made up the other three beds, shut off the AC and opened all the windows to let in the cooler evening air, and turned on the television and DVD player, popping in the new copy of *Pride and Prejudice* he'd just received in the mail. Rachel had ordered it to surprise him, and when it had arrived the other day, it sent him into an afternoon of despair.

Tonight, he would play it while he took out the marble, hoping the soothing music and gorgeous scenery would somehow influence the outcome of his experiment.

He took the marble from his pocket and turned it in his fingers. The music from the movie swelled in the background and bucolic scenes from the 1800s panned across the screen.

He held the marble up in the reflection of the screen.

Cold glass.

Usually, Billy prompted the flashbacks, borne of an urgent need to communicate, peppered with frequent hot bursts of heat and flashing green that eventually ended in a trip to the past. This time Sam needed to *will* Billy into action.

How could he get to a specific point in time? Would Billy know what he wanted?

He closed his fingers around the marble and reached to Billy.

Billy. Come on. I need you.

Nothing.

He tried again, digging deeper into his inner core.

Billy. Please.

The marble warmed, a faint tingle of electricity pulsed within his fingers.

Billy. Show me Raoul.

Green light exploded from his fingers, emitting rays so strong they hurt Sam's eyes. He jolted back against the couch. Slivers of green propelled him on waves of time, pushing him back, farther back, until he arrived with a thump on a hard wooden chair.

His hands, smooth and youthful, gripped a yellow pencil. His feet, encased in red PF Flyers, stuck out from a school desk, scarred with scribed initials and hearts carved into the wood. It was all unfamiliar. He'd never been part of this class.

The schoolroom held thirty children, each in various stages of boredom. The scent of chalk dust filled the air. A flag hung overhead in the corner of the room, partially hiding a round clock ticking from the wall above the skinny teacher's head. A sign on his desk read "Mr. Dodinski." He stared at a student in the back row, brow furrowed, thick lips pursed in anger. "I asked you a question, Mr. Mercedes."

Sam joined the rest of the class and swiveled around to stare at Raoul, who slumped in his seat, staring at his desk. He wore a ratty blue shirt and scuffed black shoes. His hair, scruffy and in need of a trim, fell over his eyes.

"Mr. Mercedes. If you don't know the answer to a simple addition problem, you're in the wrong class. Perhaps we should demote you to third grade?"

A titter broke out among the students, causing Raoul's cheeks to flush brick red.

"Now. What is four plus seven?" Dodinski spit the words with anger.

Raoul's fingers tapped one at a time on his knees beneath the desk. Sam counted with him. Eight. Nine. Ten. Eleven.

"Eleven," Raoul said, his voice barely audible.

Dodinski sighed, finally satisfied.

"Well, it's about time. And I think someone needs to review his math facts before the next class."

Another round of muted laughter circled the room. Sam watched Raoul slink farther into his seat, his embarrassment so strong that Sam felt the hot humiliation in his own body. The sick stomach. The anger building. Building. Ready to explode.

Raoul pushed to his feet and ran to the door.

"Gonna be sick," he shouted.

Mr. Dodinski shook his head in disgust and turned back to the blackboard.

Chapter Twenty-Nine

The next morning, Sam sat at the table in the sun porch with Lila on his lap and a yellow pencil in his hand. He'd reached for it automatically from the collection of dozens of pens Garcia kept in a tin canister on the kitchen counter. The pencil connected him to the scene Billy showed him last night, and he imagined it giving him some of the energy from the boy he'd become in the flashback.

Who was that young boy?

Would he ever find out?

Did he really care?

He shifted in his seat and reached for the pad of drawing paper he'd found on the shelves over the washer and dryer closet. Games were stored there, and to his surprise he'd found just what he needed. An oversized pad of paper.

"I need a timeline, Lila."

She pushed her head against his arm and purred.

"And if I tape three of these together, it might be just long enough."

The tape squeaked when he pulled a long strip from the roll and laid it across the first seam.

A warm breeze ruffled the newspapers, sending one skittering across the table. Sam looked up, wondering if he should close one of the sliding glass doors. The air felt fresh against his face, sun sparkled on the water, and the comforting sound of motorboats thrummed in the distance. He decided against it, attached the last sheet of drawing paper, and drew a long horizontal line across the sheets.

"Okay, Lila. Now let's go through the whole thing. Right from the moment Raoul met Ginger. I need to know more about that time; it could be key." Sam's fingers danced over the paper. "I'll put spring break right about...here." He drew a vertical line, and labeled it. "And Susan's birth..." He walked his fingers along the timeline. "Here. Now I just need that article that laid it all out, including Raoul's arrests."

After three cups of coffee and long after Lila had deserted him for a sunny spot on the back of Garcia's couch, Sam looked up at the clock, startled.

"Damn. It's almost nine. We've got to hide this, Lila. The kids will be here any minute."

As if on cue, the shriek of young voices greeted him. Hurrying now, he scooped up the loose news clippings, shoved them in his partially filled album, and rolled the timeline into a tight cylinder. He ran to the couch and slid them underneath.

"Perfect fit."

The child noises grew louder. He smiled and walked to the side door, pulling it open with a flourish. "Well, look who's here. My man Evan, and his superhero brother, Timmy."

Evan stood in the sunlight, looking more and more like Billy every day. His hazel eyes sparkled, and honey-colored hair flopped over his eyes. He shifted a bag on his shoulder and grinned. "Hey, Gramps."

Sam opened the door to welcome them. Timmy barreled inside and rammed Sam with his stocky body. "I Superman!" he shrieked. "I not Timmy!"

Sam crouched beside him and pulled him close, inhaling the sweet scent of baby shampoo and holding him much too long. Timmy wiggled out of his grip and stared out the front porch. "I wanna go swim! Papa, take Timmy swimmin'!"

He raced to the sunroom and placed both hands on the screen, leaning his whole weight against it. Sam imagined the screen giving way. "No, Timmy. Don't touch!" He drew Timmy away from the screen and led him back to the living room area. "Here. Sit with me a minute."

Evan rolled his eyes and laughed, plopping into the overstuffed chair. "You've gotta be kidding, Gramps. He won't sit still."

Sam tried anyway, but Timmy launched himself from his grandfather's lap and stood beside him on the couch, reaching for the display of fish figurines that decorated a set of white shelves on the wall. "Fishies!" he screamed. "I wanna pway with dem!"

"No, buddy. Those are breakable. We can't play with them."

The sound of rolling suitcases made him glance up. Andy and Maryellen entered, hefting very large wheeled valises over the doorstep.

"I told you we packed too much, Maryellen," Andy said. He turned to Sam, wiping sweat from his forehead. "Hey, Dad. We made it."

Sam lifted Timmy down from the couch. He raced toward the stairs and began to clamber up them. Maryellen smiled a flustered hello to Sam and followed her son. "Timmy! No! Wait for Mama."

"The boys can sleep upstairs in the second bedroom," Sam said, laughing. "You and Maryellen can take one of the downstairs bedrooms. Beth and the baby can have the other. Think that will work?"

Andrew laughed. "Are you sure? You know what a handful Timmy is. Especially just before bedtime."

Sam smiled. "I know, son. But you two will be more comfortable down there, and I've done it before. Many times."

"Okay, Dad. I'll just get these bags into the bedroom, then."

Evan hopped up and grabbed his bag. "I get a whole room to myself?"

Sam had pictured the two boys sleeping together on the big bed in the room beside his. But Evan's eyes shone with such hope that he capitulated.

"Sure you do, sport. Timmy can sleep with me."

Evan whooped for joy and ran for the stairs, hanging over the railing as he called to Sam. "Thanks, Gramps! I never had my own room!"

Sam chuckled. "You're welcome, pal. Now go get unpacked and put on your swimsuit. The lake's calling."

A wide smile crept over Sam's face. He picked up Lila from the couch and cuddled her in his arms. She butted his chin with her nose, and patted the side of his face with one soft paw.

"Lila. This is gonna be fun."

She purred in agreement and snuggled onto his shoulder.

After the boys unpacked their things, or rather stuffed their tee shirts and shorts into bureau drawers, Sam changed into his still damp suit and brought them both outside, leaving Andy and Maryellen to relax in the air conditioning.

Sam grabbed Timmy's arm when he barreled down the cement steps with his water shoes on, screaming "Swimming!"

"Wait a minute, buddy boy." Sam drew the boy's face close to his. "Remember the rules?"

Timmy looked at him as if they hadn't just discussed the safety rules ten minutes earlier. "Nope."

Evan dug into a white pail that contained their swimming gear. He brandished yellow and green inflammable armbands. "You have to wear these, Tim. Papa just told you inside. Remember?"

The child pouted and tried to pull toward the water. "Nope. Wanna swim!"

Sam and Evan exchanged an amused glance, and Sam scooped the boy under his arm, legs kicking. "You don't go near the water without your swimmies and without Papa."

Evan smiled. "Or Mom or Dad. Any adult is good, right, Gramps?"

Sam struggled to blow up the flotation devices while still holding onto the boy. "Right. Now slip these on your arms, like that."

Sam snagged three towels from the iron railing when he set Timmy down. He raced after the boy, tossed the towels over the Adirondack chairs, and made it to the boy's side just as Timmy screeched to a stop with his toes in the water.

"It's cold."

Sam chuckled and grabbed a large purple inflatable raft. "You get used to it. Wanna go for a ride?"

Evan laughed, ran down the dock, and nearly jumped when Sam stopped him with both hands in the air. "Wait. I can't watch you both at the same time. Stay to this side of that second post."

Evan sidestepped three feet toward Sam. "Here?"

"Yes. Perfect. I know it's not over your head there."

With a banshee like cry, Evan jumped into the water, making a splash that traveled in a ten-foot circle. Evan popped up from the green water and frowned. "Geez, Gramps. It's only up to my waist here."

Sam chuckled. "Okay. Maybe you can go halfway to the next post. But I don't want it over your chest. Got it?"

Evan vaulted up onto the dock like a grasshopper. "Okay. Let's try it from here."

When Sam turned, Timmy had run back to the white pail and donned a pair of orange goggles with a snorkel attached. He trotted back to the shore. "I ready."

Sam leaned down to him, adjusting the goggles so they didn't dig into the boy's eyes. "Okay. Do you want a ride on the raft?"

"Uh huh."

They walked into the water, hand in hand, laughing when Evan jumped and splashed them—over and over again—and mounted the raft when the water reached Timmy's chest and Sam's thighs. Sam sat behind the boy, balancing with his water shoes on the slippery stones of the lake floor. Timmy smiled behind the snorkel and goggles, giggling every time Sam bounced him up and down.

When they were blue-lipped and prune-wrinkled, with a few whimpers, the boys finally agreed to get out. He dried them off and sent them scampering into the house.

Sam followed two sets of wet footprints up the cement walk to the sun porch and slung his damp towel over the iron railing beside the front door. Evan, wrapped in his towel, headed for his bedroom to change. Maryellen chased Timmy around the room, trying to catch him.

"Timmy! Come back here and put some clothes on!"

He tossed his towel and wet bathing suit across the room, squealed with laughter, and jumped on the couch like a bucking bronco, legs flying and feet kicking.

"I naked!" Thrilled at the prospect of devilish disobedience, the boy once more escaped his mother's frustrated grasp and barreled down the hall to his parents' room. "I naked!" he shrieked again.

Maryellen disappeared, chasing Timmy down the hall. Sam chuckled and picked up the bathing suit that dripped from the back of a dining room chair, the towel that had already dampened the couch cushion, and stepped outside briefly to hang them on the railing to dry.

He nodded to two fishermen whose boat nudged Garcia's dock, grateful they waited to move in until after the kids finished swimming. They cast in and around the pilings, quiet and content in their pursuit for the big bass. Garcia told him her dock was a favorite spot of local fishermen, having produced some of the biggest fish in the lake. In a strange sense of ownership, he suddenly hoped they didn't hook any of the gilled members of his private aquarium.

Wandering out toward the water again, a strong pull lured him to the shore. He settled in one of the Adirondack chairs, his bare feet resting on the smooth warm stones. Skipping stones. Perfect skipping stones.

I'll have to show the boys how to throw them.

The fishermen floated past, casting and recasting close to shore, their trolling motor barely audible. When they disappeared around the bend, Sam walked to the end of the dock again and sat, his feet dangling in the cool water. The lake had turned glassy—a smooth mirror that made it difficult to see the fish below. He rolled onto his stomach and trailed his fingers in the water, making ripples in the surface.

There! A large bluegill flashed below. And beside it, a school of small perch. He smiled and stared, mesmerized by the scene. An image slowly formed in the water. Sam rubbed his eyes and looked again. Faint shadows outlined hair, eyes. A face.

Rachel.

The image crystallized and moved. Rachel's lips formed words, and in his head he heard her calling him.

Sam. Help me. Bring me home.

A breeze stirred, chopping the image into just water again, making him reach for the lake with his heart and hands.

Rachel. Don't go.

A sense of desperation filled his soul, as if this momentary connection and new loss freshened his grief.

Rachel. Come back to me.

He dangled one hand in the water, hoping to stir up the image again.

Nothing.

Heavy-hearted, Sam lay on the dock and closed his eyes. The warbling heartrending call of a loon lulled him to sleep.

Chapter Thirty

"Dad? Are you okay?"

The intruder's voice shattered Sam's dream, where he and Rachel were riding Cricket and Bucky on The Flats. It was summer. Scorching hot July. Rachel smiled toward him, then galloped off on her chestnut mare with a haunting laugh.

Disoriented, Sam lifted his head from the dock and tried to focus in the bright light. He checked his watch. Noon. *Geez. I've been sleeping out here for over a half hour.* He sat up slowly and shaded his eyes, squinting toward Beth's voice. Through zigzag heat waves, he made out a silhouette of his daughter standing next to a taller woman, with Isabel on her hip.

Waving, he shouted toward them. "I'm fine. Be right there." *I'm lucky they didn't see me zonked out and call the ambulance, thinking I collapsed or something.* He heaved himself to his feet using one of the posts, groaned when his knees protested, and headed down the dock, swiping at the prick of embarrassment that tingled his cheeks.

The first thing he noticed was Beth's expression of rapture. Her eyes danced with delight, reminding him of the old days, when she'd won so many swim meets in high school. Better yet, they shone like they had on the day Isabel was born. And although his daughter was a relatively happy person, expressions of this magnitude were rare. His pulse quickened as he hurried to meet the woman who stood with her arm around his Bethie.

He smiled at Penelope and leaned forward to hug and kiss his daughter and Isabel.

"Dad, this is Penelope." She turned to her partner. "Penelope, my father, Sam."

The woman held out a lean hand. Sam shook it and smiled into dark amber eyes, absorbing the essence of the woman through them. Probing, yet compassionate, they sparkled and connected with his.

"Dr. Moore. What a pleasure to finally meet you." Her grip was firm and warm.

Penelope stood several inches taller than Beth. Probably about five-foot-six, Sam guessed. Straight black hair shimmered down her back, captured in a wide silver barrette. She wore a cornflower blue sundress and no shoes, reminding him of Pocahontas in the Disney movie. Strong. Proud. Beautiful. No sense of embarrassment flickered in her eyes, and for that, Sam was glad.

"Please, call me Sam," he said. "I've been wanting to meet you for a long time."

Her eyes shifted and almost glowed while she held his hand for much longer than a typical handshake. Compassion rose from their depths. "I know. Me, too. I'm so sorry for your loss."

She released his hand and reached up to gently hug him, whispering in his ear. "Everything's going to be okay. It will all be settled soon."

With a faint sense of euphoria and puzzlement, Sam stepped back and gazed wide-eyed at Penelope. "Thank you." He wasn't sure what he was thanking her for, but felt certain she'd seen into his soul, his future, and that her assurance of a resolved outcome made some kind of crazy sense.

Isabel dragged him out of his trance. "Tikka!" She played with her mother's beaded necklace, jingling it in her chubby hands. "Ditty nob!"

"Let me hold my granddaughter," he said. "I haven't seen her in forever."

Beth handed her over. The child squealed and wiggled, then laid her head against his chest as if she were tired. He kissed her soft curls and rubbed his hand over her back, reveling in the comfort of this tiny girl who trusted him so implicitly.

Penelope motioned to a cardboard box on the steps behind her. "I hope you like white wine. We stopped at this winery—"

"Eaglecrest?" Sam asked.

She nodded. "Yes! It was so quaint, near that beautiful old seminary complex that overlooks the lake. The monks used to make wine there, did you know that?"

Sam smiled. He'd been there many times. "I did."

"Anyway, we thought one of the white wines they served at the tasting was the best. It's called Diamond."

Sam shot a surprised look at Penelope. "Really? That's one of Rachel's favorites." His voice cracked, and he looked away. "I mean, it used to be."

Beth and Penelope locked eyes, concern ping-ponging between them. Beth took her father's hand and pressed it. "Must be why we liked it so much, huh, Dad?"

"Must be. Guess you inherited that good taste from your mother."

The baby's head popped up, and she reached for Sam's watch. "You like that? See? Shiny." He took it off and let her hold it for a few seconds, then shifted her to his left hip and put his arm around Beth.

Penelope pointed to the wine and chuckled. "We bought a whole case 'cause it was on sale. I hope you don't think we're lushes or anything."

Sam snorted a laugh. "Heck, no. I'm thrilled. I meant to pick some up on the way down, but Lila and I got into such a great conversation about the state of affairs in Europe that I forgot." He pointed to the cat who wrapped around his legs. "Penelope, meet Lila."

She crouched down to pick up the cat, cuddling her. Lila relaxed in her arms and purred—clearly in kitty heaven while Penelope scratched behind her ears and stroked her soft white belly. "So, you're an expert in foreign affairs, eh, Lila?"

Sam smiled. Another point for Penelope. She earned the stamp of approval from a very picky feline. He nodded toward the wine. "With this crowd, we'll probably go through a few bottles at dinner every night. It won't go to waste, I assure you." He hesitated, then glanced at Beth. "Assuming you both can stay the week?"

Beth slipped an arm through Penelope's. "I can. And Nel is going to commute to the hospital from here. She'll be with us most evenings."

"Excellent. You'll have to tell us more about your practice over dinner tonight." He shifted his attention to the baby and caressed her curly blonde hair with his rough fingers, then suddenly squeezed her to him again. "I missed you, sweetie."

She struggled this time, chattering like a magpie. With a swift motion, she reached up to grab Sam's hair and pulled hard. "Numby dooey huh."

He exploded in laughter, untangling her sticky fingers from his hair. "Hey! That stuff's attached to me."

Beth's nose crinkled in a laugh. "She missed you, too, Dad."

When they reached the door, Penelope motioned them inside. "Why don't you go inside and visit? I'll get the bags."

"You sure?" Beth's eyes searched her lover's, swimming with playful intentions. "I can help."

Penelope laid the back of her hand on Beth's cheek. "I'm sure, sweetie. Stay with your father. He's missed you. You two need time together."

They didn't go inside immediately, but watched her walk away, padding on the cement walk with sure-footed confidence that vaguely reminded Sam of the feline fluidity of his Lila. Long bronze legs and arms swung in easy rhythm, and her glossy hair moved in counterpoint to her steps.

Beth sighed with pure pleasure, leaning on her father's arm. "What do you think, Dad?"

"She's a fascinating woman. I like her a lot."

Beth's eyes searched his. "You really do?"

"Oh, yeah. She's a keeper."

She let out a long sigh. "I'm glad you think so, Dad. I don't plan to throw this one back."

"She's a lot better than the last one."

Beth's face fell. "I sure hope so."

Sam felt bad as soon as he said it. Zafina had posed as a medical student and had burrowed her way into their family. She'd broken Beth's heart and nearly killed them all. "I'm sorry, baby. Didn't mean to bring her up. But this woman is gold. Pure gold. I have a really good feeling about her. There's something almost mystical in those amber eyes."

"You sense it, too?"

"I do. And she's obviously crazy about you."

Beth beamed at him, then collected herself. "Let's go inside, Dad. We have so much to talk about."

He opened the door with his free hand. Lila streaked inside. "That we do, my dear. Come on. Let's get this baby out of the sun."

Chapter Thirty-One

Sam flipped thick pieces of swordfish over with a long-handled spatula, squeezing more lemon juice over the filets as they sizzled on the grate. Garcia's gas grill was huge—big enough to cook all the steaks at once. He shook his head and laughed out loud, mumbling to himself. "This is gonna spoil me. I'll never want to go back to my dinky little charcoal grill."

A voice startled him from behind. "Now I know what you'll be wanting for Christmas, Dad." Beth squeezed Sam's shoulder and grinned.

"Hmm. Not a bad idea."

Sam closed the grill cover to keep the fish moist. He stepped back and sat on a nearby plastic chair. Beth joined him, plopping into the seat and stretching her tanned legs out before her. She kicked off her flip-flops and sighed. The sun sank lower on the western horizon, blocked now by the house and trees.

Sam looked back toward the house. "Nel's a real sweetheart."

"I'm so glad you see her like I do, Dad. I think this is it. Finally."

Sam squeezed her hand. "You're probably right, sweetheart. But give yourself time to be sure. There's no rush."

Beth looked at her father with surprise. "That's exactly what she said."

"Well, she's right. Good things are worth waiting for. There's no hurry if she's the one. You've got plenty of time. Your whole life."

Beth picked at a loose thread on her cutoff shorts. "I know. I tend to jump, don't I?"

Sam got up and opened the grill cover, poking at the swordfish again. "Sometimes. But something tells me, this time you're right." He cut one of the chunks in half with the side of the spatula. "I think these are done. Want to run inside and tell Maryellen?"

Beth jumped up and headed for the house. "Okay. See you in a few."

As Sam piled the fish onto an oversized platter, he gazed out at the water. A flock of Canada geese swam into view and landed on the shore. A mother and father led seven silver goslings across the pebbles, pecking at the stones for juicy snacks. Sam watched them, admiring their beauty, but well aware of the mess they'd leave behind if they decided to roost there. He chuckled when it struck him—the purpose of the metal bucket and small shovel Garcia had placed near the shore end of the dock became clear.

After shutting down the grill, Sam hefted the platter and brought it inside. Maryellen had been busy while he'd been outside. A large bowl of tabouli salad with fresh parsley from Sam's garden anchored the center of the table. Andrew carried in a steaming bowl of buttered German noodles, and Penelope buckled Timmy and Isabel into the collapsible high chairs brought from home. Each plate held sliced papaya and kiwi, topped with the fresh black raspberries Sam picked earlier from Garcia's woods behind the garage. Beth laid napkins and glasses of ice water at each place setting as everyone crowded around and settled in amidst a clamor of conversation and laughter.

Evan and Timmy devoured their swordfish in minutes. Both boys stared at the platter wide-eyed. "Can we have seconds, Gramps?" Evan asked.

Sam smiled. "Of course. There's plenty, boys."

Andrew laughed when Sam served them each another piece. "You guys better slow down. You'll get stomachaches."

The boys grew quiet, shoveling the fish into their mouths.

"Evan?" Sam asked, draining the last of his first glass of wine.

"Yeah, Gramps?" Evan started in on the noodles, slurping them up like spaghetti.

"Would you like to go for a walk with me tomorrow morning?"

Evan nodded. "Sure. And when we get back, can we do some fishing? Timmy's dying to catch a fish."

Sam stabbed a piece of papaya. "You bet."

Timmy reached over Sam's plate and grabbed five black raspberries with one chubby fist.

"Yum," he said, mushing them into his mouth. He smiled at Sam with purple teeth.

"Hey!" Sam laughed. "You can't steal Papa's berries."

While Maryellen scolded him, Sam handed Timmy his napkin, then poured another glass of wine for himself and Penelope, exchanging a glance with her.

"You love being a grandpa, don't you, Sam?" She reached over to wipe Isabel's mouth with her napkin.

Warming to the thought, he answered her slowly. "I do, Penelope. I really do." He pushed back from the table. He'd eaten too fast, just like the boys. The swordfish had melted in his mouth, flaky and buttery.

She shot him an understanding glance, then reached to grab Timmy's water glass before he tipped it into the noodles.

"Whoops. Caught it!" She laughed.

Beth beamed at her, barely able to focus on her meal. "Good catch."

Evan chimed in. "Yeah. You should be on my baseball team, Penelope. We need a better catcher."

A round of laughter percolated across the table. Sam took another sip of his wine and watched his family interact.

This is what it's all about. All we need now is Rachel.

The marble pulsed in his pocket, as if in response.

Tonight. I'll do it tonight. Rachel's coming home.

Penelope glanced at him as if she'd heard his inner thoughts, then nodded like she agreed with his plan. He swore he heard her voice in his head.

Go for it, Sam.

ꟈ

The family retired early after an evening of Scrabble and Disney's Robin Hood movie. Sam tucked a sleepy Timmy into bed, watched until he fell asleep, then headed outside to the Adirondack chairs beside the lake. The moon hid behind scattered silver-blue clouds, darkening the shore. Mist settled along the edge of the dock and around the cove, while crickets chirped in the distant woods behind the garage. He pulled a thick blanket around his shoulders.

The marble glowed in Sam's hand. Checking to be sure no one could see him, he gripped it hard and concentrated on the night he met Ginger Kennedy.

Chapter Thirty-Two

Jack and Ronnie shoved Sam toward the girl with the long copper braid. Sam's young body moved with the agility of a twenty-two year old, but the thoughts circling his brain belonged to the present.

Ginger. There she was. Long-legged and tan. Salty skin. Hair snaking down her back, swishing when she shifted her foot to the barstool rung. She lowered her eyes with false modesty and giggled with two friends. They twirled colorful paper umbrellas in their drinks, darting secretive glances toward Sam and his friends.

Pushing away the physical urges lit by licentious memories, Sam slumped toward the wall, holding his stomach. "Oh, God." He moaned and doubled over.

Ronnie grabbed his arm, concern twisting his rugged features. "You okay, man? What's wrong?"

Sam slid to the floor and did his best to feign discomfort. "My stomach. I think I'm gonna be sick."

Jack looked with longing at the girls, then helped Sam hobble to a chair.

"Sorry, guys. You go ahead. I'm gonna go crash."

Ronnie and Jack exchanged dubious glances. "You sure, man? You gonna be okay?"

Groaning again, Sam doubled over. "I'll be…argh. Just gotta get to the room before I barf."

After his friends dropped him off, Sam called the airport and arranged for a flight home the next morning. He drew the curtains and flopped onto the thin cot set up beneath the picture window. *Just have to get through the night. If I avoid Ginger, Susan will never have been conceived.*

A knock sounded on the door.

Sam put on his sick-as-a-dog face and answered it, leaning heavily on the doorjamb. "Yes?"

There she stood, glistening skin, wide eyes, pouty lips. Her skirt ended mid-thigh. Gleaming bare legs shuffled beneath.

Ginger.

She looked apologetic. "Er. Excuse me. I just wanted to check on you. Your friends said you weren't feeling well." She twirled the tail of her braid around her fingers and flicked it against her lips.

Sam froze, his young body responding like a randy soldier on leave. "I'm okay. Just got a bad stomach bug, that's all."

She radiated charm and touched his forehead with cool fingers. "Poor baby. You sure I can't do anything to make you feel better?"

What's going on here? Is time resisting the change? Is someone or something trying to make this conception happen?

"Uh. No thanks. I'll be okay. It was nice of you to stop by, but I've gotta get through this one alone."

Her face fell.

"Oh. Okay. Well, feel better."

She fluttered her fingers briefly and turned on her heels, the red braid swishing as she swiveled her hips down the walk.

He collapsed onto the cot, staring at the white ceiling tiles.

It's done.

He rolled over. The thin woolen blanket scratched his skin and the lumpy pillow was useless. Tossing and turning, he tried to relax.

Focus.

Get through the night. Get on the plane. Get out of here. Then summon Billy to take me back to the present.

ഇ ന

The flight home took forever. Fogged-in airports, overbooking, and pure bad luck put Sam behind by five hours. During the cramped flight, he closed his eyes and sent thoughts to Billy.

Don't bring me back yet. Please. I want to be sure this works. I need to see this through.

Billy didn't reply, but Sam felt his presence. In the past, he'd quickly whisked Sam in and out of scenes, usually within an hour or two. But this time, Billy had let him stay for almost twenty-four hours. At least in twenty-four hours passed in this time frame. He had no idea how long he'd actually been gone. Regardless, it comforted him knowing his little brother was involved and listening.

After taking a cab back to the University of Rochester dorms, he ran into Pete Baldridge in the deserted lobby. Pete rubbed a spot on the top of his beak-like nose and flashed teeth encased in metal braces. His green eyes peered at Sam.

"What the hell are you doin' back here, Sam?"

Sam plunked down on a Naugahyde couch across from Pete and sighed.

"Didn't feel well. That's all."

Pete leaned forward, his knobby knees almost touching Sam's.

"You look okay. Feeling better?"

Sam avoided Pete's scrutiny. "A little, I guess."

"Well, I'm glad you're here. It was damned lonely. I'm still pissed that I couldn't go with you guys. Stupid work. Anyway, I was just about to head over to the pharmacy for my shift. Wanna walk with me?"

Sam stretched his legs and arms; his muscles still felt tight from riding in coach.

"I guess so. But isn't it a bit early for your shift? Don't you start at six o'clock? It's just five now."

Pete turned crimson.

"Uh...Yeah. I like to get there a little early."

"Wait a second. Does this involve a girl?"

He stuttered. "Y...yeah. Louise. She's really neat."

Sam felt a stab of sorrow. Poor Lou. He should've been kinder to her. "Does she like you too?"

Pete stood and stuffed his hands into his pockets, squirming. "Don't know. I don't think so. But I haven't had a chance to really talk to her much. She's the owner's daughter. And she works like a dog."

"I know her. She's in my sociology class. I think she's in pre-med, like us."

Pete brightened. "Really? I didn't know. Then we have something in common," he said.

"You sure do. Come on. Let's head over."

ꕥ

Peter and Sam entered the pharmacy and headed for the soda fountain, where a willowy blonde wiped down the counter. With short, feathered hair, she wore a blue butterfly barrette over one ear. A large medallion dangled from her neck, set off by a white turtleneck. Jeans and an apron fashioned from a towel completed the ensemble.

She shot Pete a glance, but did a double take when she saw Sam. "Hello, boys."

Pete slid onto a barstool and Sam settled beside him.

"Hi, Louise," Pete said. "Been busy today?"

Sam nodded hello and busied himself with a menu, trying to ignore the feeling that Louise would somehow have inside knowledge about what would happen in the future.

"Real busy. Hey, Sam. Thought you went on spring break with Ronnie and Jack."

Sam looked up with a start, surprised she'd kept tabs on him. "Uh, yeah. I did. But I came home early."

Lou's eyes sparkled. She moved closer to Sam, rubbing circles with a wet rag. "I've heard it's overrated."

Pete jumped in. "It is! I went last year and it was nuts. Too damned hot. People partying all night, drinking themselves into comas, and sleeping with anything that moved."

Lou snorted. "Some people would think that sounds good."

Sam rolled his eyes. "Believe me. It's definitely overrated."

Pete leaned on his elbows, his eyes riveted on Lou. Sam tried to swing the subject back to Peter.

"Peter's at the top of our class right now. He's tutoring me in advanced bio."

Lou smiled briefly in Pete's direction, then returned her gaze to Sam. "Cool. That's great, Pete. So Sam, how's your last year of premed going?"

Sam put the menu down and stood. "Pretty well. But I've gotta fly. Just came by to walk Pete here to work. Got some unpacking to do."

Lou's face fell. "Okay. Well, if you get lonesome, come back. Pete and I are probably the only ones left in town. We're holding down the fort. And I make a mean root beer float."

He shuffled back toward the door, longing to disappear. This felt too much like his last conversation with Lou in Clara's diner. "Thanks. I'll keep that in mind."

On the way back to the dorm, the marble heated in his pocket. It was time to go home.

Chapter Thirty-Three

Sam awoke in the Adirondack chair, draped in a dew-soaked blanket. Shivering, he looked around in confusion.

Morning, already?

He scratched the stubble on his chin.

Feels like a day's worth.

The lonely cry of a loon echoed across the mist-enshrouded lake. Three hills at the south end hunkered beneath cobalt-blue fog, their peaks hidden. A family of ducks floated into view, quacking in syncopated rhythm.

Tossing the blanket aside, Sam stood and spun around to face the cabin.

Did it work?

Dizzy for a moment, he steadied himself with the chair back.

Wait a minute. Why am I still at the cabin? If Rachel hadn't died, wouldn't I be home with her? How the hell does this work, anyway?

A voice hailed him from the nearby cabin.

"Mornin,' Sam."

He turned to see a young man casting his line into the mist from the end of the neighboring dock. Sam half smiled and waved, noticing a mini-van and trailer in the nearby driveway.

Who is he? And when did he arrive? Has my messing with the past changed everything?

Turning back to Garcia's cabin, he noticed some changes. The A-frame glowed white in the golden morning light. Yesterday, it was brown.

The hedges that were neatly trimmed around the foundation were gone. In their place—white marble stones and several ornamental statues.

He ducked around the back of the cabin to check his Highlander and his children's cars.

All gone.

In their place, a small green Miata.

What the hell?

Nervous now, Sam approached the cabin. Checking his watch, he noted the time, six-forty-five. The aromas of coffee and toast greeted him. His heartbeat raced as he turned the doorknob.

Rachel!

Could it be?

He pushed the door open slowly, noting the different furniture arrangement. Television on the east wall. Red sofa and chairs, not plaid.

"Hello?" he called softly.

As if each step were mired in mud, Sam made his way inside, a spark of hope flickering from his heart to his throat.

"Good morning, sweetie." The figure faced away from him, busied over dishes in the sink. "Did you catch anything?"

Sam froze. That voice. It wasn't right. The hair. The height.

His insides slithered to his feet in a panicked sludge.

She turned and smiled. "What's the matter, Sam? You look like you saw a ghost."

Sam stared at Lou and paled, his weakened legs shaking. He leaned against the couch and fell back onto the unfamiliar fabric. He reached frantically for the marble, but couldn't find it.

Wrong pocket?

"Sam, honey? What is it?"

He looked around nervously. "Where is Beth? Andy? The kids?"

She frowned and wiped her hands on a dishtowel. Striding purposefully to his side, she laid her hand against his forehead. "What's the matter with you, big fella? Are you sick?"

"Beth?" he asked, looking at her. "My daughter?"

The frown deepened and she reached for the phone. "Honey. Something's wrong with you. You know we don't have a daughter. And who's Andy? What kids?" She dialed 911. "I think you're having a stroke, Sam. I'm calling the paramedics."

"No!" Sam got up and took the phone from her hand. "I'm fine. I was dreaming. I fell asleep outside on the chair. Sorry for alarming you. I'm okay, really."

Lou released her grip on the phone and scrutinized Sam, touching his forehead with the back of her hand. "Are you sure? I've never seen you like this."

He forced a smile and gently disengaged himself, backing toward the stairs. "I'm just going upstairs to clean up. Be down for breakfast in a sec."

With a dubious glance, Lou picked up her dishtowel and turned back to the sink. "Okay. See you in a bit."

Sam hurried upstairs, trying to still the pounding in his heart.

NO. NO. NO. NO. NO!

Beth. Andy. Evan. Timmy. Isabel.

Erased?

Lou's back? Married to me?

No. Wait. This wasn't supposed to happen.

He shut the bedroom door and flopped on the bed. New memories flooded his brain. Hanging out with Lou in the soda shop. Her persistent attentions finally won him over. She'd dropped out of med school to help him with his new family practice, acting as both secretary and accountant. He'd never hired Rachel.

The quest for children had been riddled with dozens of fertility tests and consultations. In vitro. Five times. Nothing had worked.

Another memory flashed through his mind. A newsflash. Three local girls died in a car crash. Rachel had been one of them.

What the hell have I done?

Not only have I eliminated my daughter, Susan, I've taken out all of my children and grandchildren. And Rachel died anyway.

He pounded the pillow beside him, his body coiled in anger.

NO!

Frantically reaching for the marble, he fished it out of his pocket and clutched it to his heart.

Billy! Help me. Please help me.

UNDO IT!

The marble heated in his hands, enveloping Sam in a cyclone of green sparks. Dizzy with the motion, he corkscrewed through time.

Images flashed before him, fading as quickly as he moved past them. Finally, Billy appeared in a wash of green.

Try it again, Sam. Don't give up.

Hazel eyes glowed in the green light, simultaneously beseeching and comforting.

Don't give up.

Chapter Thirty-Four

THE MORNING SUN WARMED SAM'S FACE. HE SNUGGLED DEEPER INTO THE feather pillow and stretched, listening to the sound of the waves splashing on the shore below the opened window.

"I wet."

Sam opened one eye, then the other.

"Timmy? Buddy? Is that you?"

Timmy pointed to the mattress. "I wet da bed."

Sam choked back a relieved sob, reaching for the boy. "Oh my God. My sweet boy. You're here!"

"I wet, Papa." His rosebud lips pouted and copper-colored eyebrows drew into a frown, trying hard to get the simple facts through to his dense grandfather. He pointed to the circle of moisture on the sheets below him. His soaking shorts emitted an acrid smell.

"No problem, buddy." Sam got up, almost giddy with excitement. If Timmy was here, then so was Andy. And most likely Beth, too. "Come on, sport. Hop down. Let's get you in the tub. And Papa put a waterproof sheet underneath, so all we have to do is throw this stuff in the washer. But we've gotta be quiet. It's only six and everyone's still sleeping."

Timmy echoed Sam's serious tone. "Seepin'."

"That's right, buddy." Sam took Timmy's chubby hand in his as the boy toddled beside him to the bathroom. He started a warm bubble bath, peeled off the sopping clothes, and wrapped them in a pile on a towel, ready to throw in the washer when everyone was up. Timmy stepped into the tub, sliding on his belly and zooming back and forth from end to end. Sam laughed and dabbed at the drips that splashed over the rim. He squirted some tear-free baby shampoo on Timmy's red hair and scrubbed it gently.

"I do it," Timmy insisted. He rubbed his scalp half-heartedly, then ducked under the faucet until it was rinsed clean. He resumed sliding back and forth, sloshing water dangerously close to the rim. "I a fishy."

"You sure are. Look at you swimming in there."

As if he suddenly remembered they were at the lake, Timmy popped up and tried to climb out of the tub. "I done. Can we catch fishies now?"

Sam snorted a laugh, wrapping a fluffy towel around the child. He lifted him out and dried him off, hugging him extra long. "Pretty soon. After breakfast." He dried Timmy's hair and tucked the towel around his middle. "Your hair smells so good, baby."

"I not a baby!"

"I'm sorry, sport. I know. Papa just missed you, that's all."

Timmy crinkled his face as if his grandfather was nuts, then changed the subject abruptly. "I hungry!"

Sam picked him up and carried him back to the bedroom, rummaging around in the drawer for some clean shorts and a tee shirt.

"Are you now? Well, looks like Papa will have to make you a nice big breakfast. What do you want, buddy?"

Timmy put one finger on his lips and looked off in the distance, as if pondering the world's fate. "Panacakes."

He slid a clean tee shirt over Timmy's head and helped him step into shorts.

"Panacakes? Is that what you want?" Sam's smile widened. "Okay. Panacakes it is."

Trying to forget the fact that he'd almost destroyed every member of his family, Sam shoved the disturbing thought aside, telling himself he'd have to be much cleverer next time. "Come on buddy, let's go downstairs. I'm feeling pretty hungry, myself."

Timmy shrieked when Sam released the small sunfish from the hook. "I do it!"

Carefully, he let the child hold onto the wiggling fish to "help" toss him back in the water. "Good job, pal."

The boy tugged at his life vest and eyed Evan, who stood on the shore skipping stones. "I throw rocks."

Sam grabbed his hand. "Wait. You hold Papa's hand, little man. And we need to get our pole. Can't just leave it here on the dock."

Timmy pulled hard on Sam's hand, ignoring his request. "I throw rocks!" he screeched.

Evan raised one eyebrow in their direction and shook his head. "He's gonna blow, Gramps. Watch out."

Sam scooped the little volcano into his arms, holding him tightly against his chest. Timmy thrashed in Sam's grip, his face reddening. "I THROW ROCKS!"

This time the cries turned to screams. Loud, piercing, lake-echoing screams that turned fishermen's heads and brought Maryellen to the doorstep.

"Everything okay out here, Papa?"

Sam stepped over the fishing pole and hung onto the boy, whose legs and arms flailed in all directions. "It's okay. Just a temper tantrum. I've got him. You can go back to what you were doing. I've done this before, you know."

Maryellen looked dubious. "Okay. Let me know if you need me."

"Will do. Thanks."

"I THROW ROCKS!"

Evan hurried to help his grandfather, steadying him as he stepped from the dock onto the lawn.

"It's gonna be a bad one," Evan said. His eyes widened and he bit his lower lip.

Sam stumbled to the lawn and sank to a crouch, trying to comfort the wailing child, who threw himself to the grass face down. Pummeling with small fists and feet, he beat the turf until his wails faded to softer sobs. Sam rubbed his back in slow circles, speaking comforting words as the child finally calmed. When he slowed almost to a stop, he allowed Sam to pick him up and hug him.

Sam picked loose pieces of grass from Timmy's hair and face as Evan rose from the nearby Adirondack chair to join them.

"You doin' better, pal? Here, let's wipe your eyes," Sam said. He used the hem of his tee shirt to dry the child's face, then rocked him for a while.

As he fell asleep, Timmy mumbled, "I throw rocks."

"Later, my boy. Later," Sam said.

Evan smiled and reached for his brother.

"I'll take him inside, Gramps. He was up so early with you, looks like he really needs his nap today."

Sam carefully transferred the child to his brother, then stood, massaging his lower back. The boy had topped forty-five pounds. "Thanks, Ev. Hey, when you get back, do you want to pick black raspberries?"

Evan tossed a smile over his shoulder. "Can't. Dad's taking me to the library. They have free internet there."

"Okay, sport. Maybe another time."

Evan shifted his brother to a more comfortable position. Met by his mother at the door, he managed to get the sleeping child indoors without waking him.

Intrigued with the idea of more alone time, Sam grabbed a bucket from the side of the house and headed for the berry patch. Penelope hailed him, emerging from the side door with her own container.

"Going to pick berries?" she asked.

Sam stopped short. "Wow. You read my mind."

"I know." Her smile widened beneath eyes dancing with delight. She loped toward him with easy grace, catching him in four strides. "Hope you don't mind the company."

Her amber eyes caught his, pinning him momentarily with searching intensity. She wore braids today, which lent a stronger Native American appearance. Penelope's high cheekbones and strong chin framed an intelligent face. Her golden skin glowed in the dappled sunlight. Sam linked arms with her.

"Not at all, my dear. I'd love to have you join me."

They walked side by side to the parking area, crossed the lane, walked behind the garage on the opposite side, and headed for the woods. Garcia's land, a narrow strip of one hundred and fifty feet wide, extended back toward West Lake Road for almost a half mile.

Clustered pines emitted shafts of light on the forest floor, where wild black raspberries grew in profusion.

"Look at all the berries!" Penelope said, bending to pick and sample them. "Oh my God. They're delicious!"

Sam chuckled, enjoying her childlike wonder. He followed suit, picking and eating until he'd satisfied his lust for the sweet fruits.

"I guess we'd better save some for the pie, Sam."

He grinned and nodded. "You're right. Look. There's a really good patch back this way." They stepped carefully through the prickly briars, following a path Sam had made the day before. "They're loaded back here."

"Wow. You weren't kidding."

They picked for the next twenty minutes. Sam stopped when the marble began to warm against his thigh.

Penelope stiffened and turned, looking pointedly at the pocket that held the marble. Sam automatically covered it, but realized there was no green glow to give it away. She'd sensed it, not seen it. "Beth told me about Billy," she said calmly. "I'm so sorry you lost him when you were boys."

Sam stared at her, speechless.

"But he's never really gone. You know that, right? He's always with you. You need to trust him. Let him guide you. He'll show you the way, Sam."

"I…" Sam's jaw dropped, incapable of normal speech.

"Here. Let me take your berries inside. Why don't I tell them you're taking a walk in the woods? Looks like he wants to talk to you, Sam." She pointed to the green glow that now shone through his shorts. "You'd best take care of business."

Sam stuttered as she reached for his pail and turned on her heels to stride back to the house.

"Th—thank you."

She tossed a hand over her shoulder.

"Don't mention it."

He shook himself and headed for the darker woods. He needed cover. Deep cover.

Chapter Thirty-Five

SAM FOUND A SPOT TO SLIDE BENEATH A LARGE BLUE SPRUCE AND PROP himself against the trunk. The low hanging branches brushed the ground ten feet from the trunk and hid him from view. Deep in the woods already, it was unlikely that he'd be seen even without cover, but in case someone hankered for a shady walk, he'd be safe from their eyes.

"Take me to the ceremony in the woods, Billy."

Sam surprised himself by saying it out loud. He cupped the hot glass in both hands, holding it up to his lips as he spoke into the green light. The hard bark behind his back faded to nothingness as he spiraled through time once again.

Billy dropped Sam outside a ramshackle house surrounded by woods and the nearby hedonistic shouts of the gathering cult. A deep violet sky dotted with stars shimmered in the east. Sparks from the pyre glowed in the clearing.

Tall, dewy grass moistened Sam's sneakers. He froze and listened. The shrieks of crazed mania resonated in the woods, frightening and fascinating him.

Another sound joined the cacophony, softer, and closer to him.

A child cried. It came from inside the house.

Susan.

Sam flattened himself against the house, looking over his shoulder to insure he wasn't seen by the bodies gyrating around the fire. There, a window. Next, a door. He crept toward it and turned the knob. *Unlocked.*

Sam pushed into the dimly lit interior, glancing sideways and beyond toward the bedroom door.

A wooden table sat in the center of the kitchen, covered in blistering green paint. Discarded coffee cups littered its surface next to overflowing ashtrays. Dishes filled the sink and hid the shelves. The room reeked of stale cigarettes and rotten food.

A white wall phone hung near the refrigerator. Sam picked it up and heard a welcome dial tone.

Another cry came from behind the door. Sam hurried toward the bedroom, turned the key in the lock, and found Susan in the same position Billy had shown him earlier.

Dressed in pink and purple, the child huddled on a ratty blanket on the floor, sobbing and calling for her mother.

Sam called her name. “Susan?”

She looked up through dark tangled locks, then scooted backwards against the wall.

“I won’t hurt you, honey. I’m here to help.”

She cried louder now, panicked at the sight of him. Sam backed away. “Don’t be afraid. I won’t hurt you, I promise.”

He hurried back to the kitchen and picked up the phone, dialing “zero” for the operator. When she answered, Sam got right to the point.

“Operator? I’ve found a child abandoned in a locked bedroom in a shack in the woods. There are naked dancers cavorting around an open fire, and I think they’re about to commit a felony—looks like they’re planning on a human sacrifice.” Sam looked around the room and found a pile of papers shoved into the corner. He grabbed a utility bill and read the address into the phone.

“Yes, operator. I’m serious. Please send the authorities to this address. Immediately.”

Sam checked his daughter again, smiled at her, and nodded. “See you in the future, honey. Hang tight. Help is coming.”

℘

When Sam came to, his head spun in confusion. Squinting in the dingy light of a cramped, hot apartment, he jumped up from a rickety kitchen chair and held the edge of a Formica table until the dizziness passed. The room smelled of rancid grease and stale coffee.

What the hell? Billy? Where am I?

Sam checked the newspaper on the table and staggered.

Today’s date.

He’d come to the present. The new present. The one changed by the phone call he’d made just minutes ago…or forty years ago.

Where am I?

He flipped the newspaper over, scanning the name on the address label.

Sam Moore.

Not Dr. Sam Moore.

And definitely not Dr. Sam and Rachel Moore.

Mail lay stacked on the table in tall, neat piles. He flipped through several, noting three or four months' worth of electric, heating oil, and phone bills. All in his name.

Panicked now, Sam searched the apartment, looking for signs of his family. He raced from the tiny kitchenette to the single bedroom off the threadbare living room.

There. On the shabby bureau. A family photo.

Sam moved closer and studied it.

Ginger and Susan filled the frame. Ginger, with a frayed smile, gazed at the lens. Susan, on her lap, must have been four. She smiled at the camera, but not with her eyes. Something was off. Something was missing.

New memories began to fill the vacuum that had become his brain, running like a ragged 8mm filmstrip at warp speed.

He remembered that while Raoul was being arrested, he had helped Ginger escape from the melée when the cops arrived. He'd grabbed her and Susan, and had gotten the hell out of there.

After dropping out of med school, he'd married her within a month. Now, after forty years of flipping burgers and cooking fries, he'd graduated to head fry cook at a Florida truck stop. Ginger had divorced him a year after they'd married, and now bled him dry each month for alimony and child support.

Could it be?

Sam dragged aside the curtains in the bedroom and blinked.

A brick wall.

Returning to the living room, he pulled open the sliding glass door and stepped onto a narrow balcony.

The view—shopping malls and highway—depressed him. A few skimpy palm trees grew in the center of an expansive parking lot.

Cars jammed the roads and asphalt lots. Dingy gray clouds glowered in the distance. Not a breeze stirred.

Returning to the kitchen, Sam flopped onto the chair again, holding his head in his hands. A cockroach scuttled out of the sink and along the countertop.

What have I done?

This time, he'd not only lost his entire family, he'd erased his entire medical career and ended up in a disgusting hovel.

No family. No gardens. No friends.

No nothing.

God. I stink at this.

He reached for the marble in his pocket and willed it to glow.

Billy.

Get me the hell out of here.

Undo it, again.

Please.

Undo it.

Chapter Thirty-Six

Sam woke on his side in the woods with pine needles pressed into his face. He slowly sat up and rubbed the bumpy impressions they made on his skin. A blue jay cawed overhead and swooped down to nab a blackberry. Cackling, the bird ascended to a tall perch to enjoy his find.

I'm back. Thank God.

And thank Billy.

The overhead pine branches swayed in a sudden gentle breeze, sighing in musical tones. Like a wind-filled dervish, the air swirled and moaned, rising in crescendo until the sounds crystallized.

Saaaaammmmmm.

He glanced up. Had he imagined it?

Saaaaammmmmm.

The cloud pattern swirled above the treetops, morphing and shaping itself into the face of a woman.

Rachel.

His heart clenched and the pain inside grew and spread until his whole body hurt. He stared at her image and whispered to her. "I'm trying so hard, honey. Don't give up on me."

His heart squeezed tighter. His Rachel. His only love. The voice returned, whispering through the branches and the wind. *Saaaaammmmmm. Bring me home, baby.*

He squeezed his eyes shut and concentrated.

One more time. I've got to try. One more time.

Billy. Please help me make this right. Show me the way.

A sense of peace descended on him, filling his empty, raw voids with warm comfort. The marble pulsed once in his pocket, then quieted, and the image overhead dissipated into the sudden calm that spread wispy clouds over the cobalt sky.

With sore bones, he hobbled to his feet and steadied himself on the trunk of the pine, accidentally touching gooey sap that made his fingers stick together. He smiled and lifted them to his face, inhaling the pungent aroma.

I'm back. This is real. But is everything still the same?

The lake glistened in the distance, just beyond Garcia's house. There, in the parking lot, was his Highlander and the rest of the family fleet. Shouts of laughter came from the shore—Timmy and Evan.

Sam relaxed and headed for the lake, where everyone had congregated. Maryellen and Beth sat together, chatting like magpies. Beside them, in a portable playpen, rosy-cheeked Isabel played with toys, wearing a beach hat far too large for her. Andrew and Penelope stood ankle deep in water, skipping stones with the boys.

Sam flipped off his sandals and sat on the edge of the dock, dangling his feet in the cool green water. Timmy rushed to his side. His tee shirt and shorts dripped with lake water. Even his hair lay in wet ringlets.

"Papa! I throw rocks!"

Sam laughed and shaded the bright sun from his face. "Show me how you do it, pal."

The boy beamed from ear to ear and scuttled away to find a skipping stone, followed closely by Andy. The shore was littered with flat slate stones, perfect for the task at hand.

Evan glanced sideways with a smile. "Hey, Gramps. I skipped one ten times."

Sam feigned shock. "Whoa. I think that's a record, Ev."

A proud smile crept onto Evan's lips as he picked up another flat smooth stone and sent it skipping along the surface.

Evan furrowed his brow. "Darn. Seven. I can do better than that."

Penelope waded toward him, her long brown limbs glistening with drops of water. She wore white cutoffs and a faded pink tee shirt, half-soaked from frolicking with the boys. Her braids were pinned up onto the sides of her head, reminding Sam of an old Heidi movie.

"You okay?" she asked as she slid onto the dock beside him.

Her amber eyes caught his, probing him. Strangely comforted, he sighed and relaxed, whispering his response.

"I screwed up. I have to try again."

Somehow, though they hadn't discussed the details of his trials, he knew that she understood. The flitting magic simmering in her eyes was enough. She held a connection with the otherworld, something new and different from his and Billy's connection, but it was there. It felt as if she reached inside his brain and absorbed the rocky landscape, raw and aching, as screwed up as it was. She understood. She empathized. She knew how he suffered.

The academic part of his brain rebelled, wondering for the zillionth time if he was in a psychotic episode. Her eyes flitted to his again, meeting his gaze square on.

"You're not crazy, Sam."

He jumped, then breathed deeply. "Thanks, Penelope. I needed to hear that."

She tucked a loose lock of hair behind her ear and splashed water onto his legs with her foot. With a smile, she squeezed his arm. "I know."

Beth watched them surreptitiously from the shore, eyes following every movement. Delight streamed from her smile.

Sam turned back to Penelope. "I'm so glad you and Bethie met."

She stretched back in the sun and closed her eyes. "Me, too. She saved me."

"Saved you?"

"Uh huh. I was so alone, Sam." She sat up and rubbed her forehead. "I didn't think I'd ever find my soul mate."

"Did you have many girlfriends before Beth?"

She grimaced. "Not really. I had my work; drew strength from it—from the babies I delivered, those healthy little bundles of life. It felt right. But I was always a bit different. Estranged from humanity, in a way. Being gay and prescient is a pretty rare combination. I didn't date much."

"It must've been so hard."

"It was. I always felt so different, completely removed from the norm. Until I met Beth, that is."

Sam smiled. "She's pretty special, my girl. A lot like her mother." A pang of depression stabbed him, spreading hurt through his body and soul.

Penelope touched his arm again. "You'll get her back, Sam. You just need to be more subtle. Small steps. A whisper of a change. Nothing too dramatic."

He looked at her with renewed respect. "You really do understand, don't you?"

She looked down at the rippled water and nodded. "Yeah."

They exchanged a glance full of shared knowledge. Penelope jumped into the water to rejoin Andy and the boys, and Sam let his brain simmer in the fresh air and sun.

Think. There has to be a way.

Chapter Thirty-Seven

After a dinner of Penelope's fresh pesto and capellini, Sam invited Evan for a walk. "It's the Sandy Bottom Nature Trail," Sam said, "just up the road."

Evan popped one last meatball into his mouth and pushed back from the table. "Can I bring my camera?" He ran halfway across the living room before Sam could answer.

"Of course, pal. I'm bringing mine." Sam shot a look at Maryellen, asking for permission with his eyes.

She smiled and waved a hand in his direction. "You boys go have fun. Andy and I have the dishes tonight."

Andy rolled his eyes and snapped a dishtowel at his wife as she scuttled past him. "We do?"

Maryellen shooed him toward the sink, laughing. "Yes. Now get back to work."

Sam and Evan headed for the Highlander, and drove two miles north on West Lake Road in comfortable silence. When they parked near the north end of Honeoye Lake, Evan jumped out of the SUV and trotted toward the trail that snaked north through the woods.

"Hey! Wait for me," Sam hollered. He locked the car and followed at a fast clip, thinking about what Penelope had said earlier.

You need to take smaller steps. A whisper of change.

Smaller steps? Was that really the way to go?

He made long-legged strides toward Evan's disappearing back and imagined various scenarios in the past.

I can't prevent Susan's birth. That's as bad as killing her. As bad as what she did to Rachel.

But a substantive change, such as getting Raoul arrested, completely changed Sam's life. Not only did he marry Ginger in that version of his past, but Rachel died, regardless.

He frowned and concentrated harder.

Evan ran along a boardwalk that wound eastward beneath overhanging beech and maple trees. "Come on, Gramps! This is so cool!"

The sound of his feet pounding along the planks echoed across the grassy meadows, woods, and smooth-surfaced stream that sparkled and wound toward the head of the lake. A flock of starlings gathered overhead in a cottonwood tree, swelling together as one chattering entity that rose and dipped against the ochre clouds.

Sam watched until they disappeared over the eastern horizon, then stepped up onto the boardwalk and joined Evan on the bridge, where they snapped dozens of shots of the pink sky reflected in the calm water.

Sam slid an arm around Evan's shoulders. "Nice time of night, huh?"

Evan nodded. "Mmmhmm. And I just saw some really cool dragonflies over there. They were all sparkly and metallic looking. Black and turquoise."

"Yeah?"

"Uh huh. Wonder if I can catch any of them with my camera."

Sam froze and pointed toward the water below. "Look!"

Evan squinted in the direction Sam pointed. "What?"

"Over there. Two otters!"

Evan spotted the smooth-coated water babies and watched with fascination as they frolicked in the clean stream. He remembered his own camera and took a few shots before the animals swam lazily toward the setting sun.

Evan's hazel eyes and sandy hair reminded Sam—once again—of his brother Billy. The same look of lively intelligence sparkled from his eyes. The same open sense of wonder appraised the world.

"You look so much like Billy," he said. "Sometimes it's uncanny."

Evan lowered his camera and smiled indulgently. "I know. I've seen his picture, Gramps."

Sam pointed to the trail ahead. "Let's keep going. The sun's really gonna give you a show tonight. Just look at those colors, pal."

Rose and saffron smeared the horizon as if splattered by an impatient child. Lavender splashed the sky, accenting it with streaks. For a moment, Sam wondered if Rachel was responsible for the vibrant display.

They continued along the boardwalk and came to an L-shaped design leading to a small shelter with built-in benches and open walls. Situated in a grassy meadow surrounded by woods, it provided the perfect reprieve from worldly woes.

"Cool," Evan said, running toward the shack.

Sam followed him at a leisurely pace, unable to stop thinking of the night to come and his next attempt to rescue Rachel.

God, I feel so insane.

He leaned on the guide rail and watched Evan squatting on his haunches to take shots of cat-o-nine tails swaying in the waning light.

What makes me think I can really bring back the dead? Or change the past? Am I so delusional that I'm completely detached from reality?

Sam swayed a little, then steadied himself and rapped the railing.

Am I really here? Is this boardwalk real or imagined? Or am I still in that loony bin, high on drugs, envisioning scene after scene?

He shook himself and straightened.

No.

I'm okay. I'm here. This is real.

He gripped the wooden rail and closed his eyes.

Evan. The marble. Billy. The past.

All real.

A crow cawed overhead, startling him out of his reverie. Evan rejoined him, and they continued along the trail.

I need a plan, he thought as they rounded the last bend and headed back to the SUV. *A really good plan.*

Chapter Thirty-Eight

Sam lay back against his pillow and sighed. "Go to sleep, Timmy. It's late." The clock clicked over to ten-thirty-two.

"I not sleepy. I Superman. You be Superman's doggie."

Sam rolled his eyes and tried not to smile. "I'm a super doggie?"

The idea ignited the child. He bolted straight up in bed and began to bounce on his knees. "Papa's a super doggie!"

"Whoa there, little man. It's too late for this."

Timmy flopped on Sam's chest and sniffled, tears perilously close to the surface. "I wanna pway."

Sam stroked his copper hair and rubbed small circles on his back. "I know, buddy. I know. Bedtime is hard, isn't it?"

The boy lay quiet for a few minutes, then popped his thumb in his mouth and rolled over to his own pillow.

"That's a good boy." Continuing to rub his back, Sam almost held his breath, hoping this would do the trick. "That's right," he whispered. "Sweet dreams."

Timmy scrubbed his feet against the blankets, then snuggled closer to Sam's chest. "I wanna pway."

The voice trailed to a whisper as sleep finally took hold. Sam lay motionless for five full minutes, waiting to be sure the child didn't stir.

Gently disengaging himself, he pulled himself to a sitting position and waited. Soft snores came from Timmy's pouty lips. Moonlight streamed in the window, dancing lacey white patterns across the boy's soft cheeks. Sam put one leg over the bed and tested the movement.

Still quiet.

He slid to the edge of the bed and waited, looking out over the lake. The moon cast a silver trail on the surface, spraying light on black rippled water.

Billy's voice resonated inside his head.

Sam.

"Are you there, little buddy?" Sam whispered.

His brother's voice responded, as clear as if he'd been sitting on the mattress.

I'm here. It's time, Sam.

He rose from the bed and padded into the hallway, grabbing his flannel shirt and reaching into his pajama pocket for the marble that warmed his thigh. The glow of the marble in his fingers lit his way downstairs. The refrigerator hummed in the background, and indicator lights shone from the dishwasher and coffee maker. The curtains lifted in the lake breeze, fluttering like beckoning fingers.

Outside.

Sam nodded as if Billy were two steps ahead of him.

"Okay, Billy."

His bare feet whispered against the pale carpet as he made his way toward the front door. He swiped a blanket from the couch and headed outside.

The lake. Go to the lake. It's quiet there.

He skirted along the cement path that mated with Garcia's tiny lawn. Dewy grass felt cool and slippery beneath his feet. Heart thumping now, Sam hurried to the shale shore, gingerly stepping over the cold stones.

Two Adirondack chairs waited side by side. He wrapped himself in the blanket and turned back when a light flared in the window. Penelope waved, then placed a hand over her heart in silent good wishes. Smiling, she turned off the light and pulled the shade. Sam wiped moisture from the chair, then settled in.

Formed by mist rolling off the cold water, an image appeared in the chair beside him. Wide open eyes. Innocent countenance. Lips curved in a smile.

Billy.

Sam reached toward him, his eyes wide. "Is that really you?"

The figure held up one hand as if in warning. *It's me, Sammy. But you can't touch me or I'll evaporate.*

Sam withdrew his hand and leaned forward, eyes scanning the familiar landscape of his little brother's features. "Wow. It really is you. I'm not dreaming, am I?"

Billy's moist form shifted. He nodded and seemed to smile. *No. You're wide awake. I just wanted to wish you good luck.*

The marble rippled effervescent green waves.

"Thanks," Sam said. A sense of peace filtered into his being, sifting soft and serene as a grassy glen at dawn.

You'll be okay, Sammy. I know it. I told you I'd take care of you, didn't I?

Sam's throat constricted. "You did, little buddy. You sure did. But…"

The foggy figure held up one hand, stopping Sam's words. *Listen to the whispers.*

Sam frowned. "Whispers?"

Leaning closer, Billy's form vibrated in the moonlight. His eyes glowed with green mist, searching Sam's. *All it takes is a whisper.*

Confused, Sam allowed himself to relax and trust his brother's words. He had his plan, and he needed to get to it. "Okay, I'm ready. Take me to the day before I met Ginger."

The figure swirled and disappeared into a pinprick of green light as the marble's heat intensified, propelling Sam in Billy's wake.

Chapter Thirty-Nine

Sam hovered just over the floor, following Billy's vaporous form through the crowded airport. He waved his arms in front of his face, then looked down at the ground. No feet. No legs. No nothing.

I'm not in a body this time. How the hell am I going to tweak the past without a body?

Billy turned back, gesturing for him to follow. *Come on, Sam. It's okay. I'll show you.*

Sam veered toward a snack stand and smacked a bag of chips clipped to a metal rack. The bag lifted and rustled. "Cool."

He heard his own voice, and the Middle Eastern clerk behind the counter looked up in surprise, twisting his body in rapid circles. "Huh? What's cool? Who said that?"

Come on, Sam. Billy pointed toward the gate. *Over there.*

They floated toward US Air Gate 11, where Raoul leaned down to peck Ginger on the cheek.

"Don't let me hear 'bout you playing around with any of those rich beach bums." The threat was real, menace lurked behind his half smile and flat black eyes.

Ginger tossed her braid, hitched her carry-on bag over her shoulder, and laughed like a schoolgirl. "Don't be silly, honey. I'm going for a girls' weekend getaway. Nothing more. Mags and Sal and I are gonna sip umbrella drinks by the beach and soak up the sun."

Raoul grumbled. "I'll have to order out while you're gone. I'm not cooking."

Ginger rolled her eyes and shrugged, a trace of exasperation in her voice. "Hey, that's your choice. It doesn't take a rocket scientist to slap a sandwich together."

His face darkened and he gripped her wrist hard. "Somebody's gonna get slapped if you don't come home on time, I'll guarantee you that, chica."

She paled, gathered control, then forced a wobbly smile. "Okay. Gotta go. My friends are already on the plane."

He shoved his hands in his pockets and walked away in silence, heading to the bar beyond the gate, where an unhappy contingent of delayed travelers sipped drinks in misery.

The brothers followed Raoul and sat beside him at a round café-style table. For a moment, Sam wondered if Raoul could hear them breathing. His eyes flickered up, searched the area briefly, then settled on a one-page menu of drinks and appetizers.

Sam waited, knowing Billy would cue him when the time was right.

A waitress appeared at Raoul's left, smacking her gum and tapping the order pad with a stubby pencil. She reminded Sam a little bit of Susan, but then he realized she wouldn't have even been conceived yet. "What'll ya have?"

"A Corona and nachos. Make the beer cold and the cheese hot." No smile. No eye contact. Just the command. He shook out a cigarette and squinted in the resultant cloud of smoke.

"Got it." Behind his back, she rolled her eyes.

Raoul glanced across the room, dismissing the odd mix of waiting passengers. He took a long drag on his cigarette.

Sam held his breath, afraid he'd cough in the noxious fumes. Billy rose and drifted toward the bar, hovering near a blonde in a turquoise jumpsuit. She flashed a diamond ring and barked a tinny laugh at the bartender. "You're such a card," she squealed, thumping the bar with one hand.

The platinum hair seemed coiffed to hairsprayed perfection, frosted at the tips and obscenely molded in place. Sam floated closer, watching her sip on the pink lipstick-smeared rim of her Bay Breeze. Her ripe body oozed sensuality—the kind found on vodka billboards—not the kind real men valued. Squirming as the chair swiveled back and forth, she eyeballed the bartender's crotch. "You work out?" She crooned slurred words in his direction.

"A little," he said, polishing a glass. He winked at her and flexed a bicep, then took another glass from the sink. His tip jar brimmed with dollar bills.

She rose and swayed. "Back in a sec. Gotta visit the little girls' room." She tottered toward the restrooms, past Raoul, leaving a cloud of fruity perfume. He didn't look up.

Billy spoke. *She's the one.*

Sam nodded and waited in the aisle near Raoul's table. Minutes later, she returned, noticing Raoul's white suit and dark glasses.

Sam leaned toward her as she passed, whispering in her ear. "Nice ass."

She stopped dead and turned, feigned offense shadowing her pout. "What did you say?"

Raoul glanced up with slight interest. "Nothing. I'm not a man of many words, sugar."

Grinning now, she leaned down, revealing plump breasts nestled in a plunging neckline. She drummed a jeweled hand on his table. "Buy me a drink and you'll see how sweet I really am." She purred in his direction, twisting one high-heeled shoe on the sticky linoleum floor.

Raoul reached beneath the table with his foot and shoved a chair back. "Have a seat."

Billy hovered for a moment longer, then motioned for Sam to follow. *That's it, Sammie. We're done.*

The surf rolled on the beach, smothering Sam in a sense of salty sensuality. He looked up at the stars embedded in the black sky as Ginger climbed off him, sweaty and spent.

"Oh, Sam..."

He sat up and looked for Billy. He'd disappeared into the frothy surf, swimming away on his back, sleek as the otters Sam had seen earlier in the day.

Sam rolled over, glad that Billy hadn't seen this part.

This is the night Susan was conceived.

The scene repeated itself.

Seagulls quieted, and waves lapped softly against the lavender sand. Sam and Ginger lay on a soft white blanket, hidden from shore by a cluster of massive boulders.

Would anything change this time?

As if watching a TV rerun, Sam anticipated the evening before him.

Ginger flopped her head to the side after a long crest of orgasms. "Sam. You're killing me."

There it was—that same sleepy-cat-smile he remembered. It crept onto her lips and spread across her face.

She unwrapped her long legs from their tight hold around him, then stretched and pointed her toes toward the sea. "I'm tingling all over."

Sam regained his breath and traced his fingers along her sandy skin, once again almost moved to tears by the pure physical joy.

"I'm killing you? You're dehydrating me!"

Inside, he froze as each movement, each word, marched on with frightening familiarity.

She turned her pouty lips to his and sighed. "Sorry, Doctor. Do you want me to leave you alone now?"

Sam lay on his back, facing the stars. "Hell, no. I wish it could last forever."

She sat up slowly and blew the sand from his body, lingering over the sensitive areas. He rolled his eyes and begged for mercy.

"Geez, Ginger. Aren't you hungry? How about a burger at the grill?"

She laughed, twisted her chunky topaz ring on her finger, and wrapped a bright orange sarong around her body. The wet fabric illuminated more than it should, sending another shudder of desire through him.

He pulled on his swim trunks and tee shirt, shook out the blanket, and followed his willowy lover's swinging red braid up the hill.

They settled outdoors in a café with metal tables and chairs. He remembered the feeling of the cool surface beneath his legs, the fireflies that winked in the parking lot, and the red and white Coke sign on the side of the burger shack. Before their order was up, Ginger excused herself to make a phone call.

This time, as last time, Billy amplified the memory, and Sam heard both sides of the conversation.

"Honey? It's me. Just calling to check in."

A rough voice answered. "Oh, it's you."

Sam looked up. This was different than the last time. Hadn't he been mad at her for calling late before?

A woman's voice laughed in the background, on Raoul's line.

"You don't sound too happy to hear from me," Ginger said with a pout.

"Er...yeah. Listen. I'm busy, Ginger."

Ginger froze. "With who?"

Raoul laughed, low and vicious. Another giggle erupted on the line.

"I might as well tell you. I've met someone else." He hesitated, then blurted out, "It's over, Ginger."

Her shoulders slumped and her lips quivered. "So that's it? Just like that?"

Raoul grunted. "Yeah. Just like that."

"What's she got that I don't have?"

He answered immediately, without a trace of sympathy or guilt. "A great ass. And about two million bucks."

Ginger dropped the phone and slumped against the wall. The receiver bumped against the booth with a rhythmic sadness, as if echoing Raoul's words. *It's over. It's over. It's over.*

Sam watched as she closed her eyes and shuddered.

Was she relieved? Glad to be out of the toxic relationship? Or did her insecurity make her want him in spite of the abuse?

The scene faded before Sam could find out, twisting him back to the new present in a humming sunburst of blinding green light.

Chapter Forty

PAPA. CATCH IT!"

Sam lay on his back on the lawn behind the house and opened his eyes to bright sun. Timmy stood silhouetted in the rays overhead, ready to release a maple tree seedpod.

"Catch it!" he squealed.

The semi-dried whirlybird floated lazily on the warm air currents, circling toward Sam's chest. He raised one hand and caught it mid-flight.

"Good job, Papa. I get more." The boy scuttled toward the swing set to scour the lawn for more treasures. Rising on one elbow, Sam tried to orient himself.

Am I really home?

He'd definitely left Garcia's place on the lake. In the distance under a cerulean sky stood his old white farmhouse flanked by the red barn. To his left, the vegetable gardens grew riotous with produce. Dozens of tomatoes hung heavy on the vines. Corn tassels rustled twelve feet high just beyond in the old paddock garden fence. Overhead, the two-hundred-year-old maple rustled green leaves in a sheltering canopy that sighed and shifted as if imbued with a unique spirit of its own.

No calls came from the clouds. No entreating words from Rachel.

Rachel.

He sat up and rubbed soil-worn hands over his eyes, casting a furtive glance toward the porch and kitchen door. His heart beat faster.

Did I fix it?

The clean scent of mint distracted him. Evan plopped down beside him and smiled, his hazel eyes sparkling as he crushed a leaf beneath Sam's nose.

"Here you go, Gramps. Thought you'd like a sprig." He handed Sam a leaf. "Is this the apple or chocolate? It's a test."

The game of identifying the multitude of mint varieties Sam grew in his overrun herb garden had been a longstanding challenge. In a moment of sheer insanity, he'd purchased and planted peppermint, spearmint, apple mint, chocolate mint, pineapple mint, and orange mint. How he'd forgotten about their insatiable spreading habits had mystified him, but in one short season, they'd taken over the entire corner of the garden.

He rubbed the leaf and inhaled. "Is this a trick?" He squinted at his long-legged grandson.

Evan plopped down beside him, followed closely by Timmy. "What do you think?"

The aroma of peppermint filled the air. Sam popped a leaf in his mouth and chewed. "Definitely peppermint, my boy."

Evan's face split into a grin. "Can't fool you, can I, Gramps?"

Timmy reached toward them. "Me want mint!"

He grabbed a leaf and stuffed it in his mouth, chewing with familiar pleasure. "Mmm. Smell my bret." The boy blew minty breath toward Sam's face, then blew toward Evan.

"Wow, nice." Sam laughed and squeezed the boy against his chest, swinging him back and forth and smacking his cheeks with kisses. "I love you, baby boy." Amidst protests that he "wasn't a baby," he swung Timmy to his side and grabbed Evan around the shoulder, pulling him to him. "And you too, big fella."

Unlike most boys his age, Evan indulged his grandfather and hugged him back.

"Kitty!" Timmy screamed, wrestling away from Sam's embrace.

Lila trotted toward them from the back woods, mewing plaintively and running a serpentine path around Timmy to reach Sam safely.

"Well, look who's come to say hello," Sam said, stroking her back and tail as she propped both paws on his chest and butted her nose against his chin. He held Timmy at bay to protect her, then let the boy sit on his lap beside the cat. "Gently, now."

Timmy pushed his face into Lila's and smiled. "Kitty likes me."

Sam and Evan exchanged a knowing glance. Lila usually ran when Timmy came near.

Evan rose and stretched. "I'm starving."

Sam looked toward the house as Timmy dragged on Evan and asked him to help him find a "lucky" clover.

What, or rather who, would he find in the house?

He glanced down at his feet and noticed an unfamiliar brand of sneakers. Reeboks? He usually bought New Balance.

In the parking lot, the Highlander sat squarely parked by the barn. He looked closer.

It's blue, not green.

His palms began to sweat.

"Guys. I'm going inside. Gonna check on lunch. Ev, can you watch your little brother?"

"Sure thing, Gramps. We're gonna look for four-leaf clovers, anyway. Come on, Timmy."

The boys dropped to their knees and crawled on all fours, raking their hands through the clover.

Sam stood and wobbled in place. His legs felt weak and shaky, but he managed to gain his balance and headed toward the house. The cell phone in his pocket vibrated. He fished it out, flipped it open, and answered. "Hello?"

The voice on the other end was familiar.

"Sam? Did I catch you at a bad time?"

His heart jumped. He walked a few steps toward the glider behind the barn. "Lou? Is that you?"

"Of course it's me. Who else would call you about work on a nice Sunday morning?"

A laugh escaped his lips, quivering with a touch of near-lunacy. He recovered and forced a normal tone. "You're right. Especially since I'm retired now. No one calls me about work anymore."

"Yeah. Sorry, Sam. But I have this case I wanted to talk over with you. You free this afternoon?"

Sam looked at his grandsons, his garden, and toward the house. Whether Rachel waited there or not, he didn't want to give up a day to grisly discoveries with a woman who may still harbor affections for him. "Actually, Lou, I'm busy today. But I'll give you a buzz in the morning and we can go over it on the phone if you'd like?"

A humming bird flitted past Sam and landed on a patch of butterfly bushes beside the barn. Sam watched the lime green fluorescent feathers sparkling at the bird's neck. After a brief pause, Lou answered.

"Oh." Disappointment seeped into her words. "Okay. Well, it's not like the victim's going anywhere soon. I'll chat with you tomorrow?"

"Tomorrow it is," Sam nodded and stood. "And Lou?"

"Yeah?"

"Listen. Do something good for yourself today. Spend some time with your grandkids. You work way too hard. Life is really too short for this kind of stuff."

She emitted a hoarse chuckle. "I guess you've got a point there, Doctor. It is Sunday, after all."

"Good. Go play with some little ones." Sam hung up and pocketed the phone. In a sudden flash of panic, he swatted at his pocket, searching for the marble.

There it was. Safe and sound. He fingered the polished cold surface, wrapping it in his hand and holding it tight.

Billy.

A short pulse of warmth flickered from the glass.

Go inside, Sam. Billy's voice was soft and persuasive.

"I'm going," Sam said.

A trickle of nerves flickered along his spine as he approached the porch steps.

One. Two. Three steps.

The top step groaned and creaked, as it always had. The screen door screeched when he pulled it open and was enveloped in a cloud of delicious aromas.

Pot roast. Cinnamon applesauce.

She sat in her wheelchair with the refrigerator door open and her back to him. Sam's heart thumped a primal beat in his chest. He approached her, crouching down beside her near the fridge. "Can I help?"

Rachel turned to him, her rich brown eyes swimming with affection. She placed a hand on his cheek and smiled. "Just look at you. You're covered in dirt, Sammy."

Unable to control his joy, Sam's eyes spilled with tears. He reached for his wife and held her to him, saying her name over and over again.

"Rachel. You're back. Oh my God, baby, I missed you so much."

Rachel allowed his display of unchecked emotion and finally pulled back with concern. "What do you mean, honey? You've only been outside for a few hours. I didn't go anywhere." A frown of concern creased her forehead beneath soft gray bangs. "Are you okay, Sam? Did you get too much sun?"

He pulled himself back, dampening the quaking waves of emotion with sheer will. "No. I'm fine. I just had a dream last night that I lost you. It seemed so real."

"Oh, you poor baby. Come here." She rocked him and patted his back as if he were a child. He held her tight, inhaling the familiar scent of her, reveling in the physical presence of the woman whose death he'd mourned just weeks ago.

He pushed back and rose from his haunches, wiping at his eyes. "Sorry. I'm such an idiot."

"Don't say that." She shushed him and wheeled back from the fridge. "Hey. How about a nice tumbler of your amaretto?"

Sam looked at her with a blank expression. "Huh?"

She pointed to a square glass bottle of DiSarrono Amaretto on the counter. "Your amaretto. You know, the drink you have had every single day since we got married?" She drew her brow downward. "Are you sure you're okay?"

Sam recovered and nodded. "Oh. Right. Sorry, baby. I'm just a little out of it today. Yeah. Let's have a glass." He stared at the unfamiliar amber liquid. "With ice."

She relaxed a little and rolled toward the kitchen table. "The glasses are on the dish drainer."

Sam grabbed the tumblers and plopped four ice cubes into each. He filled them halfway, then settled at the table with his wife. "Here you go."

Sam sipped the cold liqueur, enjoying the warmth and almond flavor as it trickled down his throat. "Mmm. That's really good."

She raised an eyebrow. "You sound as if you never tasted it before, honey."

He shot her a guilty look. "I know. Silly of me. But I do love it." He tilted back in his chair and took another warm sip. "So, who's coming for Sunday dinner?"

Relieved to be back on familiar territory, Rachel clasped her hands together and smiled. "Everyone. Beth, Penelope, and the baby. Andy and Maryellen, of course. And Susan's bringing her new fiancé."

Sam thumped his chair down hard on the linoleum. "Susan?"

Rachel nodded. "Of course. Now, Sam. I don't want you to give this young man a hard time. She met him in pharmacy school seventeen years ago, and he's just transferred up here to work. He's a nice young man. Never married. Ginger says…"

Sam's eyes widened. "You talked to Ginger?"

Rachel leaned over to touch Sam's hand. "Sammy. You're really starting to worry me. Of course I talked to Ginger. I talk to her every Saturday morning, you know that. It's how we've kept in touch all these years. And she counts on us to keep her up with Susan's life. You know since Susan moved up here she never calls her mother enough. It's the least I can do."

Visions of his changed life flashed past his mind's eye. Susan. Cared for by Ginger and supported by Sam. Summer visits. Private schools. College.

"Right. Susan lives in Rochester. She's a pharmacist," he said.

Rachel squinted with suspicion. "I'm starting to think you had a stroke. You're acting so strange."

Sam stood, ran a hand over his thick gray hair, and smiled. "No, baby. I haven't had a stroke. I'm just happy. Ridiculously happy."

He leaned down and squeezed her again, then kissed her lips, holding her face tenderly in his hands. "I love you, Rachel. For keeps. And everything's going to be just fine."

"I'm glad you think so, honey." Her glance was tentative, suspicious. "You sure you're okay?"

He kissed her again. "More than okay, baby. I'm fantastic."

She smiled with a mischievous glint and pushed him away. "Okay, you fantastic man you. Go wash those grubby paws. I'm just about to make you a chocolate cake. As if you deserve it." A snort of laughter burst from her lips. "You're such a nut."

Sam swigged the rest of his amaretto, pleased with this minor addition to his life. He wondered what other changes had taken place, what surprises awaited him. As he trotted upstairs to wash up, the marble warmed in his pocket. He reached down and patted it.

"Thank you, Billy. I owe you, big time."

A sense of warmth invaded his bones, filled him with the bright vigor of a young boy. Billy's voice echoed in his brain.

You're welcome, Sammy. Be happy.

Sam reached the bathroom and turned on the hot water. He soaped his face and hands and toweled them dry. Looking in the mirror, he smiled at his own reflection, glad no ghosts lurked in the glass.

"I will, little buddy. You can count on it."

The End

About the author

Aaron Paul Lazar wasn't always a mystery writer. It wasn't until eight members of his family and friends died within five years that the urge to write became overwhelming. "When my father died, I lost it. I needed an outlet, and writing provided the kind of solace I couldn't find elsewhere."

Lazar created the Gus LeGarde mystery series, with the founding novel, *Double Forté* (2004), a chilling winter mystery set in the Genesee Valley of upstate New York. Like Lazar's father, protagonist Gus LeGarde is a classical music professor. Gus, a grandfather, gardener, chef, and nature lover, plays Chopin etudes to feed his soul and thinks of himself as a "Renaissance man caught in the 21st century."

The creation of the series lent Lazar the comfort he sought, yet in the process, a new passion was unleashed. Obsessed with his parallel universe, he now lives, breathes, and dreams about his characters, and has written ten LeGarde mysteries in eight years. (*Upstaged* – 2005; *Tremolo: Cry of The Loon* – 2007 Twilight Times Books; *Mazurka* – 2009 Twilight Times Books, with more to come.) The author is currently working on his seventeenth novel.

One day while rototilling his gardens, Lazar unearthed a green cat's eye marble, which prompted the new paranormal mystery series featuring Sam Moore, retired country doctor and passionate gardener. The green marble, a powerful talisman, connects all three of the books in the series, whisking Sam back in time to uncover his brother's dreadful fate fifty years earlier. (*Healey's Cave,* 2010; *Terror Comes Knocking,* previously titled *One Potato, Blue Potato,* 2012; *For Keeps,* 2012) Lazar intends to continue both series.

Lazar's books feature breathless chase scenes, nasty villains, and taut suspense, but are also intensely human stories, replete with kids, dogs, horses, food, romance, and humor. The author calls them, "country mysteries," although reviewers have dubbed them "literary mysteries."

"It seems as though every image ever impressed upon my brain finds its way into my work. Whether it's the light dancing through stained-glass windows in a Parisian chapel, curly slate-green lichen covering a boulder at the edge of a pond in Maine, or hoarfrost dangling from a cherry tree branch in mid-winter, these images burrow into my memory cells. In time they bubble back, persistently itching, until they are poured out on the page."

The author lives on a ridge overlooking the Genesee Valley in upstate New York with his wife, mother-in-law, two dogs, and three cats. He finds grandfathering one of the most precious and important times of life.

Lazar maintains several websites and blogs, was the Gather Saturday Writing Essential host for three years, writes his monthly "Seedlings" columns for the *Voice in the Dark* literary journal and the *Future Mystery Anthology Magazine.* He has been published in *Absolute Write* as well as *The Great Mystery and Suspense Magazine.*

Contact him at aaron.lazar@yahoo.com.

Novels by Aaron Paul Lazar

Gus LeGarde Mysteries

Double Forté, author's preferred edition 2012
Upstaged, author's preferred edition forthcoming 2012
Tremolo, 2007, Twilight Times Books
Mazurka, 2009, Twilight Times Books
FireSong: an unholy grave, 2011, Twilight Times Books
Don't Let the Wind Catch You, forthcoming 2012

Sam Moore Paranormal Mysteries

Healey's Cave, 2010, Twilight Times Books
Terror Comes Knocking, 2012, Twilight Times Books
For Keeps, 2012, Twilight Times Books

Tall Pines Paranormal Mysteries

For the Birds, 2011, Twilight Times Books
Essentially Yours, 2012, Twilight Times Books
Sanctuary, forthcoming 2013 Twilight Times Books

See excerpts and reviews here:
http://www.lazarbooks.com
http://www.legardemysteries.com
http://www.mooremysteries.com
http://www.murderby4.blogspot.com
http://www.aplazar.gather.com
http://www.aaronlazar.blogspot.com

Don't miss any of these other
exciting mystery/suspense novels

- *Essentially Yours*
by Aaron Paul Lazar
(1-60619-168-3, $17.95 US)

- *FireSong*
by Aaron Paul Lazar
(1-60619-164-0, $16.95 US)

- *For the Birds*
by Aaron Paul Lazar
(1-60619-166-8, $16.95 US)

- *Healey's Cave*
by Aaron Paul Lazar
(1-60619-162-4, $16.95 US)

- *Mazurka*
by Aaron Paul Lazar
(1-60619-160-8, $16.95 US)

- *Terror Comes Knocking*
by Aaron Paul Lazar
(1-60619-170-5, $17.95 US)

- *Tremolo*
by Aaron Paul Lazar
(1-933353-08-2, $16.95 US)

Order Form

If not available from your local bookstore or favorite online bookstore, send this coupon and a check or money order for the retail price plus $3.50 s&h to Twilight Times Books, Dept. GB812 POB 3340 Kingsport TN 37664. Delivery may take up to two weeks.

Name: ______________________________

Address: ____________________________

____

Email: ______________________________

I have enclosed a check or money order in the amount of

$___________

for _____________________________________ .

If you enjoyed this book, please post a review
at your favorite online bookstore.

Twilight Times Books
P O Box 3340
Kingsport, TN 37664
Phone/Fax: 423-323-0183
www.twilighttimesbooks.com/